Ballyrourke

Linda O'Brien

JOVE BOOKS, NEW YORK

BALLYROURKE

A Jove Book / published by arrangement with
the author

PRINTING HISTORY
Jove edition / October 2002

Copyright © 2002 by Linda O'Brien
Cover art by Bruce Emmett
Cover design by Marc Cohen

Visit our website at
www.penguinputnam.com

ISBN: 0-515-13409-0

A JOVE BOOK®
Jove Books are published by The Berkley Publishing Group,
a division of Penguin Putnam Inc.,
375 Hudson Street, New York, New York 10014.
JOVE and the "J" design
are trademarks belonging to Penguin Putnam Inc.

PRINTED IN THE UNITED STATES OF AMERICA

10 9 8 7 6 5 4 3 2 1

To my daring O'Brien relatives
who crossed the ocean in 1836 to come to a new land;

To my wonderful, supportive husband, Jim,
and my children, Jason and Julie,
for putting up with my long hours spent at the computer;

To my family and friends
for their encouragement and patience;

To my agent, Linda Hyatt, for her faith in my talent.

Thank you all.

One

County Wicklow, Ireland
June 1893

Colin MacCormack braced his hands on the crumbling brick sill, leaned out the arched window high up in the ancient round tower, and inhaled the rain-freshened air, glad to be back on his own land after three weeks away. *His land.* The very sound of those words was a battle cry to his embittered soul.

No matter that it now had a British owner, by rights Ballyrourke *should* belong to his people, the O'Rourke clan— every rolling hill and emerald pasture, gurgling stream and fragrant heather, fertile farmland and thatched cottage, and even the big house, occupied now by the English Lawthrops.

The last owner, or landlord, as the British preferred to call them, Sir Lionel Lawthrop, had passed away a year ago, and his wife Millicent had died recently. Now a search was on by their solicitors to find the heir named in Lady Lawthrop's will.

The entire clan was holding its collective breath to see who that heir would be, fearing Ballyrourke would fall into the hands of Sir Lionel's only son Horace, who was despised by them all. For Colin, that hatred was even more intense, for it was due to Horace's own actions that his mother and sister had died.

"Colin!" a young voice shouted from below, breaking into his musings. "You're back! Have you heard the news?"

Colin glanced down at the bright red head of young Dermot O'Rourke. "What news?"

"They've found a second will, Colin. A *new* will! We're gettin' our land back!"

"Are you telling the truth?"

"Didn't I just hear my mam talking about it? Will ye come, then?"

"I'll be right down." Colin's heart swelled with fresh hope as he gazed out at his beloved Ballyrourke. A new will? Was it possible? Could it be that they were to be spared ever seeing that devil's face again?

When Horace Lawthrop left suddenly last year, all of Ballyrourke had rejoiced. No one knew the reason behind his sudden departure, nor did they care, still they all thanked God for it. Yet after he'd gone, had the O'Rourkes taken steps to reclaim what was theirs? No. They'd done nothing.

Colin's frustration at their complacence grew by the day. It seemed to him that in losing the land, they'd lost their self-respect, too.

O'Rourkes had first settled there in A.D. 1100, and by the very dint of their hands had worked that land until, by the sixteenth century, it had become one of the wealthiest estates in county Wicklow. Sean O'Rourke, then the clan's patriarch, had built a fine brick home for his large family, which he'd filled with the ancient artifacts and family treasures passed down from those early ancestors.

But in the seventeenth century, O'Rourke and all the other Irish people of means who wouldn't swear allegiance to the English crown had been stripped of their estates. The estates had been given to foreigners, mostly Englishmen loyal to the queen, reducing the Irish to sudden poverty. Most went west to Connaught, but the O'Rourkes stayed out of a fierce devotion to their land. They built cottages and grew crops to pay their rent. They became tenants on their own soil. Colin's gut roiled each time he thought of the terrible injustice of it.

Well, if no one else would take a stand, if no one else would fight the injustice, then, by all the saints in heaven, he would. He took pride in his strength of conviction and unswerving devotion to his people. He'd take back what was rightfully theirs so his family could live as they were meant to—masters of their own land.

This news of another will made Colin want to shout for joy. It seemed a higher power had taken his side at last.

Colin followed the lad to the cramped, thatched-roof cottage where Patrick and Eileen O'Rourke and their two children lived. As the eldest O'Rourke male, Patrick was the head of the clan, but it seemed that everyone looked up to Colin for leadership.

The small cottage smelled of straw and peat, and onions simmering in a peppery lamb broth in a huge pot Eileen was tending.

"Is it true, Eileen?" Colin asked, ducking his head to fit his six foot height through the doorway. "Is there another will?"

Eileen pressed a hand in the small of her back as she stirred the contents of the iron pot. Eight-and-a-half months pregnant, she was a small-framed woman with a dusting of freckles across her cheeks and a ready smile. Today, however, she looked weary and wan. "'Tis but a rumor, Colin. Don't get your hopes up."

"A rumor!" Dispirited, he sank down on the bench at the trestle table.

"Aye," she said with a regretful sigh. "One of the maids up at the house swore the old lady wrote a new will, but it has yet to turn up. Besides, the Lawthrop heir has been found and is on her way."

"*Her* way?"

Eileen turned to gaze at him. "They've found Garrett and Suzannah's daughter Katie living in America."

"Saints be praised," Colin said with scorn.

"Aye, Colin, saints be praised, for it's not Horace! And don't forget, Katie is an O'Rourke as much as she is a Lawthrop."

Colin scoffed in disdain. In his mind Katie was pure Lawthrop. What else could she be? Her mother Suzannah had been Sir Lionel's only daughter. She had raised Katie alone after her husband Garrett O'Rourke had died on a return trip to Ballyrourke many years ago. Suzannah had cut off all ties with the O'Rourkes after that, no doubt out of spite.

"Sure, Katie won't want to give up her easy life in America to come here, now will she?"

"Wishful thinkin', Colin, but this moment they're readying the house for her. And what makes you think Katie's had an easy life, with no father to support her? Now the poor child has lost her mother, as well. She has no one but us, so be kind."

"The *poor child* is all grown now, Eileen, and still has her dear uncle Horace. Anyway, she's never considered us kin, nor we her. Why would she want us now?"

"If it's an argument you're wantin', Colin, go have a pint with your friends down at Teach O Malley," Eileen chided. "I'm just about to serve up the stew. Will you have a bowl with us?"

"Thank you, but I've got work to do."

"You'll not do anything foolish, will you, Colin? You'll forget about that silly rumor of another will."

Colin winked. "I'll be good as gold."

"I don't believe you for a moment," Eileen called as he slipped out the door.

Colin followed the worn path from their cottage to Kilwick Road, which led straight to Lawthrop House, where he intended to find out about the rumor firsthand. As the Lawthrop's estate manager, he had the run of the place, having taken over that position from his father James MacCormack, who'd been killed by a stroke just two years before.

He strode up the wide, curving stone steps leading to the main entrance of the redbrick house. Ordinarily he'd use the side entrance that led straight into the kitchen, but today he wanted to imagine himself as owner of this grand home. He stopped at the door and turned to gaze at the park, separated from the house by the brick drive.

The park was enclosed on its outer three sides by a low fieldstone wall. A garden took up the center of the park, its four square flower beds crisscrossed by brick paths and punctuated by a circular pond in the center. The pond was enclosed by benches, with a fountain in the middle.

What a beauty it was, too, designed and built by O'Rourke hands, as were the rest of the grounds. With a contented sigh, Colin turned and rapped on the door with the heavy iron door knocker. It was opened by a young, black-haired maid in a starched white apron and gray dress.

"Colin! What are you doing at this door?"

"Morning, my sweet Doreen," he said, doffing his cap. "Might you have a cup of tea for me?"

The maid giggled at his endearment. "Always have a cup for you, Colin."

"And where's that old workhorse Grainwe this morning?" he asked, chucking the young woman beneath the chin as he slipped past her into the marble-floored hall.

"Right behind ye, laddie!" a booming voice announced.

"Didn't you think I knew that?" He swung around and pinched the cheek of the elderly housekeeper who stood with her ample arms crossed over her white-aproned chest. "What's this I hear about a new will?"

"You'd have to ask Mary Flynn about that," Grainwe said of the upstairs maid. "Mary swears Lady Lawthrop wrote it on her deathbed. Well then, I ask you, where is this will?"

"Have you searched for it?"

"Have ye lost yer mind?" Grainwe retorted. "We can't go rummaging through her ladyship's personal effects."

"We can if it means getting back our land." Colin started up the winding staircase on the right of the foyer.

"Where do you think you're going?" Grainwe called.

"To find Mary."

"Ye won't find her up there. She's quit."

"Then I'll go see her at her mother's house," Colin said, starting back down.

"Her mother has moved to Dublin, and ye won't find Mary there, either. She eloped with Danny O'Doyle."

"Then I'll have a look through the room myself."

Grainwe hiked up her long skirt and went after him. "Over my dead body ye will, Colin MacCormack! We've got Mistress Katherine due any time and the room's been prepared. I'll not allow the likes of ye to disturb it. Besides, Lady Lawthrop's personal effects have been moved out, and I'd have seen a will had there been one lyin' about."

"The likes of me?" Colin asked in mock chagrin. "A hardworking manager who thinks you're the loveliest woman on the face of the earth?"

Grainwe grabbed his arm and pulled him to a stop. "Yer charm is wasted on me, ye arrogant pup. We've got too much to do without havin' ye in our way."

"Where have you put the personal effects, then?"

"None of yer business."

Colin glanced down at pretty little Doreen, standing at the bottom gazing up at him with interest. If Grainwe wouldn't divulge the information, he could always coax Doreen into telling him. He had a way with women.

He hooked his arm through the older woman's and walked down with her. "So what do you know about the fair Mistress Katherine?"

Grainwe's cheeks flushed red. "Nothing but that she's coming, and to ready the house."

"Now, Grainwe, what is it you're hiding?"

The housekeeper yanked her arm away. "Why would ye think I'd hide something from ye?"

"I know you, old woman. Out with it."

Grainwe stopped at the bottom and faced him squarely, her rheumy eyes searching his. "Horace Lawthrop is coming back, too."

Colin felt the old bitterness burn in his gut as he took his horse from the stall and saddled up. Grainwe's last words echoed again and again in his mind: *Horace Lawthrop is coming back.*

He led the mare out of the stable, swung up onto the sad-

dle and headed for the lane, where he started off at a gallop.
The wind tousled his hair and took his breath away as they
dashed across the rolling terrain, man and beast, riding as
one. For a few blissful moments he forgot about Horace, but
as Colin brought the exhausted horse to a stop near a stream
and dismounted, the image of the devil's sharp-beaked face
returned to haunt him, as it had so often when Colin was
young.

He'd been but twelve years old when the prices of agri-
culture across Ireland plummeted, causing many tenant
farmers to fall into arrears. Those who couldn't pay their
rents were mercilessly evicted from their small cottages, including most of the O'Rourkes, who were personally driven
out by Horace, acting on Sir Lionel's behalf.

Colin's family, the MacCormack branch, had put aside
enough money to see them through, but Horace had cleverly
and diabolically sabotaged their efforts and evicted them
anyway. Colin's mother and seven-year-old sister, both ail-
ing, had died soon afterward from malnutrition and disease.

Eventually, conditions had improved, and the families
had been able to return to their cottages, but Colin had never
again trusted the Lawthrops, nor had he ever forgiven
Horace for his cruel deed. In Colin's eyes, Horace Lawthrop
had murdered his family the same as if he'd shot them
through the heart.

In an attempt to protect the O'Rourkes from Horace after
Sir Lionel had passed on, Colin had made an offer on behalf
of the clan to buy the estate a piece at a time, paying as they
could afford. Lady Lawthrop had turned him down, saying
only that they would have to sacrifice too much for too long
to raise that kind of money.

However, Colin had come up with another plan.
Lawthrop House contained art purchased by Sean O'Rourke
centuries ago, originally displayed in the house but now rel-
egated to the attic, replaced by the Lawthrops' personal collection. That ancient artwork was now highly desired by
collectors, according to the art dealer Colin had met in
Dublin. By rights that art should still belong to the clan.

Didn't he then have the right to sell them for the good of the clan?

If the new will turned out to be a fabrication, then Colin still had his plan. And if that plan failed, he'd come up with another. This was a battle he was determined to win.

Colin was jarred from his thoughts when his horse nudged his shoulder. He stroked her velvety nose. "Had enough of a rest, Lizzie?"

The clop of horses' hooves brought his head around with a jerk. In the distance he saw a hired coach heading toward Lawthrop House.

"Well, Lizzie," he muttered grimly, "seems it's time to meet our new landlord."

TWO

Azure-blue skies. Fluffy white clouds. Rolling green pastureland dotted with grazing sheep. The scents of sweet grass and heather. And in the background, a sweep of mauve-hued mountains. Katherine sighed as she took it all in from the window of her carriage. Breathtaking was the only word to come to mind. Positively breathtaking!

She still couldn't believe her sudden fortune. She was an heiress! If only it hadn't come with such a painful price.

Only a month ago Katherine had believed herself to be the daughter of British-born parents, both from hardworking farm families. Then she'd answered a knock on her door, and her world had turned on its ear.

On the stoop of her Chicago apartment a harmless-looking gentleman had stood dressed in a gray three-piece suit and white shirt. He'd doffed his bowler and smiled, a friendly smile in a bespectacled, middle-aged face. He'd held a leather case in one hand, his hat and walking stick in the other.

"I'm looking for Katherine O'Rourke," he'd said, with the precise, clipped accent of the British.

"I'm sorry, sir. You must have the wrong address."

"Is your mother Suzannah, father Garrett?"

"Why, yes, but the name is Rourke, not O'Rourke."

"Ah, it is indeed a pleasure to find you at last, Miss"—
he'd hesitated, as though unsure of what name to use—
"Rourke. We've been looking for you for a long time." He'd
given a crisp bow. "Jasper Firth, from the law firm Dawes,
Holmes and Firth; London. Our firm has represented your
mother's family for three generations. May I come in? I have
something for you from your maternal grandmother Lady
Millicent Lawthrop."

"From my grandmother? That would be highly peculiar,
Mr. Firth, since my grandmother has been dead for over
twenty years."

"In truth, Miss—er—Rourke, she passed on only a few
months ago." He'd patted his leather case. "I have the proof
right here."

Katherine had been certain he was wrong. After all, her
mother had distinctly told her that both her grandmother
and her grandfather had died the year she was born, eigh-
teen seventy-one—twenty-two years ago. She doubted her
mother would have been mistaken about their deaths.
Katherine had even noted that fact in her journal. It had
seemed important to do so because it was one of a very few
bits of information she knew about her mother's family. Her
mother had intensely disliked speaking of the past.

Her curiosity roused, Katherine had admitted the attor-
ney to her tiny parlor. Mr. Firth had settled on the blue bro-
cade sofa, opened his leather case, and taken out a thin
stack of papers. Katherine had poured him tea, then perched
on a stuffed chair and waited for him to begin.

"Ah," he'd said blissfully, after taking a sip of tea, "the
first decent cup I've had since arriving in America. And biscuits, too. Your mother taught you well, Miss Rourke."

Katherine had felt an instant tightness in her chest, a
grief still sharp after two months. Her mother had been
merely forty-two years old when she'd been struck down by
pneumonia. Her passing had left a void in Katherine's life.
She had no siblings and merely vague recollections of her
father—she had been just six years old when he'd aban-

doned them. "Etiquette was very important to her," Katherine had replied quietly.

"I'm sure you miss her. Please accept my condolences on her sudden passing."

"Thank you. Now, about this proof?"

Firth had set the cup in its saucer, picked up a document and handed it to her. "This is your Grandmother Lawthrop's certified death certificate. Please note the date."

She'd looked it over twice and still hadn't known what to make of the news. This all didn't seem possible, yet there it was, in black and white.

"I also have here a copy of your grandmother's will, in which she left your mother a sizable inheritance. Since you are Suzannah's next of kin, you are the beneficiary. I'd like to read it aloud, if I may."

A sizable inheritance? Katherine had blinked in astonishment. "Please do."

Firth had picked up the top document, cleared his throat and read, "I, Millicent Lawthrop, being of sound mind and disposing memory, do hereby give, devise and bequeath to my daughter, solely, the estate known as Ballyrourke, county Wicklow, including Lawthrop House and all its contents."

"Isn't County Wicklow in Ireland?" Katherine had asked.

"It is."

She'd blinked hard, trying to grasp the astounding information. What would dyed-in-the-wool British farmers have been doing with an estate in Ireland?

"Further," the solicitor had read, "it is my wish that any items of personal property or furnishings in the residence that my heir chooses not to retain shall then be gifted to the National Museum of Ireland."

There were items worth gifting to a museum?

Firth had continued: "To my son Horace Lawthrop I do hereby give, devise, and bequeath the sum of ten pounds, as he has previously been dealt with most generously by me. Witnesseth this 16th day of November, 1892."

"My mother has a brother?"

"Yes. He lives in London. If you like, I can give you his address so you can write to him."

She had an uncle! The news astounded her. "And just how big is the estate, Mr. Firth?"

His brow had wrinkled as he'd pondered the matter. "The size of a small village, perhaps."

Katherine had stared at him as she attempted to absorb his words.

"I do apologize if this is unsettling, Miss Rourke," Firth had said, glancing up at her. "You have quite a bit of information to digest, and I'm sure you'll have many questions. I'll be happy to answer any now; moreover, I've taken a room at the Palmer House and shall contact you in a few days to answer any remaining questions. In the meantime, you'll undoubtedly want to arrange your travel plans, as you'll need to dispose of your inheritance."

"Dispose of it?"

"Unless you'd want to live there."

"No, of course not." Katherine's mind had instantly begun to fill with ideas. "Then I can sell the estate and use the money as I choose?"

"You may do whatever you want with it. It's yours."

Katherine had clasped her fingers together excitedly as a plan formed in her mind. "How much would you say it's worth?"

"Dear me! You'd have to have it appraised."

"Would you think there would be enough money from the sale to build an orphanage?"

His eyebrows had lifted in surprise. "An orphanage?"

"You see, I'm a member of the Ladies' Society for Abandoned Children. We've been raising funds to build a new orphanage, but it will take years before we'll have enough. If I can sell this estate and use the profits, we can build right away."

He'd seemed unsure of how to answer, so she'd hastened to explain: "This isn't merely charity work for me, Mr. Firth; it's much more personal. After my father abandoned us, and the last of our money was gone, my mother and I were given shelter at an orphanage not far from here. It wasn't their *habit to take in young women with children, but they were desperate for help.*

"For almost a year we lived in conditions that would sicken you, with my mother scrubbing floors and laundering clothes in exchange for our beds. She abhorred every moment of it, and even more, hated that I had made friends there. We were Lawthrops, she would remind me. We had breeding, refinement. It was a mistake to fraternize with those children.

"One day she took me away, to this very house, without even letting me say good-bye. Suddenly we had money and clothes and day help. She wouldn't say who had given her the money, only that it was a gift. Several times after that she was approached by the ladies' society to help the orphanage, once when an influenza epidemic hit, killing many of the children I had befriended, but she always shut the door in their faces. It was as if she felt degraded by her experience and wanted no association with them.

"My mother's callousness has always caused me great shame, Mr. Firth. My work with homeless children is my way of rectifying the past."

"Your goal is quite admirable, Miss Rourke; however, I think it would be best if you had a look at Ballyrourke yourself. If you'd care to accompany me, I shall be leaving for Ireland at the end of the week." He'd put the documents in his leather case and looked up with a smile. "Any other questions I may answer before I leave?"

Katherine had thought of so many, she hadn't been able to sort through them fast enough. "Would you tell me, please, why you initially referred to me as O'Rourke, and why I'm the sole beneficiary of the estate when my mother's brother is alive?"

"O'Rourke is your true name. Your parents undoubtedly dropped the 'O' when they came here from Ireland, as many did at the time. You'll be pleased to know you have a number of family members still living at Ballyrourke."

"But my mother distinctly told me that both she and my father had been born and reared in England."

"I don't mean to contradict your mother, Miss Rourke,

but your father was most definitely Irish. And your mother lived in Ireland for many years herself."

Katherine had been dumbfounded, as the initial excitement over her inheritance faded. If Firth's information was accurate, then what little she'd been told about her family was a lie.

"As to your mother's brother, Horace Lawthrop," the solicitor explained, "your grandmother was very insistent that he be given only ten pounds and no more, and that her daughter Suzannah, or her direct lineal descendant, inherit the rest."

Katherine had stared out the window, turning the information over. To suddenly find out that her father was Irish, that her grandmother had been alive all these years, and that her own mother had deceived her was more than she could comprehend. She'd had no words to express the immense betrayal she felt.

The thought of making that long voyage hadn't pleased her. Nevertheless, she had to go. Her mother had hid the truth from her, and Katherine had to know why.

Three

Katherine tore her gaze from the beautiful scenery to glance over at her uncle Horace, who lounged lazily in one corner of the hired carriage. His face was a study in apathy, with only his pale eyes revealing his displeasure. He was a tall, angular man, with her mother's fair coloring and thinning light brown hair. He had a high forehead; a long, curved nose; and weak chin, all of which gave him the appearance of a parrot.

Mr. Firth had kindly arranged for Katherine to meet her uncle in England, before the second leg of their voyage to Ireland. Horace had been delighted to make her acquaintance, and had seemed quite amazed that her mother had never mentioned him, since apparently he and Suzannah had been close at one time. Clearly, there was a whole lot her mother had never mentioned.

Horace had immediately offered to accompany Katherine to Ireland "to guard her interests," although she had assured him that Firth could do the job.

Yet he had insisted. "The O'Rourkes are a deceitful lot," he'd warned. "I learned long ago not to trust them."

Life had been miserable for him at Ballyrourke, with the peasants persecuting him at every opportunity. They were bitter because the Lawthrops had saved Ballyrourke from financial ruin, something the O'Rourkes had been unable to do, and because the Lawthrops had been given the estate by the queen.

Sir Lionel had been immune from their ill treatment, but Horace, as merely the son, had been the perfect target. Indeed, it had been a major factor in his decision to go to England.

Horace had questioned Katherine extensively about what she knew of her background, yet all he would say about her parents was that Garrett O'Rourke had been a reckless hothead who had been more devoted to his clan than to his own wife and daughter, and that Suzannah had been better off without him.

Suzannah should never have married beneath her, Horace had said. The Lawthrops had a distinguished past, a sterling reputation. She could have married well and lived a happy life. Instead, she'd been swept off her feet by a fast-talking blackguard, and where had that taken her? To an early grave.

"Don't make her mistakes," Horace had warned. "Remember your proud English heritage." His admonition had been eerily similar to her mother's.

About his own past he'd been vague, apparently disliking any reminders of it as much as her mother had. Indeed, he'd grown irritable each time she'd mentioned it, until Katherine had finally given up in frustration. Someone at Ballyrourke would be able to give her answers.

But all that was pushed aside as Katherine turned back to gaze through the glass, completely enchanted by the landscape. Indeed, she'd never felt such a stirring for a place she'd never seen before.

They rode up a long, curving dirt road edged with leafy trees and low stone walls, past tiny white cottages topped with thatched roofs that looked like brown velvet in the midday sun. The cottages, her uncle explained, belonged to the peasants that farmed the land. In the distance she saw a magnificent home sprawling across a bright green lawn. "Look at that grand house, Uncle!"

He glanced out the window and replied in a bored voice, "It's *your* house, Katherine. This is Ballyrourke."

She opened her mouth and stared. "I'd no idea!"

The home—if it could be called merely a home—was built of red brick and gray stone, and had three floors and a center front entrance that was two doors wide. She counted the windows across the top floor—ten! How many rooms could it possibly have? And chimneys! Why, there were six stacks with four chimneys each that she could see! And what a beautiful entranceway, with its curving stone steps accented with pots of colorful flowers.

As the carriage came to a halt, the park on the opposite side of the drive became visible. Katherine stepped down from the carriage and immediately crossed the brick path straight to the fountain in the center. She stared up at the magnificent sculpture of a lady pouring water from an urn, then turned slowly in a circle, taking in the exquisite vista. This was all hers?

"Are you coming, Katherine?" her uncle called impatiently.

Lifting her skirts, she hurried back across the drive and up one side of the stone steps as the front door opened and a tall, sturdy woman dressed in servant's clothing stepped out. The woman curtsied and dipped her gray head.

"Welcome to Lawthrop House, mistress," she said in a thick Irish brogue, "and to ye, sir."

Katherine gave her a warm smile. "Thank you so much. I'm Katherine Rourke, and this is—"

"Everyone knows who you are, Katherine," Horace drawled, stepping past the servant and into the house.

Katherine was embarrassed by his curtness. "I'm sorry, your name is . . . ?" she asked kindly.

"Grainwe O'Rourke," the servant said, again curtsying. "If ye please, mistress, come inside and we'll see you settled in."

Katherine felt foolish as she entered the elegant entrance hall. This elderly servant was an O'Rourke, and if Firth was correct, that meant Katherine was being served by her own kin. It gave her a very uncomfortable feeling.

That feeling was replaced by one of awe as she gazed around the hall, with its black-and-white marble floor, persimmon-colored walls, and ornately carved white trim. There were even crystal sconces on the walls to light both the hall and the staircase.

Then her gaze sharpened, and suddenly she saw beyond the grandiosity to obvious signs of neglect: a water leak that had ruined one large area of the high, plaster ceiling; threadbare carpeting on the beautiful, curving staircase; carved trim in need of scraping and painting, and badly mildewed window sashes.

As she turned to hang her hat on a mahogany coat tree, she suddenly noticed a young, pretty, dark-haired girl in maid's dress standing to one side, waiting with obvious eagerness to be introduced.

"This is Doreen," Grainwe said. "She'll serve ye faithfully, mistress, and she's a wonder with hair, is our Doreen. She can fasten up a row of the tiniest buttons in the blink of an eye. When ye want her help, give three tugs on the bellpull. Two will bring me. I'll introduce ye to the rest of the staff in a bit, but I'm sure ye'll be wantin' to freshen up now after yer long trip, so I'll show ye to yer room."

Katherine didn't have the heart to tell Grainwe she wouldn't need Doreen's services—she simply wasn't the type to fuss with her hair; a plain bun was sufficient. As for dressing herself, she wore front-buttoned bodices, as did most American women of modest means.

Horace was down the hall, poking his head in doorways, as though checking to see if anything had changed in his absence. As Katherine started up after the servant, he called, "Come down for tea when you've freshened up."

"Mind the drip pots," Grainwe said from above her. Katherine carefully stepped around a copper pot on the landing, then glanced up to see where the water was coming from, almost stepping in the next one on the stairs.

She followed Grainwe to the second floor and then down a long hall lined with doorways and another pot. "Are these all bedrooms?"

"Yes, miss. Six in all." Grainwe led her to the very end

room in the left wing and opened double doors. Katherine stepped inside and stopped, gazing around with indrawn breath.

"Beautiful," she breathed, taking in the pale yellow walls and white lace curtains; yellow, green and white floral satin bed covering; ornate iron bedstead with intricate filigreed headboard; and lovely old, pastel-colored Persian carpet.

The room was immense, at least as large as three normal-sized bedrooms, and even had its own desk, plus a reclining sofa and matching chair facing a handsome green marble fireplace at the opposite end of the room. A bay window on the long wall overlooked another garden.

"This was yer grandmother's room, miss," Grainwe told her, a hint of longing in her voice. "We freshened it all up for ye, with new sheets and towels. Yer private bathing chamber is through that door," she said, indicating a door to the right of the fireplace. "Yer dressing room is through that door." She pointed to a matching door on the left. "Yer trunks will be brought up shortly. There's fresh water in the pitcher, and I'll have tea ready downstairs in the pink parlor, second door on the left. Is there anything else I can do for ye before I go?"

Katherine loved the way Grainwe said "tay" for tea and "penk" for pink. She found the Irish accent charming. "Thank you, but I can't think of anything right now."

As soon as Grainwe had gone, Katherine went over to one of the open windows in the bay and knelt on the cushioned window seat beneath it, leaning out to gaze down at the land—*her* land.

She turned, spied the high brass bed, and had the most astonishing urge to flop backward onto it. Instead, she sat carefully on the end, as a lady should do. She stroked her palms across the satin bed covering, relishing the feel of it. Her grandmother's very bed, Katherine thought with a wistful sigh.

Feeling a child-like excitement bubbling inside, she peered in at the bathroom, or bathing chamber, as Grainwe had called it, admiring the deep soaking tub with its brass handles. But there beneath the tub were old water stains and signs of warping. She wondered if the floorboards had rotted.

"Good heavens!" she uttered, gazing at the large, mirrored dressing room, now empty of everything but thick wooden hangers. How many dresses had her grandmother owned?

A soft scratching at the bedroom door interrupted her musings. She hurried out of the dressing room and opened the door to the young maid Doreen.

"Miss, shall ye come down to tea now? Yer uncle is waitin'."

"Yes, I shall come right now." Katherine followed after her, down the staircase to the entrance hall, mindful of the drip pots. This had once been her mother's home. Why hadn't she wanted her daughter to know about it?

Katherine entered the second room on the left, the pink parlor. And indeed, it was pink—rose pink, with rose-colored tapestries lining the walls and rose draperies hanging on the four tall windows. She spotted her uncle sitting on one of a matched pair of sofas by a white marble fireplace, now darkened from soot damage. He was watching her, his fingers drumming on the back of the small sofa.

"I'm sorry to have kept you waiting," she said, taking a seat on the sofa opposite his. She picked up a tall silver pot and poured tea for both of them. "I had no idea Lawthrop House would be so big," she paused to glance around the room, "or so in need of repairs."

"My mother let the house go after my father died. Now I'm afraid it will cost a great deal to fix it. Of course we'll have to let the new owner worry about it. I'm sure you aren't planning to stay months to see it completed."

"How sad to see it in such a state, though." She gazed around, imagining how beautiful it would be when it was redone. She almost wished she *could* stay.

Horace paused to sip his tea. "One thing I feel I must point out, Katherine, is that servants don't expect you to be friendly. They are here only to serve you, and if you try to befriend them, they soon forget their place."

"I can't be rude to them."

"There's a difference between rudeness and propriety. Remember, you are a Lawthrop, the mistress of this house. They will respect you only if you behave as such. And never forget that these people are not to be trusted. Now," he said, "as to the disposition of the property. If you wish, I will wire a listing agent in Dublin, an Englishman of my acquaintance, who will come out to appraise the estate for you."

"I thought Mr. Firth would handle that."

"He'll merely point you toward a listing agent anyway."

"Then please do. The sooner the better." Katherine's excitement about the prospects of building her orphanage didn't stop her from feeling a tiny pang of regret. She'd owned Ballyrourke for just over a month, and suddenly she had to think about selling it.

"Also, I shall contact the museum curator to let him know you might wish to donate some artifacts. In the meantime," he said, rising, "I'm sure you'll want to inspect the artwork to decide what, if any, you'd like to take back with you as a souvenir." He started out the door, and then looked back. "When did Firth say he would be here?"

"In two weeks."

"That long?" With a sharp sigh, Horace left.

Katherine sipped her tea and contemplated her uncle's words. Remember her place. Act like mistress of the house. Don't trust the servants. Easier said than done. She wasn't accustomed to treating people as though they were beneath her. It was, in fact, a foreign and unpleasant concept.

She let her gaze roam the beautiful room. What would she take home with her? She saw movement outside the window and went to look, spotting a gardener pruning shrubs in a rose garden. The sunshine and bright colors beckoned invitingly, and she went outside to investigate.

"How lovely," she said, peering over the old gardener's shoulder as he clipped a bush of apricot-colored roses.

He looked around with a start, then quickly rose and doffed a tweed cap. "Yes, miss, 'tis lovely indeed." He stood staring down at the ground, until Katherine realized he was waiting for permission to continue with his work.

"I'll just wander around a bit," she said awkwardly, backing away, "so you can get back to your clipping.

"Thank ye, miss," he said shyly.

Katherine meandered along the brick path toward the pond in the center, stopping to examine various roses, deciding that her favorite was a deep, deep red. As she bent to smell it, a bee came buzzing out. She jumped back with a gasp and hit a solid object directly behind her. To her surprise, the object turned out to be a man—a handsome, dark-haired man with vivid blue eyes and a smile that could charm the skin off an apple.

"Hello, beauty," he said.

Four

Beauty? Katherine glanced behind her to see who he was speaking to, and discovered with a jolt of surprise that it was her. She would have thought to blush if she hadn't been so astonished.

Gads, what a handsome man he was, with shoulders broad enough to stand on, and a waist as trim as any soldier's. And what regal bearing. He stood tall and proud, with back straight, arms folded and feet braced, making Katherine's heart beat at a rapid pace and show no signs of wanting to slow.

"Did that nasty bumbly bee frighten you?" he asked, speaking to her as if she were a child. Like a magician at a carnival he produced a knife, cut one of the stems, stripped the flower of its thorns, and handed it to her. "Here you go, beauty. Not a stinger on it."

Katherine grasped the stem gently and gave it a tug, but he didn't let go. Instead, he moved his fingers down to cover hers and stepped closer, surrounding her with his clean, earthy musk, a scent that made her slightly dizzy with excitement.

In a husky, lilting voice that sent shivers of pleasure racing each other to the tips of her toes, he said, "Take this to your mistress with compliments of Colin MacCormack." Then, with his gaze fixed on hers, he lifted her hand to his lips, flower still in her grasp, to press a lingering, feather-light kiss on the back of her knuckles.

Katherine's nerve endings quivered with exhilaration, sending tingles from her hand straight into the depths of her very being, causing her heart to gallop awkwardly in its frantic pace and making it difficult to breathe, let alone speak. She'd never had such an intoxicating experience.

Still holding her hand, he tilted his head to avoid her hat brim, then lowered his mouth toward hers, closing the space between their lips as though to kiss her. Wordlessly, she gazed back at him, deep into his eyes, caught in a spell of enchantment that drew her ever nearer his firm, handsome mouth.

Then, like a warning bell sounding in her head, his words sank in. She stepped back in confusion. "My *mistress*?"

Colin's eyebrows drew together as he studied her for a long moment. "Yes, lass, your mistress. Katie O'Rourke."

Katherine glanced down at her clothing. What was it about them that gave him the idea she was a servant? Her dress was rather plain, but in a crisp navy that she thought complemented her fair skin. Her hat wasn't in the latest fashion, either, but certainly wasn't servants' wear. However, she had forgotten her earbobs and her gloves, and she probably looked a bit wan from traveling.

But a servant? How presumptuous! To think she'd nearly let him kiss her. Why, for all this man knew, she could have been married. Had he inquired first? Absolutely not.

"Thank you for the rose, Mr. MacCormack," she said, and turned away.

Colin stood with hands on his hips, frowning as she strolled casually away from him along the path, bending to sniff flowers. She was a beauty indeed, and with such a lusciously inviting mouth that he wouldn't mind at all having a romp with her. But the poor thing seemed a bit lacking upstairs. "The rose is for Katie," he explained, striding after her, "Or Katherine, if you like that better."

She swung around, her blue-green eyes assessing him. "I

have it, Mr. MacCormack." She lifted the flower so he could see it.

"Yes, I see that, but—" He stopped as her words registered, the surprise of his discovery rendering his glib tongue silent. This very lovely, very Irish-looking lass, with her dark red hair; large, expressive eyes; round-tipped nose misted with fine freckles; and creamy skin, was the very English-bred Katherine O'Rourke. His sworn enemy.

"Was there something else you wished to say, Mr. Mac-Cormack?" she asked coolly.

Ha! There was the Lawthrop side of her—haughty and cold, just like the rest of them. Colin bowed formally, mockingly. "I hope you enjoy the flower." Setting his mouth in a firm line, he strode off toward the stables.

To think she'd aroused his passion so much that he'd already planned her seduction. *Toss out those plans with the wash water, boy-o,* he chided himself. *You'll not be needing them—ever.* He'd have to be daft to consort with a Lawthrop.

Katherine watched him from the corner of her eye, stewing over his presumptuous attitude even while her pulse still danced madly from his touch. She stroked the rose's velvety petals along her cheek, remembering the feel of his fingers on hers. Though she was ashamed to admit that an arrogant man could arouse such emotions in her, she'd experienced a heady excitement at being that close to such a specimen of virility.

Katherine leaned over to study her reflection in the pond's surface. She certainly didn't think she was beautiful, yet he had called her beauty. Had he merely been flirting? She had very little experience on which to base a judgment. In school, she'd never quite fit in with other girls—they with their giggling, silly behavior and her with a studious bent. Later, she'd seemed to frighten off any potential suitors, though she hadn't been sure why. Now, she was usually too absorbed in her charity efforts to care.

Holding the flower to her nose to inhale its fragrant perfume, Katherine started toward the house. She caught sight of Grainwe watching from inside a glassed-in porch at the rear of the house and lifted her hand in a wave, remembering afterward that she wasn't supposed to be friendly.

"Beggin' yer pardon, mistress," Grainwe said, dipping her large frame politely as Katherine approached, "yer uncle said ye'd be wantin' these right away." She held out a sheaf of paper and a thick graphite pencil.

Katherine accepted the writing tools with a smile. "Thank you, Grainwe. What is this room called?"

"This'd be the loggia, mistress. Yer grandfather had this and the whole back portion of the house added on about twenty years ago."

"And who is Colin MacCormack?" she asked, removing her hat.

"Colin? He's the land manager for Ballyrourke. Have ye seen him, then?"

"Yes, he was just here. He gave me this." She held up the rose, feeling a blush color her cheeks.

Grainwe clucked her tongue. "Ye'd best watch out for that laddie, mistress. He's always got an eye for a pretty lass."

First Colin had called her beauty, now Grainwe had said she was pretty. Katherine decided she'd better have another look at herself in the mirror. "I thought only O'Rourkes farmed the land at Ballyrourke."

"There's O'Rourkes, and there's the O'Rourke clan," Grainwe explained. "Colin's mother married an O'Rourke the first time around. After he died, she married the land manager James MacCormack and had three children by him, two boys and a girl. That'd be Kane and Colin, and the wee lass Rosaleen. Kane left Ballyrourke many years ago, and Rosaleen—" Grainwe shook her head sadly. "Rosaleen died the very day she turned eight, and her mother with her. So sad, it was."

She paused for a moment, her gaze far away, then quickly shook her head. "Don't mind me; I'm woolgatherin'. What you're wantin' to know is if the MacCormacks are part of the clan, and the answer is yes. Now, I'd better see about supper or we'll all pay for it. We'll serve at six o'clock if it pleases ye. It's what time yer grandmother preferred."

"That would be fine." Katherine had more questions about Colin, but she hesitated to ask them, fearing Grainwe would mistake simple curiosity for attraction.

With a frustrated sigh, she looked down at the writing tools in her hand. What she really wanted to do was to talk to someone who could answer questions about her parents. Perhaps she could take a quick survey of the house and be done with it.

Her plan was to begin with the back addition, starting from the loggia, and move clockwise. But at the very next room—a music room—she glanced out a window and spotted Colin astride a handsome roan, galloping up a winding sliver of road. For several long moments she stood spellbound, watching the pair race the wind, marveling at Colin's form, remembering his captivating gaze and arousing touch. Then she caught herself and turned away, vexed.

Next she found a room that contained a collection of gold artifacts—items that definitely would need appraising. She had taught herself quite a bit about oils, but she knew very little about other media. Unfortunately, the room also had a collection of mildew growing along the baseboard of the outer wall, no doubt due to a roof leak.

Following that was the last room in the addition, a large hall that looked very similar to the front entrance hall. This great room had French doors that opened out onto the other side of the house, where Katherine discovered a fountain of leaping dolphins in the center of a small pool, with stone benches encircling it.

She studied the fountain, wondering if there was significance to it, then decided she'd have someone give her a tour of the house to explain the names and purposes of the various rooms and garden areas. She briefly considered asking her uncle, then decided against it. His antagonistic feeling for the place would color any history he gave her.

She checked the watch pinned to her bodice and gasped. It was nearly time for dinner and she hadn't written a single item on her list. She returned to her room to freshen up, and found that her clothes had been unpacked and placed on hangers. She donned a dinner dress of green silk and stopped to check her appearance in the cheval glass.

"Ordinary," she said aloud, giving her cheeks a pinch for color. Certainly not beautiful. Not like the fair-haired girls with their smooth, unfreckled complexions, nor the dark-haired, dark-eyed girls with their golden skin tones, both of whom Katherine had always admired.

Her mother had been light-haired; Katherine didn't know about her father. The one daguerreotype she had of him was a miniature, faded to shades of gray. She'd found it hidden in the bottom drawer of her mother's chest. Her mother had been too bitter over his leaving ever to display it.

Katherine proceeded downstairs, where Grainwe was waiting to lead her to the dining room. "We've got a fine, fine feast for ye, mistress," she said. " 'Tis special is yer first supper at Ballyrourke."

As usual, her uncle had arrived before her and was tapping his fingers restlessly on the tabletop. He rose when she walked in, but her attention was diverted to the massive portraits hanging on walls opposite each other—one of a king, the other of a queen, both in heavy, gilded frames. She recognized them at once.

"Oh, my!" she said, examining the one closest to her. "This is King George the third, and the other is his wife Queen Caroline, painted by"—she squinted to see the signature in the corner—"Sir Joshua Reynolds. He was painter to the king. How exciting! I've never seen one up close. And this frame is probably by William Adair, but I won't know for sure until I take it down to see the back."

"I think that can wait for another day, Katherine."

With an embarrassed blush, she went to her chair. She had to remember that not everyone was as enthused about art as she was.

"Claret?" Horace asked. At her nod, he signaled a serving girl who poured the dark red wine into a crystal glass.

"To your first day at Lawthrop House," Horace said, lifting his glass in a toast.

Katherine thanked him and took a sip of the wine, savoring its rich oaken flavor, while a maid brought in bowls of clear soup. Her mother had loved fine wine, and in the last few years of her life she would buy a bottle for special occasions to instruct her daughter on the correct way to serve and drink it. She had always insisted Katherine learn how to comport herself like a lady. It was how a Lawthrop should behave.

"Like the room?" Horace asked.

She glanced at the ornately carved cove molding that encompassed the large room and heavy satin draperies at the tall windows, noting that the trim needed to be scraped of its peeling paint and the faded, dusty draperies replaced. The baseboards had rotted in the corners near the windows, too. Everywhere she looked, there was work to be done.

"My mother decorated it," he said dryly. "Lavish, isn't it?"

Katherine picked up her spoon and quietly ate her soup. She couldn't tell if her uncle was being complimentary or not. He showed so little emotion. But then her mother had been like that, too.

"How is your list coming along?" Horace asked.

"I haven't even begun. There's so much to see."

"I fear you will be overwhelmed with all your new responsibilities, Katherine. As I've said before, I can easily take care of all this for you, and you can be on your way home in a matter of days. You don't want to keep those orphans waiting, do you?"

Katherine felt suddenly ashamed. Still, she had come all this way to find answers, and she wasn't leaving without them.

"I appreciate your offer, Uncle, but now that I'm here, I'd like to find out more about my heritage. I'm going to see if I can find someone who will tell me about my parents."

Her uncle's features seemed to turn to stone, all but the pupils of his eyes, which shrank to pinpoints, almost as if in fear. But surely she was mistaken. The tone of his voice remained as monotonous as ever. "I doubt you'll have time."

She'd make time, that's all.

When they had finished their soup, the bowls were removed and platters of food were set before them. Katherine started to reach for the potatoes and was sharply rebuked by her uncle.

"Let the maid do that."

She dropped her hand to her lap and waited as she was served helpings from each bowl. She watched the servant do the same to her uncle, then blinked in surprise at the quick look of scorn on the serving girl's face as she cast a backward glance at him. Did they look at her like that, too?

As they finished their meal with cups of honeyed tea, Horace again commented on her idea. "I really think you shouldn't go digging up the past, Katherine. It will only serve to inflame the peasants."

"By peasants, do you mean my relatives?" she asked pointedly. "Why would it inflame them?"

"There were bitter feelings on both sides when your father and mother married. And I don't mean to insult you, but these people *are* peasants—farm laborers—who depend on us for their living. You must accustom yourself to the fact that there has always been and will always be resentment between peasant and landlord."

"Why do you refer to the Lawthrops as landlords when they owned Ballyrourke?"

"It's an old term. Ofttimes, owners preferred to live in England and merely act as landlords, renting out parcels of farmland to tenants, with a manager to oversee things. My father chose to live here and run it himself." Horace finished his tea. "Remember this canon, Katherine: Landlords and tenants should never fraternize. It upsets the balance of things."

Katherine didn't pursue the matter; she doubted if anything she said would change his mind, anyway. His haughtiness, however, dismayed her, reminding her very much of her mother's attitude toward the orphans. But surely her mother hadn't felt as Horace did about the O'Rourkes, or she wouldn't have married one.

"How long did my mother live here?"

"Perhaps eight years."

Eight years that her mother had never wanted to talk about. "Did she marry my father here?"

"They eloped, then left afterward for America. I really don't know much more about it." He finished his tea and rose. "It's been a long day, so I'll say good night."

"Good night, Uncle." She sat back in her chair and eyed the portrait of King George, with his arrogant expression and hard, almost unfeeling, gaze. It reminded her very much of Horace.

Five

Katherine yawned as she made her way up the broad staircase to her bedroom. Grainwe had turned down the bed for her and was fluffing her pillow when Katherine walked in.

"Did ye enjoy the meal, mistress?"

"It was delicious. My compliments to the chef."

The elderly woman cackled. "Molly will get a tickle from that, she will. No one's ever called her a chef before. Yer bath's ready, miss, and I've put out fresh linens for dryin'."

Katherine had to admit that having a bath drawn for her was truly a luxury she could get used to. She emerged from the bathing chamber a short while later and found Grainwe waiting patiently for her beside a dressing table.

"If ye'll sit down here, miss," she said, "I'll brush out yer hair as I used to yer grandmother's."

Feeling wickedly sinful at such indulgence, Katherine nevertheless obliged her by perching on an upholstered bench in front of the table. She watched in the mirror as Grainwe unpinned her hair and began stroking a brush through her long tresses, as though it was the most natural thing in the world for her to do.

"Such thick, healthy hair ye have. 'Tis O'Rourke hair, ye

know. Now yer grandmother, Lady Lawthrop, had hair the color of flax and as *foin* as satin."

Katherine closed her eyes as the brush's soft strokes lulled her. "Tell me about my grandmother, Grainwe."

"Well, I'd have to say Lady Lawthrop was a proud woman, a just employer, and as honest as they come. She loved her family and she loved this house. It was her fondest wish that her family live in it with her, but that wasn't to be. Fair broke her heart when yer mother left. Her ladyship would have gone to fetch her back, but yer grandfather, his lordship, wouldn't hear of it. Now he was a stubborn, cold man if ever there was one, beggin' yer pardon for sayin' so. When he died last year, how her ladyship did search for ye and yer mother. Wasn't it merciful that death took her away before she could learn her only daughter had passed afore she did."

"My grandmother knew about me?"

"That she did, miss. She'd get an occasional letter from yer mother, and we'd hear news of ye now and then from friends who'd traveled to America. Yer poor grandmother lived for those bits of news. But then they stopped." With a heavy sigh, Grainwe shook her head. "'Twas as if you'd dropped off the face of the earth."

"When was this?"

"About a year or so after ye lost yer father."

Grainwe did not mention *how* she'd lost her father, Katherine noted. Clearly she was too kindhearted to say that he'd walked out on them. Besides, she was an O'Rourke, too, and wouldn't want to speak ill of a relative.

But Grainwe's information raised another question. Katherine could understand why her mother would have stopped corresponding with her father's family after he abandoned her, but why with her own?

"Had there been a rift between my mother and my grandmother?"

"I wouldn't know, miss."

"Was my grandmother close to anyone here? Someone to whom I could direct my questions?"

"Other than some of her neighbors—Lady Tarkinton

comes to mind—I can't say. I know she took tea with the lady quite often. What I can say is that yer grandmother would be very pleased to know ye'd come back; she wanted ye to live here. 'Tis yer rightful place. Ye belong here."

Katherine shifted her gaze away guiltily as Grainwe put down the brush. "I'll say good night now, mistress, unless there's anything else."

There was so much more Katherine wanted to ask, but she could see the weariness on the old servant's face. "Thank you, I'm fine."

As Grainwe quietly let herself out and shut the door, Katherine went to one of the open windows to gaze up at the heavens. The sky was dark with clouds and a misty wind blew into the room, bringing with it the scent of roses. Had her grandmother sat at this window at night, wondering what had happened to her daughter and granddaughter?

"She loved her family and she loved this house. Fair broke her heart when yer mother left," Grainwe had said. *"How her ladyship did search for you and yer mother."*

What would have made her mother turn her back on a woman who loved her that much?

Katherine woke in the morning refreshed and ready to tackle her list. Her plan was to be finished by noon, then hopefully have a meeting with Lady Tarkinton afterward. She breakfasted alone—her uncle had not yet risen—then gathered her pencil and paper and went to her task.

Working in her usual systematic way, she started clock-wise with the first room on the left, a large, formal drawing room decorated in a Victorian style. Each room, she found, had a unique style, but what fascinated her most were the oil paintings.

"Mistress," a maid called from the doorway, "would ye care for yer mornin' tea now?"

"Yes, thank you, I would. Has my uncle come down yet?"

"No, miss. I haven't seen him. Would ye like yer tea in the mornin' parlor, as her ladyship always did?"

"Yes, thank you." Where was her uncle? She'd hoped he

would set up the introduction to Lady Tarkinton for her. She put down her pencil and paper and turned to follow the maid to the morning parlor, only to find the servant had gone. Now how was she to find the parlor?

Katherine decided the most likely place to find the maid would be the kitchen. But where was the kitchen? She stood in the hallway and sniffed, then followed the aroma of roasting meat down the hall to an enormous room filled with three gigantic black cooking stoves manned by three hardworking cooks, four worktables, a wall of open fronted cabinets, racks of pots and pans, and meaty aromas that hinted of a scrumptious luncheon to come.

On the far wall she spotted a door that opened to the side of the house near the rose garden. Standing at the door was Doreen, talking to none other than Colin MacCormack.

Katherine felt her heart lurch at the sight of him, which, once she got her breath back, instantly annoyed her. Colin was nothing more than a presumptuous, arrogant rake. Why on earth would his presence cause such a strong reaction?

The young maid who had come to fetch Katherine cleared her throat loudly, causing both Colin and Doreen to glance her way. Doreen gave a gasp of surprise, grabbed a basket of linens and sat herself down at the nearest table to fold them, while Colin stood there as bold as brass, looking for all the world as if he owned the place.

Poor Doreen. Her face was pink with embarrassment, and her hands shook slightly as she worked. Katherine could hardly blame the girl for being attracted to someone with Colin's masculine appeal when her own heart had surged at the sight of him.

"Good mornin', Miss O'Rourke," Colin said, bowing with exaggerated formality.

"Is there something I can do for you, Mr. MacCormack?" she asked, displaying a coolness she didn't feel inside.

"I always stop by of a morning to see if there's any special task to be done."

"I see." Katherine clasped her hands behind her and gazed down at the floor, wondering what to say next, unwilling, for some odd reason, to let him go. "Well, in that case, I have some questions about the gardens. Perhaps you can answer them for me."

"I'm always at your service," Colin replied, his words contradicting the defiant flicker in his blue eyes.

Noticing that the kitchen had suddenly gone quiet, Katherine turned to find the servants working industrially at their jobs. Although none of them looked at her, she was sure they were listening with great interest.

Remembering her uncle's advice, she straightened her shoulders and assumed the mantle of mistress. "Shall we continue this conversation in the garden, Mr. MacCormack?" To the maid she said," I'll have my tea when I return. Would you bring my hat to me, please?" and closed the door behind her.

Colin watched in bemused silence as Katie, as he preferred to think of her, showed off her uppity manners, even stopping to put on a hat, as if she were going to church instead of taking a walk in the park. He was surprised she hadn't asked for her gloves, as well.

'Twas a pity she was so cold and formal about things, for her Irish features bespoke a warm nature. Her coldness wouldn't stop him from turning on the charm, however. He needed to be on her good side. A little insurance for his plan.

"Well, then," Katie said, and gazed up at him as though waiting for something. He suddenly realized she expected him to offer his arm. Reluctantly, he did, though he'd much rather have strode off ahead of her and kept distance between them.

With her arm tucked in his, Colin was too aware of the suppleness of her flesh, the soft, powdery scent of her skin, and the way her pretty mouth moved when she spoke. Had she been the simple maid he'd first thought her to be, their little stroll through the flowers would be one she'd talk about dreamy-eyed for a long time to come.

"Do you know much about the gardens?" she asked.

" 'Tis my job to know. We'll start with the rose garden." He led the way along a flagstone path, trying to keep his mind to the subject of flora, and away from fauna of the female variety. "So you're a gardener, are you, Miss O'Rourke?"

"Unfortunately, no. There's only enough yard behind my house to grow a few petunias. I've studied art, however, and have even worked as an assistant to an art historian at a museum in Chicago."

"Assistant art historian," he mused, rubbing his chin thoughtfully. "Dealing in paintings and the like." That wasn't good news to Colin's ears. He hoped she hadn't come across that stash of oil paintings in the attic. He'd have to clear them out soon, in case he didn't find the will. If *she* found the paintings first, she'd surely claim them as hers.

"I hear 'tis a big place, is Chicago," he said, to change the subject. "Full of people in fancy dress, and carriages fit for kings."

Katie gave him a smile that lit her face and brightened her eyes. "I'm afraid you've heard some exaggerations, Mr. MacCormack. The majority are hard workers who live quite modestly."

'Twas a true Irish smile, he decided, and not at all what he wanted to see. It would be harder to do what he had to do if he thought of her as a genuine O'Rourke.

"Watch your step now," he said, leading her down five stone steps to the path that encircled the oval-shaped area. "This particular style of garden is called a parterre. It was laid out in the seventeenth century as a copy of a garden designed by the Earl of Bantry.

"The shape is similar to a concert hall," he continued, "and the roses are set out in beds of various sizes to fit the curves."

"Yes, I see. Like balconies overlooking a center stage." Katie let go of his arm to stoop beside a bush of deep crimson roses and inhale their fragrance. "This is my favorite," she told him, bending to pick up a petal that had fallen to the ground.

"It's called royal prince."

She gazed up at him in amazement. "You know all the roses by name?"

"Not all," he answered. A slight exaggeration, since he

knew just the one, and that one because it was his favorite, too. But he didn't want her thinkin' he was soft.

Colin watched with rapt attention as Katie lifted the petal to her nose to inhale its perfume. A blissful smile appeared on her face as she closed her eyes and rubbed it against her cheek. Her actions were so sensuous that he had to glance away, not wanting to admit how they made him hunger for her.

"Was the garden planted here so that it would be under the bedroom windows?" Katie asked, breaking into his musings.

Collect yer wits, boy-o. 'Tis a dangerous path you're on, having such lusty thoughts about yer enemy.

"It's a possibility," he replied, dragging his mind back to the subject, "although I think it had more to do with the view from the drawing room and parlors. The loggia was added on this side to take advantage of the view."

She rose, the petal lying softly in her open palm, a palm he suddenly had the strongest urge to kiss. "I understand my grandfather had the back addition built about twenty years ago."

Colin's fantasy dissolved, his good mood replaced by irritation. Any mention of what the Lawthrops had done to the house made his blood boil. "Did you want to have a look at the dolphin fountain, then?"

He led her around to the opposite side of the house, where three leaping dolphins sprayed water into a circular pool. Katie sat on the stone bench that encircled pool, turning so she could see both the fountain and Colin.

"Your grandmother had this sculpture shipped from Italy," he told her, propping one foot on the bench. "If you look toward the house, those French doors there are where her fancy grand hall is, where her ladyship entertained. The fountain can be seen from inside."

"Did she entertain often?"

"Fairly often until your grandfather died, then she kept to herself, for the most part."

"The outside of the house is beautifully maintained."

" 'Tis my responsibility. I take pride in its beauty."

Katie gazed down at the water as she trailed a fingertip through it. She seemed to be pondering something, but Colin didn't much care about that. The way her lips formed a pout when she was thinking was much more interesting.

Katie tilted her head to gaze up at him. "Did you know my parents?"

"I was only a boy when they left Ireland. I have just a bit of a memory of them, mostly of your father. He was a legend to us lads—brave, strong, and never one to shy away from danger. That's about it, I'm afraid."

"A legend?" she asked, her face mirroring her disbelief. "*My* father?"

"Why do you find that odd?"

Those lovely lips from which he couldn't draw his gaze turned downward. "Because that's not how I would describe him."

"And just how *would* you describe him?"

"Certainly not in complimentary terms." She shook the water off her fingers, as though suddenly annoyed. "Is there anyone around who *would* remember them?"

Colin puzzled over her strange remark. Other than his foolish choice of marrying a Lawthrop, Garrett O'Rourke was a hero in his eyes. How could she think less of him? "Eileen would be the one to ask, I suppose. She's your aunt, married to your father's brother, Patrick."

"My aunt," she said, as though amazed to learn she had one. "How do I find her?"

"I can take you to her."

"I'd like that very much. Perhaps later this afternoon, if you have the time."

Colin hesitated, oddly torn between wanting to please her and needing to move forward with his plan. He had decided to work straight through the day to finish his duties early so he could meet with his friends that evening. "Tomorrow afternoon would be better."

"All right, then, let's say tomorrow just after lunch."

The way Katie was looking up at him, with her skin glowing and her eyes sparkling, he wanted her so badly he felt his manhood begin to harden. But he had only to glance over at the addition to the house to remind himself of who she was.

"Now, about this particular fountain . . ."

Katherine couldn't stop watching Colin as he continued to talk. What solid, masculine features he had. His face was clean-shaven, yet she could see a faint shadow where his beard would be. And such thick, glossy dark hair. She had the oddest urge to comb her fingers through it, to stroke her hand along that hard jawline and feel the stubble of his beard.

Katherine felt herself blush as Colin sat down and peered at her, his face so close she could see her reflection in the deep blue of his eyes. "What were you thinking just now, Mistress Katie O'Rourke?"

Thinking? Why, she'd rather die a horrible death than tell him she was admiring his looks. That wouldn't be proper behavior at all. She gave him a quick, sidelong glance. "Only that my grandmother did a fine job with her gardens."

A surprising look of irritation flashed across his handsome features. "*Her* gardens, you say. Did you know that, with the exception of this fountain and the addition, the gardens and parks and even the house were built by O'Rourkes a long time before the Lawthrops were here? And did you know, too, that this was O'Rourke land for over seven hundred years before the Lawthrops came? And that all the old treasures in the house belonged to the O'Rourkes, as well?"

Katherine pressed her lips together to prevent herself from retorting that it was the Lawthrops who had kept the house and all those treasures from being sold to pay off the debts. But her mother's etiquette lessons won out, though at great cost to her sense of justice.

A male voice called sharply, "Katherine, what are you doing?"

Startled, she glanced over at the loggia, where her uncle stood glowering. She looked back at Colin, shocked to see pure loathing reflected in his eyes.

Sensing a conflict, she answered quickly, "I had questions about the gardens, and I asked Mr. MacCormack to answer them. Have you met Mr. MacCormack yet?"

"He knows me," Colin said through clenched teeth, getting to his feet.

"I need to speak with you at once, Katherine," Horace called.

Her uncle's rudeness not only rankled her, but most certainly insulted Colin. "I'll be in when we're finished," she replied firmly.

"Never mind," Colin told her, his eyes turning an icy blue. "We're finished now."

Six

Katherine watched Colin stride off, then she turned and marched toward her uncle and said in a tone that surprised her for its rancor, "Your rudeness was uncalled for."

"Come inside, Katherine, and let's have a talk."

She sat down on a black wrought-iron chair in the loggia and folded her arms. She was inches from letting loose with a torrent of anger, which was very unlike her. She had never lost her temper in her life.

Horace crossed his arms and peered down at her over his nose. "I realize this is your house now, Katherine, and that you may do as you see fit, but I would be remiss in my duty if I didn't warn you to stay away from that man."

"Why?"

"I fear for your safety. He has a violent streak in him and should not be trusted."

A violent streak? Katherine nearly scoffed out loud. "Mr. MacCormack has no reason to hurt me."

"Ah, but he believes he has every reason to hurt me, and therefore you are also at risk. To put it frankly, he would very much like to see me dead."

"For what reason?"

"Mr. MacCormack blames me for his mother's and sister's deaths."

Katherine's eyes widened in surprise. Grainwe had mentioned their deaths, but hadn't connected Horace to them.

"I suppose back then, to his childish mind, he thought he had just cause to hate me," Horace explained. "It was my unfortunate job to inform the peasants of their evictions, his family included. But I was merely following my father's orders. What else could I have done?"

"When was this?"

"Fifteen years ago, perhaps."

"Why were they evicted?"

"They couldn't pay their rent; so you see, we really had no choice. An estate needs money coming in to pay expenses. I suppose being so young I wasn't as patient as an older, more experienced person would have been. But I had no control over their finances. I was very sorry to hear of the deaths, but I didn't cause them. To carry that hatred all these years is the sign of a disturbed man."

Katherine could understand how someone of Colin's presumptuous nature might blame the handiest authority. After all, he'd suffered a tragic loss. But her uncle was right; carrying that bitterness for so long was not healthy. "I'm sorry. I didn't know the full story. However, I wish you could have been more tactful. Mr. MacCormack was here at my invitation."

"His kind doesn't understand tact, Katherine."

His kind. The peasants. With that attitude, it was no wonder the O'Rourkes disliked her uncle.

Horace patted her hand. "Please do remember my warning. I'd hate to see you hurt."

She would remember his warning all right, but she would not let it deter her from finding answers, no matter what their source. "Uncle, how would I go about meeting Lady Tarkinton?"

"Why do you want to meet her?"

Katherine was hesitant to tell him, remembering his previous reaction to her quest for information. "She was a friend of my grandmother's, wasn't she? I thought it would be courteous to have her over for tea."

"That's a splendid idea, Katherine. The Tarkintons were indeed friends of my parents." He tapped a long finger against his nose. "In fact, we should invite several neighbors over and let the word get out that the estate is for sale. I'll send cards of introduction around this afternoon."

Her uncle started for the door, then paused long enough to say, "Oh, yes, I nearly forgot. Edward Calloway, the listing agent I mentioned earlier, wired to say he will be here to meet with you tomorrow after lunch."

After lunch? That was when she'd asked Colin to take her to meet her aunt and uncle. Katherine hurried through the addition and down the long marble hallway, looking for Grainwe. She had to get word to Colin so he could arrange another meeting time.

"Grainwe, how do I find Mr. MacCormack?" Katherine asked, poking her head into the formal drawing room.

The elderly woman kept her eye on her work as she dusted a fragile glass sculpture. "No tellin' where he'd be, lass. His duties take him all around."

"He promised to take me to meet one of my relatives tomorrow, and now I must cancel."

"I'll send one of the help to tell him, if ye'd like."

"Thank you. Let him know I'd like to go another time, as soon as possible."

"I can have someone else take ye," Grainwe offered.

Katherine pondered how to reply. The truth was, she didn't want anyone else to take her. "There's no need. Mr. MacCormack has already offered."

At that Grainwe stopped dusting and turned to gaze at her with eyes full of doubt. "Are ye sure ye know what yer doin', lass?"

First her uncle, now Grainwe? "I don't fear for my well-being, if that's what you mean."

"There's all different ways to be hurt. Remember this: Colin is not above breaking hearts or laws to get what he wants."

"What is it he wants?"

"Ye'd better ask him that yerself."

Grainwe's words haunted Katherine all afternoon. She'd now been warned twice about Colin, yet she still didn't believe he would harm her. Could both her uncle and Grainwe be wrong?

Horace left the loggia in high temper, though he was confident no one would ever guess. He prided himself in his unfailingly composed demeanor. It was a Lawthrop hallmark, a symbol of their superiority. Katherine had come dangerously close to losing hers with her little fit of pique, and he knew exactly the reason why: Colin MacCormack.

He had to keep Katherine away from the blackguard, and for a much more important reason than maintaining her disposition. MacCormack was a threat to his objective, just as Katherine's father had been. Now that he thought about it, MacCormack seemed almost the embodiment of Garrett O'Rourke.

And if MacCormack wasn't careful, he'd meet the same ends.

After an enormous dinner of roasted rabbit, boiled potatoes, soda bread, carrots, raspberries, whortleberries and cheesecake, Katherine decided a little exercise would be in order, and went out to investigate the park in front of the house. She strolled along paths of flowers and flowering shrubs the likes of which she'd never seen before, and found herself wishing Colin were there to answer more questions.

At the far side of the park were steps that led up to a gate in the stone wall. Katherine tried the latch, which was stiff with disuse, and finally got it to open. She stepped out onto the road that ran past the house, Kilwick Road, she thought it was called, where a low, stone wall ran along both sides for as far as she could see. Up the road a little ways was a stand of trees, and sitting on top of the wall beneath a spreading tree branch was a little girl playing with a calico cat.

"Evenin' to ye, miss," the little girl called.

Katherine walked up the road to meet her. "Evening to you."

She appeared to be around eight years old, with raven-colored hair, ivory skin, and eyes so pale blue they were nearly clear. She dangled a slender twig in front of the cat, who jumped and leaped at it.

"What a beautiful cat," Katherine remarked.

"Her name is Cali, for the calico she is, ye see."

"How clever." Katherine bent to pet the animal, who sniffed her palm, then rubbed her cheek against it. "Do you live around here?" she asked the girl.

"Down the road a way. You're Katie O'Rourke, aren't you?"

"Yes. Katherine, actually."

The child studied her through those strange light eyes. "Ye look more like a Katie."

"Then you may call me Katie. What's your name?"

"I'm called Gersha." She gave Katherine a long, scrutinizing stare. "Do ye like cats?"

"Very much. I had one a long time ago."

"See, Cali? Didn't I tell ye?" Gersha asked, turning her attention back to the cat. "Will ye live here, then, Katie? At Ballyrourke, I mean."

"I live in America."

"Nowhere's as pretty as here," Gersha declared.

"I think you may be right."

"You feel it, too, don't you?"

"Feel what?"

"The spirit of the place, of Ballyrourke. You'll not say you've never felt it, Katie. 'Tis in yer blood."

It was an oddly adult remark coming from such a young child. Katherine looked back at the house, now rapidly fading in the growing dusk, and remembered the strong feelings she'd had when she'd first seen it. She rubbed her arms, shaken by a sudden chill. "I should go back now, before my uncle thinks I've gotten lost."

"He'll not worry about ye," Gersha said, drawing the twig along the top of the wall so the cat would spring at it.

"He shouldn't, should he? After all, I'm a grown woman.

But your parents might worry about you, so I'll say good night now and let you run on home."

"Will ye come back again?"

"Of course."

"Hear that, Cali? She'll be back to see us."

Katherine left Gersha playing with the cat and hurried back to the house, where lamps had already been lit. For some reason, she couldn't get the little girl's words out of her mind. *"You feel it, too, don't you?"*

There was no such thing as a "spirit of the place," she assured herself as she let herself in the big front door. It was just a child's fancy.

She found her uncle in the library reading a book. "I'm back," she said. He gave her a blank look, as though he had no idea she'd been out. It appeared Gersha had been right after all.

Colin sat with his two friends at Teach O Malleys, the pub where the locals met when their work was done and they had a bit of coin left over. The pub had windows in the front, but the back was dark and cozy, with chairs and round tables of heavy, dark pine.

It was a place of solace for Colin, who'd been in a stew ever since facing off with Horace Lawthrop, or Ratty, as he and his friends had dubbed him. A strong gut feeling told Colin the man was up to no good, and that boded ill for the O'Rourkes.

"As soon as I saw his ugly face, I felt the urgency," Colin told his longtime friends Kevin Dowling and Michael O'Malley, son of the pub's owner. "He can't be happy his niece got the land, can he? According to Doreen, he's got a listing agent coming round tomorrow to give an appraisal. I've a powerful suspicion that the agent is in cahoots with him. Ratty will find a way to get his filthy hands on the estate somehow."

"What will happen to his niece if he does?" the soft-spoken Kevin asked.

For a moment, Colin envisioned Katie innocently trailing

her fingers through the water, her lips forming an inviting pout, and an oddly protective feeling rose up inside him.

She's a Lawthrop, and not your problem, boy-o. You've got enough troubles without adding hers to the stack.

"She'll go back to her fancy home in America and leave us to deal with the devil."

"She's selling Ballyrourke, then," Michael said, shaking his head of brown curls. " 'Tis a shame."

"Not if I can find the new will," Colin replied." I have to get inside to search for it, there's no doubt of that. But just in case it's only a rumor, we've got to move those paintings from the attic."

"And put them where?" Michael asked.

Colin sipped his pint slowly, his mind working hard. "The old monk's tower."

"And cart them all the way up the ladder?" Michael cried.

"Will you keep your voice down?" Colin whispered, as several heads turned in their direction. "I'll take them up myself to the first floor. Once they're all inside, I can move them higher as needed. I'll get a key to Lawthrop House from Doreen; she's got a soft spot for me. Let's meet at midnight tomorrow at the tower and go from there."

Kevin, ever the nervous one, leaned close to whisper, "What if we're caught in the house?"

"I'll bring the paintings down myself and hand them off to you one by one. If someone sees me, aren't I only leavin' after a midnight visit to Doreen's room?"

"I don't know," Kevin said, shaking his head doubtfully. "It feels like criminal work, to me."

"Is it criminal to walk into your own house to claim your own possessions?" Colin asked. "Those paintings belonged to the O'Rourkes long before the Lawthrops arrived, boy-o. What's criminal is that the Lawthrops think *they* own them. And what do you make of Lady Lawthrop writing a will giving it all back, heh? She felt guilty, is what."

"He's right, Kev. There's no crime in taking your own paintings." Michael lifted his pint of Guinness. "To tomorrow night then, boys. May the ten toes of our feet steer us clear of misfortune."

"Sláinte," they said in unison, clinking their mugs together.

Seven

"*Have a good* stroll, did ye?" Grainwe asked as she turned down the covers on Katherine's bed.

"Yes. The park in front is lovely." Katherine sat at the dressing table and unpinned her hair, still musing over her encounter with Gersha. "I met a neighbor down the road this evening, a little girl about eight years old."

Grainwe fluffed the pillows, then came over to brush Katherine's hair. "Must have been young Meaghan, though 'tis a far piece for her to be over this way."

"She said her name was Gersha."

"*Girseach,* ye say?"

"Yes. She had long black hair and pale blue eyes."

Grainwe's hand stilled and an odd expression flashed briefly in her eyes. For a moment she said nothing, then she began brushing again. "Ye must have heard wrong. *Girseach* simply means 'little girl'."

"I'm sure that's what she said."

"The only young girl of that age living near here is Meaghan. I'd say someone was havin' a bit of *craic*—a joke, as ye say. The Irish are well known for that." Grainwe put down the brush and patted Katherine's shoulder. "Yer bath is all prepared, so I'll say good night, unless there's anything else ye'd be wantin'."

"I'm fine. Thank you, Grainwe."

As soon as the servant had gone, Katherine undressed and stepped into the deep tub, sinking down with a contented sigh into the warm, soothing water. She let her thoughts wander as she soaked, and found herself coming back to Grainwe's odd expression at the mention of the little girl. What was it that had surprised her?

She toweled off, slipped on her nightdress and was about to climb into bed when a soft mewling at the open window caught her attention. She turned around and saw a cat's white face peering in at her. A moment later, the calico stepped inside.

"Cali! Good heavens. What are you doing here?"

The cat jumped down from the window and came straight toward her. Katherine knelt down to stroke her soft fur. "Did you follow me home? I'll bet you climbed a tree to get on the roof, didn't you? You're lucky the window was open."

Cali eyed the bed, then sprang onto it and curled up as though she belonged there.

"No you don't. Out you go." Katherine started to pick her up, but the cat merely licked her fingers, then gazed up at her imploringly with big golden eyes. Katherine scratched her under the chin, conceding the fight. "All right. You may stay the night, if you like, but tomorrow morning it's home you go."

The calico purred contentedly.

Early the next morning, Colin headed for the big house to find Doreen. He'd already decided he wouldn't tell her the whole purpose of wanting a key. The less she knew, the safer she'd be if she were ever questioned about it.

He came around the side by the rose garden and saw her following behind the gardener, a flat basket over her arm, as the worker cut flowers for the hall and dining room.

"Ah, Doreen, I almost missed you, blending in as you do with the other beauties in the garden."

The maid giggled. "Colin, you silver-tongued eejit. What are you up to?"

He led her away from the gardener. "I want to find the old lady's will, but I need a key so I can slip in the house during the night and hunt for it."

Her mouth fell open. "Colin, I would lose my job if they found out I gave you a key!" She peered around to see if anyone were watching from the house. "I shouldn't be gabbing here with you now."

"And how will anyone find out unless you tell? Will they not think I have a key myself, being the manager and all?"

"Grainwe knows better, Colin."

"Do you want to keep slaving for the Lawthrops all your life, Doreen? Don't you see the injustice of working for them, when by rights the land is ours?"

The young woman gazed up at him with lips pursed, then sighed sharply. "All right, I'll give you my key. But swear on all that's holy, Colin, that you won't tell where you got it."

He made a cross on his shirt. "I swear."

Doreen took two keys off her ring and slipped them to him. "One is for the kitchen door and one is for the attic, where they've put Lady Lawthrop's belongings. And have a care for that attic key, Colin. Grainwe doesn't know I have it."

"You're a true sweetheart, Doreen."

"You know," she said quietly, peering around again, "you could always ask Mary Flynn where the will is."

"I thought she eloped with Danny."

"She had a change of heart before she said her 'I do's.' Seems Danny boy had promised more girls than Mary that he wanted to get wed. Now she's taken a position at the Tarkintons."

"I'll look her up, then. Thanks, Doreen."

"And what do I get in return?" Doreen asked saucily.

He wiggled a dark eyebrow. "One of Colin MacCormack's famous kisses, perhaps?"

* * *

After a light breakfast of oatmeal stirabout with warm milk and honey, which Katherine shared with Cali, she put on her navy straw hat and white gloves, gathered the cat in her arms and headed for the front door. In the entrance hall she met Doreen, who was arranging roses in a crystal vase.

"Good morning," she said cheerily.

The young maid's cheeks instantly blazed with color. She averted her gaze as she mumbled a reply, bobbed politely, and hurried back toward the kitchen. Probably still feeling guilty about her kitchen meeting with Colin, Katherine decided.

As she carried the cat up the drive toward the road, her thoughts returned to the strong warning her uncle had given her about Colin. After a night of contemplation, she had decided her uncle was simply being overly cautious, as was Grainwe. While Colin may be harboring old feelings of anger, it was absurd to believe he was out for Horace's blood, or hers either, for that matter.

"Good morning," she heard a deep male voice call from behind.

Katherine turned as Colin himself strode toward her, looking as strikingly masculine as ever and, while not exactly menacing, still thrillingly dangerous. She could mentally brace herself to resist his charm, but she seemed powerless to control her physical response. Did her pulse have to leap and her heart boom like a cannon every time she saw him?

She shifted the cat to her shoulder and smiled up at Colin. "Good morning to you."

He stood before her, the sun at his back, forming a bright halo of light around his head. "You sent me a message about this afternoon."

Even with her broad brimmed straw hat, she had to squint to see his face in the bright sunlight. "Yes, I did. I can't go with you to see Eileen today. Might we go tomorrow instead? I'm extremely eager to meet her."

"I'll have to see about that. I'll get word to you later."

Katherine's happy mood dimmed. He certainly didn't seem as eager to go with her today as he had the day before.

Colin nodded toward the cat on her shoulder. "Are you collecting animals now?"

"This is Cali," she told him, shifting the wiggling cat back to her arms. "She came in my window last night. I'm taking her back to her owner. Perhaps you know her—a young girl about eight years old. She said her name was Gersha."

Colin ran his strong hand gently over the cat's head. "Sounds like someone was having a *craic* at your expense. *Girseach* isn't a name, but a description."

Katherine watched him stroke the cat's fur, gentle, rhythmic motions made by a masculine hand. A quick image blazed in her mind: Colin running that capable hand along her shoulder, down under her breasts, brushing across her nipples, then continuing down over her stomach to her thigh. She shuddered as a wave of desire swept through her, followed by a cold flash of shock. Where had that thought come from?

She glanced up and was aghast to find Colin studying her, a canny look in his blue eyes, almost as if he could read her thoughts. With her cheeks on fire, Katherine said hurriedly, "Grainwe said it was probably Meaghan."

"Bright red hair?" Colin asked.

"Black hair, with light blue eyes."

"There's no one around here like that. Perhaps from a neighboring village."

"There has to be someone around like that. She said she lives down the road. And she knows my name."

"'Twas a fairy, is all." Colin took the animal from her. "I'll find out where the cat belongs."

"She was not a fairy!" Katherine retorted as he strode away. There was no such thing as fairies. She had seen the little girl with her own two eyes. It was Colin having a bit of *craic* with her, she suspected.

Colin strode back toward the stables, shaking his head in wonder. Here he thought Katie had been on her way to church, dressed in her fancy hat and matching gloves. And she'd only been returning a cat!

He cradled the animal in one arm and scratched her behind the ears. "You look too well fed to belong to a fairy," he said. Spotting the stable boy at the far end of the long, stone building, he called out to him, "Do you know whose cat this is, Tommy?"

"I've seen it around, but I can't say whose it is."

The cat struggled to get down, so Colin set her on the ground and she scampered away. "I suppose she'll find her way home."

Colin glanced up the drive toward the road, but Katie had gone back to the house. He had to laugh, remembering how silly she'd looked wearing those gloves and hat just to take a cat home. If it weren't for those lovely eyes and that sweet mouth of hers, not to mention those voluptuous curves, he wouldn't be thinking of Katie at all, other than how she could further his plan.

But that was the problem, wasn't it? He *was* thinking of her, in ways that kept him dousing his head with water to cool off his lusty thoughts, when he had more important things of which to be thinking.

He slipped the keys Doreen had given him from his pocket and kissed them. "Thank you, Doreen," he said aloud. He now had two good chances of finding that will.

Katherine spent the rest of the morning exploring the long gallery and the spacious walnut-paneled library, whose shelves held well over five hundred volumes. She stopped midmorning to have tea in the morning parlor, a cozy, sunlit room decorated with faded floral prints and mint green walls, and had just poured herself a cup when her uncle strode in.

"We received this invitation today," he told her, handing her a beautifully scripted card. "It's from Lord and Lady Tarkinton. They're holding a ball this Saturday evening and would like for us to be their guests of honor. It will be the perfect venue to spread word about selling the estate."

"This Saturday?" Katherine looked up in surprise. "That's in three days. Why so soon?"

"I mentioned that we would be leaving shortly. There really wasn't any better time."

"Heavens," she said in dismay. "I have nothing to wear."

"The maids will help you find something. My mother had ball gowns." Horace pulled out a chair and sat across from her at one of the elegant tea tables situated beneath the tall windows. "How is the list coming?"

"I'm still reviewing everything."

"Tempus fugit, Katherine."

She sighed. "Yes, I know: time *is* flying."

"Have you thought about what you'll do with the money once everything is sold?"

"Of course. Build the orphanage."

"It's not that simple, I'm afraid." Horace folded his hands on the tabletop. "The money will need to be invested; you won't pay it all out at once. You might consider letting me handle it for you. I'm quite skilled in that area. I oversaw the finances here for many years."

"That's good to know."

He gazed at her for a long moment, as though waiting for her to agree to his suggestion on the spot. But Katherine never made decisions that weren't researched and well thought out, especially financial ones.

"Well, then," he said, "I shall leave you to your tea. Don't forget that Calloway will be here at two o'clock."

"Uncle," she called as he started for the door. "Why don't you ever venture outside to see the grounds?"

"I'm too busy. I'll see you at noon."

Katherine sipped her tea, remembering what he'd said about the O'Rourkes hating him. Was he busy, or fearful?

She was roused from her pondering by Doreen, who was still behaving sheepishly. "Would you like another pot of tea, miss?"

"No, thank you. This is sufficient. And Doreen, about your meeting with Mr. MacCormack . . ."

The girl froze, her features turning ashen. "My m-meeting?"

"Yes, in the kitchen yesterday. I can see you're still embarrassed by it, but please don't be. I know it was harmless."

The maid's color returned. "Thank you, miss."

"Do you know if my grandmother's clothing is still in the house?"

"I believe so, miss. I'll ask Grainwe, if ye like."

"Yes, please do. I need a ball gown for Saturday night."

"Ooooh! I know just the one that would suit yer coloring. It's in the attic," she said, reaching for her keys. She stopped suddenly, a startled expression crossing her face, then said, "I'll have the gown here for ye just after lunch," and darted away.

When Katherine returned to her room after the midday meal, she found a whole row of formal gowns in her closet. With Doreen on hand to help her, she went through them, weighing the merits of each one.

"Oh, miss! Look at this one. Brand new, it is." Doreen held up an ivory satin gown decorated with lace and pearls. "Will ye try it on?"

"Isn't it rather elaborate for a country ball?"

"Sure it is, miss, but wouldn't ye just like to see how it looks? 'Twas to be yer mother's wedding dress."

Katherine fingered the fine satin. Her mother's wedding gown. But of course she hadn't used it since she had eloped.

Ten minutes later, she examined her reflection in the mirrored wall of the dressing room as Doreen fastened the long row of tiny pearl buttons down the back.

"There now!" Doreen said, stepping back with a happy sigh. "Isn't that a fair sight?"

The ivory dress was the most elegant Katherine had ever seen, but there was something about it that unsettled her. She stared at her image in the mirror and tried to picture her mother as a young, happy bride, but all she could remember was her pinched face and hard expression caused by years of bitter feelings.

A sudden movement in the mirror drew her eye. There stood Colin, watching her from the doorway. And if that wasn't startling enough, in place of his usual gray work clothes, he wore a formal black frock coat, white tie and vest, and pinstriped trousers—wedding attire! She spun around in surprise.

The doorway was empty.

Eight

"*Where did he* go?" Katherine asked.

Doreen looked over her shoulder cautiously, as though expecting to see a ghost. "I didn't see anyone, miss. But that's not to say no one was here," she quickly amended.

"There *was* someone here. I saw him standing right there in the doorway."

"Did ye see who it was, then?"

Katherine started to say his name, then felt foolish. Colin, in her bedroom, in a formal suit? She must have imagined the whole thing. "Undo the buttons, please." She suddenly wanted that dress off.

Katherine finally chose a peach-colored silk taffeta gown with outsized cap sleeves over full, ruffled lace sleeves. The hem of the gown, as well as the shoulder line of the cap sleeve, was trimmed with ermine, and crystal beads in an iris motif decorated the skirt. It was decided that Doreen would remove the fur trim and take in the full skirt to bring it up to the times.

Katherine studied the décolletage, which was low and heart shaped, and decided it needed a necklace of some sort.

"Doreen, do you know where my grandmother's jewelry has been stored?"

The maid finished unbuttoning the back of the dress and helped her step out of it. "I'll ask Grainwe."

While she dashed off on her errand, Katherine put on her white shirtwaist and navy skirt, pausing to glance through the mirror to the doorway behind her. Why had she imagined she'd seen Colin? Had it been wishful thinking?

How silly! Why would she be wishing to see him?

Grainwe came in a few minutes later. "Doreen said ye'd be wantin' me."

"I thought perhaps there was something in my grandmother's jewelry collection I could borrow for the ball on Saturday."

"There's no need to borrow what's already yours, lass. Come with me."

She led Katherine up to the third floor, to a locked door at the end of the hallway. Pulling her keyring out of a deep pocket, Grainwe unlocked the door and climbed a steep flight of stairs to the attic.

Katherine followed her up, gazing around the immense space with wide eyes. The attic ran the length of the original house, with a high, slanted roof and a long row of windows facing west, through which dust motes danced on rays of sunlight. She followed Grainwe past long racks of clothing encased in muslin sacks, and open cabinets full of shoe and hat boxes, to where at least a dozen-and-a-half huge travel trunks were stored.

As Grainwe moved among the trunks, Katherine explored the other end of the attic, where oil paintings were lined up along the walls, some in elaborate frames and some just bare canvasses.

"Why are these paintings sitting up here where no one can see them?"

"His lordship had other paintings he wished to display," Grainwe said in a vague way.

She pushed aside two enormous trunks to make a path for herself, then opened another trunk and lifted out two crates full of books. She patted the top crate. "These are yer mother's journals. Ye can read them if yer ever curious about what she was like as a child."

Katherine lifted the lid and picked up one of the journals, leafing through it as Grainwe brought out a small, embossed leather trunk with an arched lid.

"And this is yer grandmother's jewel case."

Katherine put the book back in the crate and peered over Grainwe's shoulder as the woman used a tiny key on her keyring to unlock it, then unlatched the brass fasteners and opened the lid. Inside were stacks of flat jewelry cases, some covered in black velvet, some made of teak, others of mahogany, and one faded and worn box covered in blue silk.

The elderly servant stood with a groan. "Ye can go through it now and choose what suits you, or I can tote it down to the bedchamber and ye can go through it as ye like."

"I'd rather have it in my bedchamber, but you needn't—"

She was about to suggest that Grainwe let a younger servant carry it, when the elderly woman snapped it shut and hoisted it up on one shoulder as though it weighed nothing. "To yer bedchamber it goes, then."

Katherine followed behind, shaking her head in amazement. When they reached her room, she checked the time and saw it was half past one. "Drat! I've only got half an hour. I'm supposed to meet with a Mr. Calloway at two o'clock."

"Are ye sure it was two?" Grainwe asked. "Yer uncle is meeting with 'im in the library right now."

Katherine patted her hair to make sure the bun was still tidy as she hurried downstairs. Why had her uncle not informed her the agent had arrived early? Surely she could have been called. But perhaps no one had thought to look for her in the attic.

The door was closed, and from within she could hear male voices. Breathlessly, she opened the door and entered, causing both men to fall silent.

"Good afternoon," she said, nodding to the men. "I apologize for being late, but I thought we were meeting at two."

Calloway glanced sheepishly at her uncle, making Katherine wonder if they'd met early by design. She couldn't think of any other reason for the man's embarrassment, yet neither could she understand a need for a private meeting.

But Horace only said, "Mr. Calloway arrived sooner than expected," and dismissed the matter.

As soon as their meeting had concluded and Katherine had left, Horace closed the door to the library and seated himself in the brown leather chair behind the desk. He regarded his friend with the slightest of smirks. "You see, Edward, you worried for nothing. As I had predicted, Katherine is quite willing to follow my advice. I foresee no problems in implementing our plan."

"*Your* plan, Horace, not mine. Your niece is a very kind young lady. I don't enjoy cheating her."

"You mustn't look at it that way. Trust me, Katherine has absolutely no comprehension of how much the estate is worth or how much repairs will cost. Anyway, I told her the proceeds will be invested where it will be accessible as she needs it. Of course, I will manage the account." He leaned forward. "Don't forget, Edward, if all goes well, you'll receive six percent."

"And you'll have the bulk of your inheritance."

Horace made a temple of his fingers and contemplated the agent's words. At long last he'd have what was rightfully his—most of it, anyway. He'd have the last laugh on his mother, too, may she rot in hell.

"I have a favor to ask, Edward," he said. "I'd like to hire a man as my personal assistant, someone who would be absolutely discreet and unalterably loyal. Do you know of anyone like that?"

"In fact, I do," Calloway replied "His name is John Bloom. I'll bring him out with me when I come back." The agent rose and started for the door, where he paused to look back. "I'm curious, Horace, as to why you don't want to keep Ballyrourke, especially since your parents loved it so."

"I'd as soon live in a desert as live here among these heathens," he sneered. "I've hated Ballyrourke and its people from the moment my father brought us here. Once I have my money, I'll return to London and live like a king. For all I care, this house can burn to the ground and take everyone with it."

Katherine came away from the meeting satisfied that Calloway would give her a fair appraisal, though she had been dismayed to hear that Lawthrop House's state of disrepair would substantially diminish the estate's value. He had promised to return in two days' time to write up his report.

She spent the remainder of the afternoon examining the contents of the jewelry cases, carefully taking inventory of the beautiful necklaces, bracelets and earbobs. By the time dinner was announced, she had selected the perfect accessory for her gown, a simple opal pendant, taken from the faded blue box. It had been her grandmother's favorite, too, Grainwe had told her. A gift from her grandfather on their wedding day.

"I found a dress to wear to the ball," Katherine announced happily as she sat down across from her uncle at the dinner table, "and a pendant to go with it."

"Splendid." He waited until the food had been served and the servants had departed, then, putting his fork and knife to the tender veal, he said, "By the way, I've compiled a list of investment opportunities. They are excellent companies all. I recommend we sit down to go over them as soon as possible."

Katherine listened politely to his suggestions, but she wasn't anywhere close to being ready to decide where to invest the money. However, it was easier to humor Horace than to argue her point, so she thanked him for his efforts and said perhaps they could meet in the morning. She was finding out that he was a very persistent man.

On her after-dinner stroll that evening, Katherine came across Gersha sitting on a sturdy branch of an ancient apple tree beside the stone wall. Her pet cat perched on a branch nearby, long tail swishing, batting a paw at the occasional insect that flew past her face.

"Evenin', Katie."

"Good evening, Gersha."

"Climb up and sit with me."

Katherine smiled. "As delightful as that sounds, ladies don't climb trees."

"Then pretend you're a child. Who is there to know but me, and I'd never tell a soul."

It was very tempting. Katherine eyed the tree skeptically. "I'm afraid I'm not dressed for it."

"Don't be afraid. 'Tis a simple thing. Tuck yer skirts up, roll back yer cuffs and grab hold of a limb."

A simple thing for a child, perhaps. She gazed at Gersha's hopeful face, then heaved a determined sigh, grabbed a branch and hauled herself up onto a low limb. After some maneuvering and one close call, she perched gingerly on her aerie seat, one arm wrapped securely around the trunk.

"Will ye look at yerself now?" Gersha said with glee. "Sittin' in a tree like a bird."

"I feel more like an elephant than a bird. I hope this branch is strong enough to hold me."

"Ye'll not fall, Katie."

Katherine made herself as comfortable as possible, then gazed out at the rolling fields. She had to admit, the tree perch gave her a beautiful view of the land. "What do they grow out there?" she asked, pointing.

"Wheat and barley, mostly. Potatoes, too."

Katherine studied the child curiously. "Colin told me that *Gersha* means 'little girl'."

"Aye, that's true enough."

"Then what's your real name?"

" 'Tis a secret."

"A secret? Why?"

"I'm not fond of it. But if you promise never to use it, then I'll tell ye."

"I promise."

The child gave her a coy glance. " 'Tis Caitlin. Caitlin Og."

"That's a pretty name. Where do you live?"

The little girl giggled, as though she thought the question silly. "Down the road, of course, as I told you before."

Katherine felt foolish for asking. A fairy, indeed. She turned to watch the cat walk daintily along a slender branch. "I see Colin returned Cali to you. She came to see me last night. Did he tell you?"

"Cali is fond of you, is why she came to see you," Gersha said, swinging her legs. "She told me so herself."

"Did she?" Katherine laughed.

"She'd like to live with you."

Katherine plucked a leaf, amused by the child's imagination. "And not with you?"

"She likes me well enough." Gersha shrugged. "Someone needs to watch over you is all."

"Watch over *me*? Why?"

"To protect you, of course."

"From whom?"

At that moment, the cat jumped down from the tree and bounded off after a chipmunk. Before Katherine could blink, Gersha was down, too, scampering into the wheat field after her. "Cali, come back here, ye naughty girl."

Katherine turned her head to gaze out at the rolling fields, the sweep of heather in the distance, and the low mountain range far beyond, feeling once again that deep stirring in her soul.

"You feel it, too, don't you?" Gersha had asked.

She *did* feel it, though she hated to admit it. She believed in logic, facts, not something as ephemeral as a feeling.

"You've not been eating green apples, have you?" a deep male voice called.

Katherine looked down the road and saw Colin coming at a stride. Instantly, her heart beat faster, and heat colored her cheeks. What would he think of her sitting up in the tree?

"I know better than to eat unripe fruit," she assured him, trying not to look as flustered as she felt.

Colin stopped beneath her and looked up, his hands on his hips. "Is tree climbing a skill they teach you in America?"

"I climbed up here only to keep Gersha company."

"*Girseach,* again, is it? And where, might I ask, is this *girseach?*"

"She's just over there," Katherine said, pointing to the field. But the child was nowhere to be seen. "She was following her cat. They're probably over the hill."

"Would it be this cat here?" Colin said, bending to sweep up the calico.

Katherine stared down at the animal in bewilderment. "I didn't see her come back."

He put the struggling animal on the ground. The cat's tail swished angrily as she huffed away. "She was sitting here beneath the tree as big as life when I came upon you."

"That's odd." Katherine started to lower herself from the branch, but Colin decided to do the job for her. His solid hands clamped around her ribs as he lifted her and set her gently in front of him.

Katherine stared up at him as his manly scent enveloped her and his touch ignited sparks of desire deep within her that caused the blood to pound in her ears and set her heart to thumping like a kettle drum. All she could do was gaze mutely at him, feeling both paralyzed and electrified by the tidal wave of emotions flowing through her.

Colin felt it, too, she was certain. She knew by the intensity of his gaze, even by the increasing pressure of his fingers. It was as though their lives had interlocked for one brief moment in time—two people linked not just by touch, but by a stirring, soul-deep connection. It was so remarkable she couldn't think of a single thing to say.

A thank-you seemed completely inadequate for what she was feeling. Yet she couldn't continue to stand there and gape at him. Feeling suddenly self-conscious, she dropped her gaze and said shyly, "That was very kind of you."

Colin's reply was husky soft. " 'Twas my pleasure."

His hands lingered on her body, his thumbs just under her breasts, where she was certain he could feel her heart pounding. She raised her gaze slowly, wonderingly, to his, as he dipped his head down, closing the distance that spanned their lips.

Katherine held her breath. He was going to kiss her!

Nine

Have you lost your mind?

Colin took his hands from Katie's waist and stepped back, the heels of his boots sharply scraping the stone wall behind him. He barely noticed, so stunned was he by the fierce desire sweeping through him, desire that would have him lift her skirts and take her right there against the wall. At the same time he was horrified that his lust for an enemy battled so equally with the old feelings of hatred inside him.

But only one could be victor, and it had to be his hatred; it had to be nurtured and protected to keep his goal fixed. *Ballyrourke.* That was his battle cry, and every fiber of his being sang out for it.

The problem was that when Katie gazed up at him with her guileless eyes, he was of a mind to shove it all aside. But he'd come to find her for a reason, and it wasn't to satisfy his lust.

Time to use your head, boy-o, and not those other parts that would do your thinkin' for you.

Colin tamped down his fierce emotions and assumed a devil-may-care attitude, pretending nothing out of the ordinary had passed between them, though her flustered look gave him a few pangs of remorse. He hoisted himself up onto the stone wall, braced one foot on its top, and half turned to gaze out at the fields. "I understand you had a listing agent out today."

Although her emotions were in a dizzying tumble, Katherine had enough presence of mind to gather her scattered thoughts. "The agent was invited at my uncle's request."

Colin turned his head to look at her, and even though his face and voice were composed, she saw how his fingers clenched the stones. "Thinking of selling Ballyrourke, are you?"

She nodded, bracing herself for an argument.

"Then sell it to me."

"To *you*?"

Colin jumped off the wall and clasped her arms, gazing down into her eyes with a fervor that caused her breath to catch. "Not just to me, Katie. To the O'Rourkes. We don't have enough money to buy it outright, but we'll make payments to you regularly until it's paid for, I swear."

His use of her nickname surprised her almost as much as his offer. But even in her astonishment, she knew that what he was proposing wouldn't work. She needed money soon, not spread out in small increments. Still, she hated to say no outright. It would be better to let him down gently. "I'll have to think about it."

His brow furrowed. "What's there to think about? You don't want your family's land going to a stranger, do you?"

"I never make quick decisions."

"There's no time to be lost. Listen to me, Katie! This is O'Rourke land, the land of your father, who came back here to help us fight for it, and died. Would you give this land to a stranger? Would he love it as much? Would you destroy what we've worked so hard to build? Look around you at the beauty of it. Listen to your heart. You'd never want anything bad to happen to Ballyrourke, would you?"

Katherine blinked up at him, stunned by his revelation. "My father came back to fight for Ballyrourke?"

"And died for it."

She stared at Colin in disbelief. Her mother had reviled

her father for abandoning them. Not once had she said why he'd left or even how he'd met his end. Katherine shivered as a cold wave of outrage washed over her. It was another secret her mother had kept. "How did he die?"

"I was only twelve, not privy to what the adults knew. Ask your uncle Horace."

Her uncle knew?

Colin clutched her arms tighter. "Say you'll do it, Katie. Say you'll let us buy it. You know it's right."

A loud meow dragged her attention away from Colin's riveting gaze to the little calico sitting in the road, holding up a paw as though it were injured. The interruption gave her time to collect her wits. She stepped back from him, freeing herself of his hold. "I'll think about it."

"You do that, Katie. You think about it." Colin gazed at her for a long moment, his jaw working as if there were more he wanted to say. But then he turned and headed up Kilwick Road, calling back, "In the meantime, stay out of trees. I might not be around to rescue you next time."

Her thoughts spinning from yet another startling disclosure, Katherine knelt down beside the cat and examined her paw, but found nothing to cause such distress. Cali rubbed her head against Katherine's hand and began to purr. Katherine picked her up and held her close as a whole slew of new questions crowded her mind.

At least now she knew what Colin was after, and it hadn't been a kiss.

Katherine put the cat down and started for the house, only to have the animal follow behind. "Go home," she said firmly, trying to shoo her away. "Go find Gersha," but Cali wouldn't be deterred. At the front door the little cat strolled inside with her, just as though she belonged there.

At that moment, Horace came out of the library and started up the hall toward them. Cali arched her back and hissed, then turned and ran out the door.

"Horrid creatures," her uncle said. "They should all be drowned at birth."

"Uncle, I have to ask you something."

Horace studied her for a moment, his brows drawing together, as though puzzled by her seriousness. "Shall we step into the drawing room?"

Katherine took a seat on a chair in the enormous room and clasped her hands tightly in her lap, trying to contain her agitation. "I'd like to know how my father died."

"It was my understanding he was returning here."

Then he *did* know the truth! Both her mother *and* her uncle had kept it from her. "Why was he returning?"

"To see his family, I would suppose."

"Not to fight for Ballyrourke?"

"There wasn't a war going on, Katherine."

"Then how did he die?"

"No one ever determined that."

"Was his body found?"

"Katherine, what is this about?" Horace asked sharply, clearly peeved.

She twisted her fingers together. "If his body wasn't found, how do we know he died?"

"I don't understand what your point is. Why are you even raising this subject?"

"The point," she said, her voice rising in frustration, "is that I know nothing about my family. Nothing! And no one seems to want to tell me. I thought we were English. I thought we had little money and that my grandparents were all dead long ago. I thought my father simply walked out on my mother, and that's why she would never speak of him. Now it seems that's a lie, too. I want the truth!"

"Katherine, you're upsetting yourself. I knew I shouldn't have let you come to Ballyrourke."

She pressed her fingertips against her forehead to stop the angry churning of her thoughts. "Why? So I would continue to be ignorant?"

"Of course not. Don't be preposterous. This display of emotion is very unlike you."

"What *is* like me?" she asked, standing. "I don't know who I am anymore."

"Where did you hear this story about your father?"

"Does it matter?"

"It was MacCormack, wasn't it? I warned you to stay

away from that blackguard, Katherine. He cannot be trusted. Now he's toying with your emotions to turn you against me. If you won't heed my advice, then I will have no choice but to fire him."

A quick, hot fury swept over her. She didn't like being ordered about as if she had no mind of her own. And, after all, Ballyrourke was *hers.* "If anyone is to fire him," she retorted, "it will be me." She marched out of the room and headed for the kitchen. Horace would not give her the answers she needed, but Grainwe would.

Katherine found the old woman in a storage room off the kitchen, folding table linens. "Grainwe, I must speak to you."

The servant glanced up in surprise, then quickly put down the bundle she was holding. "Yer all flustered, lass. Come into the kitchen and I'll make ye tea."

"No, please, Grainwe, I don't need tea. I need answers. Tell me how my father died."

The instant flicker of fear in Grainwe's eyes shocked her. The woman cast a quick glance over her shoulder, as if she were afraid of being overheard. "I don't know how he died. I can't help ye."

"But you must know something. You must have heard something. Surely my grandmother spoke of it."

Her mouth in a tight knot, Grainwe shelved the linens and turned away. "Blind should be the eyes in the abode of another. That's what a servant lives by. That's all I'll say on it."

Grainwe's reaction stunned her. The woman had to know more than she was saying. What, or whom, did she fear?

Horace paced his bedroom floor, fuming inwardly and thinking hard. MacCormack was stirring up trouble, causing Katherine to ask too many questions. Those questions had to be answered, he now realized, but in just the right way. He'd have to give her enough information to satisfy her curiosity, yet not enough to arouse her suspicions. It wouldn't be easy, but he was a clever man, and this was a problem he could correct.

What he could not, and would not tolerate, was MacCormack's influence on Katherine. Something would have to be done quickly to discredit him. Horace paced to the window and stopped to gaze outside while he considered various options. Almost at once, artful man that he was, he came up with a plan.

At midnight, Colin and his little band stole quietly from the round tower, skirted the cemetery and the ruins of the ancient cathedral and made their way across rolling pastureland to Lawthrop House. Colin quietly unlocked the kitchen service door and crept through the silent house, up the staircase, down the third floor hallway to the attic door, where another key let him in with a harsh scrape of the lock. He moved cautiously up the stairs and across the floor so the old boards wouldn't creak, then selected three large canvases and carried them back down.

He'd just reached the second-floor landing when he saw a sudden glow of light from the far end of the hallway. He moved down the stairs quickly, then darted through the open double doors of the formal drawing room. Resting the canvases on the floor, he watched from behind one of the doors as the light traveled down the staircase, until a form appeared at the bottom, a lamp in hand.

It was Katie! And she was coming his way.

Katherine paused in the silent entrance hall, sure she had heard someone moving about. "Hello?" she called softly, holding the lamp in front of her. No one answered.

From the corner of her eye she saw movement, a slight shift in the darkness inside the drawing room. She stepped to the doorway and glanced around, but saw nothing. As she turned to leave, she spotted something large propped against the wall, nearly hidden behind one of the doors. She moved closer and saw that it was three large, unframed paintings, such as she had seen in the attic. She couldn't imagine why they would be there. She made a mental note to have them returned in the morning.

She continued down the hall to the library to find something to read. She found a shelf filled with books of poetry and ran her fingers over the titles until she spotted one by John Keats, whom her mother had often quoted. She was surprised to find an inscription inside the book.

In bold handwriting, it said "To my lovely Suzannah. 'A thing of beauty is a joy forever.' Keats had surely been speaking of you when he wrote that in his poem. With all my heart, Garrett."

It was from her father. Katherine ran her fingers over his scrawled writing, trying to picture him. She closed her eyes, and suddenly she could hear him speaking those words, down to the resonant, lilting sound of his voice. She heard him so clearly, it was as if he were standing beside her. How had she forgotten what he sounded like?

She stared down at his distinctive signature, tears gathering in her eyes. Here in her hands was proof that he had once loved her mother. Why, then, had he forsaken her? Colin had said her father had come to fight for Ballyrourke, yet her uncle had claimed that there'd been no war. If her father had truly loved them, would anything in the world have caused him to abandon them?

Colin let his breath out slowly as Katie climbed the stairs to the second floor. He'd begun to think she'd fallen asleep back there. From now on he'd be sure to come later in the night, when she'd be slumbering soundly.

He stayed hidden until he heard the distant sound of a door closing. Then, picking up the canvases, he stole cautiously through the house and outside to where his friends waited.

"No more trips tonight," he told them, wiping his brow with his sleeve. "I was almost discovered."

"I don't think you should chance it anymore, Colin," Kevin whispered nervously.

"We'll just have to do it later tomorrow night is all," Colin suggested as each man carried a canvas toward the round tower.

"Don't count on me," Kevin told them. "I promised my

wife I'd take her to the dance in the village, and you know how late those run."

"And I'm hosting at O'Malleys," Michael added.

"All right, then, Sunday."

"That's a sacrilege, Colin," Kevin protested.

Colin set his canvas down at the base of the tower. "Monday, then, and no getting out of it." He pulled down the ladder from the opening four feet off the ground, climbed up inside, and took the paintings his friends handed to him. Once all the canvases were in, he carried them up two more flights, where he knew they wouldn't be discovered. No one ever came out to the abandoned tower, save for the occasional pair of lovers.

"'Twould be easier to find the will," Kevin pointed out, as Colin sat on the grass and wiped his face and neck with a handkerchief.

"I have a lead on it," Colin told them. "Doreen told me today she heard that the old lady's personal maid, Mary Flynn, took a job at Tarkinton Manor. I'm going there tomorrow morning to talk to her. Mary has given me a look a time or two. I think she has a soft spot for me."

"All the girls have soft spots for you," Michael teased.

Colin shrugged. "I keep telling you, it's the kisses. They're legendary among the lasses."

"Better be careful," Kevin warned. "Tarkinton isn't too fond of you since you made him a laughingstock at the festival last year. He'd love nothing better than to catch you in his house. He'd have you jailed in the blink of an eye for trespassing."

"But didn't old Tar-n-feathers deserve it, with his pompous ways, making promises to his people he didn't intend to keep?" Colin asked.

"I happen to know he's giving a ball tomorrow night," Michael boasted. "With all the commotion, it would be the perfect time to slip in to see Mary."

"Thanks for the news," Colin said, thumping his friend on the back. "That's exactly what I'll do."

Ten

As Katherine passed the drawing room on her way to breakfast the next morning, she suddenly remembered the canvases. But when she checked behind the door, they were gone.

"Doreen," she called, spotting the girl at the other end of the hallway with a stack of linen napkins in her arms, "did you find any paintings standing behind the door in the drawing room yesterday?"

"I'm so sorry, miss," she said, looking somewhat abashed. "Did you lose them?"

"I didn't lose them, exactly. Last night I found three canvases leaning against the wall behind the door. They're gone now. I'd like to know where they went."

"I'll find out for you, miss."

"One more thing," Katherine said. "Please get word to Mr. MacCormack that I need to see him."

Bobbing, the young maid scurried off.

Katherine nibbled her lip. Perhaps she was being too hasty in sending for Colin. He would think she was summoning him to discuss his offer, which was the last thing she wanted to do because she hadn't yet come up with a tactful way to turn him down.

All she really wanted was to remind him to arrange a meeting with her aunt Eileen and uncle Patrick. Yet, as Grainwe had said, there were others at Ballyrourke that could go in his place. Why not use one of them instead?

Annoyingly, she found herself thinking more and more about Colin. Even now, as she investigated the bedrooms on the second floor, arousing memories would suddenly skitter across her mind—the feel of his strong hands on her body as he had lifted her from the tree; the way he had gazed down into her eyes; the sound of his deep, husky voice; and the moment he had almost kissed her. What would his kiss have been like? How would his lips have felt on hers? Would she have swooned?

She was more likely to have kissed him back.

"Good heavens," she said aloud, shocked by her bold thought, "what am I thinking?"

"I don't know, miss. I can guess, if you'd like."

Katherine looked around to find Doreen standing behind her. "I was only talking to myself," she explained sheepishly.

"Saints be praised!" the young woman said with a dramatic sigh. "That's one worry off my mind. I never was good at guessing games."

"Did you want something, Doreen?"

"Yes, miss. Colin has sent word he's busy, but he'll come on Monday."

Katherine sighed inwardly. Not until Monday! She wasn't sure which she felt most disappointed by—not seeing Colin or not meeting her aunt and uncle before Monday.

"And none of the servants have seen any canvases this morning," Doreen concluded.

"'Twas the work of the fairies," Grainwe remarked quite seriously as she passed by with a load of freshly washed sheets.

"What would a fairy do with an oil painting?" Katherine asked. "Next you'll be telling me there are leprechauns under the bed."

"Leprechauns under the bed. That's a good one." Grainwe let out a cackle of amusement as she continued down the hallway. "Everyone knows they live beneath the trees."

"Katherine glanced at the paper in her hand and saw that she hadn't written anything yet on her list. Instead, she'd been daydreaming about a certain dark-haired, blue-eyed Irishman. That had to stop immediately!

At noon, she spent an uncomfortable half hour dining with her uncle, to whom she said little because she was still miffed.

Finally, Horace put down his fork with a clatter. "All right, Katherine. You may stop sulking. I will tell you all I know about your father, though it pains me to do so."

He pushed back his chair and went to the sideboard to spoon bread pudding onto his plate. "Six years after your parents moved to America," he began, "your father received word that his family was in financial straits due to crop failures. He then made arrangements to come back here, leaving you and your mother to fend for yourselves."

Horace returned to his chair and placed his napkin over his lap. "What the man thought he could do is beyond me—failed crops can't be revived, after all. But the O'Rourkes have always had this peculiar fealty to Ballyrourke that makes them lose sight of truly important matters. With your father, that trait was even more pronounced. Indeed, though I hate to say this to you, Katherine, Garrett was reckless and irresponsible when it came to his own family.

"Nevertheless, your father came, landing in Ireland a month after he set sail. He sent a wire to his family saying that he was on his way, but he never arrived. A search was made without success. That's all we know."

"What do they think happened to him?"

"There are any number of possibilities: an overturned carriage, highway robbers, even a sudden illness that struck while he stayed overnight at an inn. Knowing his rash nature, I suspected it was more likely he had run away with another woman. Regardless of what it was, however, his thoughtless decision left your mother a young widow with a child to raise and no income on which to do it. I'm sure you can understand why she refused to speak of him."

Katherine stirred her tea absently, weighing the information against what Colin had told her, knowing Horace's version would be tainted by his feelings toward the O'Rourkes. She tried to imagine how her father must have felt after learning of his family's plight—the helplessness, the outrage. But what *had* he thought he could do for them by returning?

If Horace's story held the slightest glimmer of truth, then, in effect, her father had chosen the land over his wife and daughter. Katherine could well understand her mother's bitterness over that, but it was still no reason to keep the truth from her daughter.

She gave her uncle a skeptical glance. "Why didn't you tell me this earlier?"

"Katherine, dear, it distresses me to tarnish your memories of your father."

At six o clock that evening, Katherine stood before the mirrored wall in the dressing room studying her reflection, while Grainwe and Doreen stood behind her, awaiting her approval. In the now modified apricot-colored dress; opal pendant; long, white gloves; delicate, white satin slippers; and with her hair fashioned into an intricate twist, she barely recognized the lady in the mirror.

It was symbolic of how she felt inside. Unrecognizable. The person she'd always thought she was had dissolved in a mist of lies, half-truths and mystery. Who was she, really?

Katherine turned and gave the women a smile, remembering to use her lady-of-the-manor voice: "I'm very pleased with the outcome. Thank you so much for your help."

They both let out sighs of relief. "Thank you, mistress," Grainwe said.

"You're fair beautiful, miss," Doreen said wistfully. "Don't I wish I were goin' somewhere so fancy. Wait till the lads see you. You'll not lack for a dance partner all night."

"Stop yer yappin', lass," Grainwe chided. "Miss, yer uncle is waiting below in the hall."

Katherine took a deep breath to gather her resolve. She

would do her grandmother proud. Tonight she was a Lawthrop.

She picked up her fan and the ivory silk shawl Grainwe had found for her in her grandmother's belongings, and proceeded down the hall to the staircase. Her uncle waited below, dressed in a dove-tailed black suit and gray vest, and carrying a black top hat and cane.

"Ready, Katherine?" he asked as she came down the stairs toward him. He made no comment on her ensemble.

The carriage ride took half an hour, during which time Horace drilled Katherine on the names of the people she would encounter. "And be especially attentive to Lord Henry Guthry. He'd make an excellent buyer for Ballyrourke. He's always looking for good property."

Colin's words pricked at her conscience: *"You don't want your family's land going to a stranger, do you? This is O'Rourke land, the land of your father, who came back here to help us fight for it, and died. Would a stranger love it as much?"*

She knew what her answer to Colin would be: No one should love a land so much he'd put it above even his own wife and child.

Seizing advantage of Katie and Horace's absence, Colin waited until the servants had retired to their rooms for the evening, then he quietly let himself in the side door of Lawthrop House and tiptoed to the hallway. Grainwe had said they'd moved the old lady's personal effects; Doreen had said the attic was the most likely spot. With any luck, he'd be able to find the will without having to trouble Mary Flynn.

The stairs seemed to creak with exceptional loudness as Colin crept up two flights; the attic key turned with a harsh grating sound; and the door hinges squeaked, as if the very house itself was protesting his furtiveness. He paused to listen, but heard no movement, no sign that anyone had heard him.

Colin placed three more oil canvases near the top of the stairway where they'd be handy for his next moonlight visit, then he moved carefully across ancient floorboards to where the huge trunks were stored. He opened the heavy lid of one of the largest and dug through its contents, flabbergasted by how much one old lady could put away for no good purpose that he could see. Keeping an eye on the time, he searched a second trunk, but was unable to find anything remotely resembling a will. He stepped back to count the number of trunks still to go and felt his heart sink.

Perhaps it would be easier to keep his meeting with Mary after all.

The carriage pulled up to the portico of a home much grander than Lawthrop House. Katherine gazed around her in wonder as they entered the large entrance hall and followed a servant to the ballroom in the south wing, where Horace was immediately greeted by their host and hostess.

"And this lovely woman must be our guest of honor, your niece Katherine," Lord Tarkinton said, gazing at her from under bushy white eyebrows. He was a short, portly man with pink cheeks and neatly combed white hair. He took her hand and bowed formally. "A pleasure to meet you."

Katherine curtsied. "How kind, sir."

His wife, a majestic woman with a large bosom and shrewd brown eyes, bussed her cheek. "Katherine, how happy I am to meet you at last. Your grandmother and I were very good friends. She would be so pleased that you've come home."

"Thank you, Lady Tarkinton. I hope we'll have a chance to talk later. I'd like to hear more about my grandmother."

"Of course we shall, dear. Oh, look, here is Henry, come to meet our guests of honor."

Katherine glanced around as an elderly gentleman approached. He was heavyset, with a large, fleshy, veined face that was red from the exertion of walking across the room. He had double chins that shook like jelly when he moved; and a tiny, spade-shaped nose that all but disappeared in his jowly face and droopy eyelids.

Katherine felt the pressure of her uncle's hand on her forearm. "Lord Guthry," he breathed in her ear.

After introductions were made, Katherine tried to engage in the conversation Guthry seemed to be having with her, except that she couldn't understand a word he said. He spoke in a mumble, with his lips together and his cheeks puffing in and out. He kept on mumbling to her even when more guests came up to greet them.

Guthry even mumbled through the formal dinner in the grand dining hall, where, thanks to Horace's maneuvers, Katherine found herself seated at the man's right. She attempted to make conversation with others near her, but Guthry kept interrupting, and once even placed his fat hand on her knee. With a shudder of distaste, Katherine removed it. If this was how she was to find a buyer, she wanted no part of it.

As soon as the dinner had concluded and the guests had returned to the ballroom, the orchestra began to play. At once, Guthry was there to partner her. Katherine suffered through two dances, with his sweaty face near hers and his damp palm on her back making her dress stick to her skin, until she felt suffocated. As soon as the second dance ended, she made up an excuse to leave the floor, then snaked her way through the dancers and out of the ballroom.

She glanced over her shoulder and saw Guthry moving through the crowd after her, so she headed down the hall toward the back of the house, tried a door, found it unlocked, and slipped inside.

The room was dark, with only a faint glow from dying embers in the hearth. Katherine closed the door ever so quietly, then leaned upon it, heaving a sigh of relief. Insufferable man! She wondered how long she could hide from Guthry.

She had just peeled off her gloves when suddenly, out of the dark, a shape came at her, and she found herself enveloped in an enthusiastic hug.

"You're a sweetheart, taking such a risk for me," a man's voice whispered near her ear, and then he cupped Katherine's face and kissed her, quick and hard.

The emotional side of her brain wobbled from shock, while the logical side quickly cataloged the experience: lips firm, masculine, and tasting of fruit—apples, perhaps? Chin rough from a slight stubble. Skin fragrant, with an aroma akin to bay rum. Arms solid, muscular. Hands broad and gentle on her shoulders. A man, to be sure. A quite forward man, at that, to be kissing an unknown female in the dark.

Katherine had barely recovered her breath when she found herself kissed once again. This time, however, another part of her anatomy took over, and she forgot all about stopping him, or making mental notes. Her nerve endings tingled, her nipples shrank, then expanded, until they pushed against the edge of her corset, and that secret inner core pulsed and trembled, wanting something far beyond her experience.

As if they had a mind of their own, her hands came up to stroke his firm jaw, where, just beneath her fingertips she could feel the slight stubble of a day's growth of beard. She combed her fingers through his hair, finding it thick and wavy, then ran her hands across his shoulders, discovering solid muscle. He was quite an exciting man, this impertinent stranger.

His tongue intruded between her lips, and she realized it was seeking entrance into her mouth. A part of her was shocked, another part intrigued and highly stimulated. The second part won.

Katherine opened her lips and let him explore, the hot rush of desire that ensued causing her to moan and press her body against his. She felt the answering pressure of his body through her layers of petticoats, and wound her arms even more tightly around his neck, hoping the kiss would resolve this urgent and desperate craving she felt inside.

Colin's groin ached from the raging lust coursing into it. He forced himself to think, his mind sluggish, drugged by lust. This was Mary? Mary who had grown up practically next door? Why had he never noticed her before? Why hadn't he thought to court her?

She hadn't seemed too pleased to see him at the kitchen door that evening, harried as she was with the party in full swing. She'd shoved him up the back staircase, whispering for him to wait for her in the first room on the right until she could slip away. He knew he could remedy her annoyance with one of his famous kisses, intended only to show his appreciation.

Never in his entire life would he have guessed Mary would be so arousing, so sensual. In truth, he couldn't remember ever enjoying a kiss this much.

Thoroughly caught up in the excitement, he backed her to the wall, pressing against her layers of skirts and petticoats, the rustling sounds muted by the blood pounding in his ears. Somewhere deep in his befuddled brain an alarm sounded, but he ignored it. He slid his mouth down her neck, to the hollow of her throat, drawing forth a tiny gasp as he continued down. She gasped sharply when he cupped one firm breast in his palm, but that only excited him further. He was so excited, in fact, that he forgot his purpose for coming there.

The will, boy-o! The will.

Right. The will. In just another moment or two.

A breathless female voice cut through the blanket of lust smothering his reason. "You must stop!"

Colin went stone still. That wasn't Mary's voice. In fact, that wasn't even an Irish voice. It was American.

Instantly, he backed away from her. Spinning on his heel, he turned and slipped out of the room. Luck was with him, for no one was in the hall. He darted through the busy kitchen and out the servants' door into the night. He didn't stop until he'd reached the Lawthrop stables, and then he collapsed in the straw, still aching from the force of his arousal. Silk and satin, skirts and petticoats—not the dress of a maid. He'd been so overwhelmed by his desire that he hadn't noticed.

He glanced down suddenly and saw a long white glove snagged on his jacket button. He yanked it free and stared at it. The glove could only belong to Katie.

Had she known it was him in the dark? Was she even now alerting her hosts?

Colin, eejit, you've done it now.

Eleven

Katherine sank weakly onto a sofa in the dark room, her limbs trembling, her heart thudding, and that secret core still throbbing from lust generated by the stranger's touch. And oh, the mortification. She'd wrapped herself around that man like ivy on a lamppost, and she hadn't even known who he was!

But that wasn't the worst of it. Heavens, no. The worst of it was that she'd wanted more.

The door opened suddenly and Katherine turned with a gasp, fearing, yet half hoping, to see her mystery man again. But it was merely a maid.

"Oh! Beggin' yer pardon, miss," she said sheepishly, and quickly backed out.

"Wait!" Katherine called, jumping up. "Did you see anyone leave this room just now?"

"No, miss. No one."

"That's all right, then. Thank you." Katherine snatched her gloves from where she'd dropped them, then dashed into the hallway. It suddenly seemed important that she find the stranger, though she hadn't figured out what she would do if she did. Would she reprimand him for his forwardness or apologize for her own?

Heavens no. She would demand another kiss.

"I have to stop thinking like that," Katherine whispered. She looked up and down the long marbled hallway, but saw only servants scurrying in and out of the ballroom. She hurried to the doorway of the elegantly decorated room, where an orchestra played a stately waltz, and peered in with dismay at the sea of faces and whirling skirts. Her hostess, Lady Tarkinton, spotted her and immediately headed her way.

Katherine quickly went to pull on her gloves only to discover one missing. She glanced down at the floor, then at the hallway behind her, then realized she must have lost it in the library. But there was no time to go back now.

"Here you are, my dear," Lady Tarkinton cried jubilantly, as Katherine stuffed the remaining glove in her evening bag. "There must be a dozen admirers just waiting for the opportunity to dance with you. You won't disappoint them, will you?"

Katherine was forced to smile and dance for another hour and a half, thankfully with different partners, as Guthry seemed to have absented himself from the ballroom.

With each new partner, however, she found herself searching his face for some telltale sign that he had been the culprit. The problem was, she knew him only by touch and taste, and she couldn't very well kiss each who danced with her. The scandal would be unthinkable.

How would she ever know her mystery man unless he were to kiss her again?

"I hear Lady Tarkinton has invited you to come for tea on Tuesday, Katherine," her uncle said.

She gazed out the carriage window into the black night and sighed dreamily. "Yes, she has."

"Lord Guthry has expressed an interest in coming to see the house this week."

"How nice."

"Katherine, you haven't heard a word I've said since we left the ball. Whatever is on your mind?"

"Nothing." *Nothing but a stranger's kiss.* She sighed

again. Who was her mystery man? Was he even now thinking about her?

"I've invited him here on Wednesday for dinner."

She sat upright and stared at her uncle. "Who?"

"Guthry."

"Oh." She sank back down. Her uncle, sitting opposite her in the carriage, continued to study her.

"Are you feeling ill?"

"A bit tired. I'm not used to dancing."

"I met with Guthry for nearly an hour this evening. You should be relieved he's showing such interest. By the way, have you had an opportunity to review that list of investments I gave you?"

"I will first thing tomorrow," she replied, and at once forgot all about it.

"Where are your gloves?"

Katherine's stomach gave a lurch. "I—I seemed to have dropped one somewhere. I have the other here in my bag."

"A lady keeps her gloves *on* at a formal occasion, Katherine."

As if she needed to be reminded. She bit back the retort she'd liked to have given him and said only, "I'll try to remember next time."

"By the way," he said casually," I heard some rather interesting news this evening. It seems there's a band of rebels operating in the area, and their ringleader is said to be none other than Colin MacCormack."

Katherine looked at him in surprise. Colin? A ringleader? "What is he accused of doing?"

"Apparently he's trying to start a land revolt by inflaming the peasants. Lord Tarkinton, for one, would like to see him jailed. MacCormack is dangerous, Katherine, as I've told you before. The wisest move would be to fire him and find a new manager before he turns the peasants against us."

Katherine could imagine Colin as a rebel. He had that fiery nature and quick temper. But would he lead a revolt against them? She doubted it. What's more, she wished her uncle would stop referring to the tenants as peasants and stop trying to make decisions for her.

"You understand that he's a threat to us, don't you, Katherine?"

She gave him a quick nod and looked out the window again. The only threat she felt at that moment was the threat of being kept awake all night wondering about her mystery man.

When the carriage stopped in front of the house, Katherine stepped down and fairly floated up the steps into the house. She continued straight up the staircase to her room, automatically dodging the drip pots, and found Grainwe and Doreen both awaiting her, their expressions eager.

"Did ye have a grand time at the ball, miss?" Doreen asked, as she unfastened the buttons down the back of the gown.

"Yes, a grand time." Katherine stepped out of her dress and gazed at her reflection in the mirrored wall as the ladies untied her corset and helped her undress. She appeared the same old Katherine on the surface, but inside she felt ethereal, celestial. All because of a passionate kiss in the dark.

When the women had gone, Katherine went to the open window and sat on the window seat, her elbows propped on the sill, staring up at the stars. She had never considered herself a romantic; romance was for dreamers, not practical thinkers like her. Yet she couldn't stop fantasizing about meeting the stranger again. She'd even given him a secret name—Adonis, the handsome young man from mythology—for that was who she imagined he looked like.

She heard a sound from below, a rustle in the shrubs, but the moon had gone behind a cloud, so she couldn't tell what had caused it. A few minutes later, Cali came daintily across the sloping roof and stepped inside.

Katherine picked her up and cuddled her. "Silly cat! It was you making that noise." She took her inside and put her on the bed, then climbed in beside her and lay stroking the soft fur, contemplating the shocking storm of desire the stranger had aroused in her. "Where were you tonight to protect me, Cali?" she asked with a yawn, turning down the lamp wick.

The calico purred softly beside her.

* * *

From his seat on a bench in the rose garden, Colin watched the lamp's soft glow fade to blackness in Katie's window, then he put his head in his hands and groaned. His plan had gone all wrong. Terribly, horribly wrong. He was supposed to have met Mary in the back parlor to learn the whereabouts of the will. He'd not only failed that, but he'd also made a muddle of his feelings.

He pulled a slender white glove from his pants pocket and held it to his nose. Ah, there was her scent, light and sweet, and as powdery soft as her skin. And now he was cursed by the knowing of her body, and by his wanting more.

He wasn't supposed to be attracted to a Lawthrop. Ha! Wasn't that a laugh? Not only was he attracted, but here he was in her garden waiting for a glimpse of her in the window like a lovesick schoolboy.

He was nearly as bad as Garrett, who had let himself be seduced by a Lawthrop and had paid for it with his own blood. In Colin's opinion, only a traitor or a fool would marry a Lawthrop. Hero though he'd been, Garrett had still been a fool when it came to love.

By all the saints in heaven, Colin wasn't about to be a fool, too. He stuffed the glove deep into his pocket, jumped up and stalked toward the stables to saddle a horse. He would not let one kiss distract him. He'd go back to Tarkinton House and find Mary Flynn. Then he'd come here, get the will and be done with the Lawthrops forever.

But the guests were leaving by the time Colin rode up, and the servants were busy cleaning up after them. He tried to get in the kitchen door, but was shooed away by weary, irritable cooks. Finding Mary would have to wait until another day.

In the bright light of morning, Katherine's reason returned. Her fantasies about a stranger she'd foolishly named Adonis were so absurd, she had to laugh at herself. She had simply been startled and overwhelmed by an impertinent cad who had accosted her, causing her to lose her bearings. What else would explain her brazen behavior?

No more would she give in to the ridiculous urge to daydream about the scoundrel. She had much more to occupy her mind than dreams of one stolen kiss.

With that matter resolved, Katherine ate breakfast, then accompanied her uncle to church. Afterward, Katherine decided to spend a quiet afternoon exploring the attic.

As she climbed to the top of the attic stairway, she noticed three large canvases stacked to her immediate right. Someone did bring them back, she thought, and lugged them one by one across the room back to where the others were stored.

She spent two glorious hours analyzing, appraising and cataloging the paintings. Yet even her enthusiasm for her task did not prevent her thoughts from drifting back to the ball, to that dark room, to a stranger's passionate embrace.

Sitting on the wooden floor with her legs curled beneath her, a pad of paper on her lap and a canvas propped in front of her, Katherine closed her eyes and ran her fingers along her lips, remembering the firm feel and fruit taste of his mouth—her Adonis—and the intimate touch of his hand on her breast. She sighed dreamily, imagining where that touch would have taken him next.

Giving herself an angry mental shake, Katherine refocused her energy on the painting in front of her, carefully listing the artist and subject on the paper before moving on to another. She examined them in detail, finding the subjects rather uninspired, but the frames of great interest. They were Sunderland frames, named after an aristocratic collector and dating to the 1600s, distinguished by a style known as *auricular.*

On Monday the household returned to its normal routine. After breakfast, Katherine told Doreen to discreetly let her know if Colin came by, then she sat down with her uncle in the library to go over Horace's list of investments. She listened as he described exactly how he would handle the money for her, then she politely informed him she'd research them fully when she returned to Chicago.

She knew her meticulousness irked him, but she refused to be pressured into any quick decisions. If she had her own way, she'd just put all the money into the bank where it would be instantly accessible.

"Don't forget that Mr. Calloway is coming this afternoon to begin his appraisal," Horace reminded her.

As soon as Katherine had gone, Horace rose from the chair and went to stand at the window, seething with frustration at his niece's stubbornness. Were she his daughter he would demand compliance to his wishes. His sister had given her too much independence. Like everything else Suzannah had done, she'd muddled Katherine's upbringing, too.

Of course, Suzannah herself had been too independent. His father, excellent though he was at running the estate, had not been strict enough with her. Had he been, she would not have dared run off with that Irish hooligan.

That his sister had ever agreed to wed Garrett O'Rourke in the first place confounded Horace no end. As the only daughter of a wealthy landholder, Suzannah had stood to gain a huge dowry by making a satisfactory marriage. She could have wed a baron or a lord; instead she chose the second son of Padraig O'Rourke, a tenant farmer with nothing to offer his future wife but a life of hard work. The only one who would have benefited from their union was Garrett. Horace had made sure that had never happened.

He turned from the window with a sharp sigh. It was of little use to dwell on the past. His immediate concern was to convince Katherine to trust him.

Katherine was busy cataloging the paintings in the drawing room when Doreen poked her head in. "Miss?"

Katherine looked up expectantly, hoping the maid had come to announce Colin's arrival.

"It's teatime."

"Thank you, Doreen." She scolded herself for feeling disappointed. Why should the mere thought of seeing Colin have such an elating effect on her?

Then she had an idea. She dropped her paper and pencil and hurried out of the room after the maid. "Doreen?"

The young woman turned in surprise. "Yes, miss?"

"I'd like to take my tea outside to the park."

Doreen's mouth dropped open. "Outside? To the park?"

"Yes. To the park. I thought I'd take in some of that rare sunshine."

"Outside!"

"Yes. Is something wrong?"

"Oh, no, miss. It's just that no one's ever done it before."

"Then I'll start a new custom."

"I'll bring it right out to ye," she said, shaking her head in wonder.

Katherine didn't tell her the main reason was that she hoped Colin would happen by. She quickly amended that thought. She hoped he would happen by so she could arrange her meeting with her aunt Eileen.

As she sat on the circular bench around the fountain, sipping her tea, she saw a petite, red-haired woman, heavy with child, coming up Kilwick Road, a basket loaded with provisions on each arm.

"Mornin', Katie," the woman called with a smile.

It still amazed Katherine that everyone knew her. She set aside her cup and walked to the gate in the low, stone wall. "Good morning to you, too," she said as she opened it and stepped onto the road.

The woman set down one basket and offered her hand. "I'm Eileen O'Rourke."

Katherine was so excited to see her aunt at last that she shook her hand a bit too exuberantly. "I'm so sorry," she exclaimed, releasing her hand. "It's just that I'm very happy to meet you. I was hoping to meet you, in fact. Would you care for some tea?"

"Thank you for the offer, but I should get home with my food so I can start the day's cooking. It was very good to meet you, too."

"May I help you carry your baskets?"

"I couldn't ask you to do that. 'Twouldn't be right." Eileen paused for a moment, then gave her a wide smile. "Unless . . ."

"Unless?"

"You stayed and had a meal with us."

"I'd be delighted."

"Now mind you, it's nothin' fancy, just colcannon and soda bread, but it's hearty and my family tells me it's the best around."

"Colcannon?"

Eileen's eyes twinkled with amusement. "Aren't I the silly one. Of course you wouldn't know what that is. 'Tis merely a mixture of mashed potatoes and cabbage, with melted butter and thickened cream, and a bit of greens and scallions tossed in for good measure."

"It sounds delicious. I'll just hurry back to the house to fetch my gloves and then I'll be right back." Katherine walked through the park as fast as was proper, fighting the strongest urge to pick up her skirts and run. Here at last was her opportunity to have some questions answered.

When she returned, she took one of the baskets and hung it over her arm, then started off beside Eileen, amazed at the quickness of her aunt's stride. "Do you always walk all the way into town?"

"'Tis only a few miles. The Lord gave me two perfectly good feet, so I may as well put them to use."

"Yes, but in your . . ." Katherine wasn't sure how to delicately phrase it, "circumstances?"

Eileen laughed. "If I let that stop me I'd get nothing done."

Her aunt chatted all the way back to her home, telling Katherine about her two children, Dermot and Cathal, and her hopes that her baby would be a girl so she wouldn't be the only female in an all-male household.

The instant kinship Katherine felt with Eileen surprised her, although it would have been impossible not to like someone with her warmth and friendliness. The cottage, however, took her aback. It was small and crude and lacked any amenities, reminding her of the conditions of the poor in Chicago.

Eileen called her sons in from the field across the lane and introduced them to Katherine, then sent them back outside to finish hoeing. She chatted away contentedly as she made biscuits and put on her colcannon to simmer, stopping only to refill Katherine's teacup. When her cooking was finished, she sat down at the table and had a cup with her.

"Tell me about yourself, Katie," her aunt urged. "You know enough about me to write a book. What is it like living in America? Do you live in a fine house there, too?"

Katherine quickly disabused her of that notion, although, considering Eileen's cottage, her little home in Chicago seemed luxurious. She told her briefly of her childhood and her charity work. She even told her of her plans to build an orphanage.

"That's a fine cause, Katie," Eileen said, gazing at her with admiring eyes. "Sure 'tis bound to take a lot of money. Will you be able to raise such a sum?"

Katherine opened her mouth to reply, and quickly shut it again, unable to tell this kind woman that she intended to sell Ballyrourke. She knew she was being cowardly. Why shouldn't she admit her plans?

Colin's words echoed in her thoughts: *This is O'Rourke land, the land of your father, who came back here to help us fight for it, and died. Would you give this land to a stranger?*

She took a sip of tea to clear his voice from her mind. "I'm sure I'll be able to raise the money."

"I admire your dedication to those poor children. Don't I know what it's like to be without a home!"

It was something they had in common, Katherine thought. "Eileen, what do you know of my father's death?"

Eileen gave her a sympathetic smile. "Not much, I'm afraid. Probably as much as you."

"What's this?" a male voice said from the doorway. "Company?"

Katherine glanced around as a stranger came into the cottage. Of average height and stocky build, with a ruddy, freckled complexion and hair the color of Katherine's, he looked vaguely familiar.

"Patrick!" Eileen exclaimed, obviously pleased to see him. "You're just in time to meet your niece Katie."

"Little Katie!" he said with a fond smile as he strode toward her.

This was her father's brother. Katherine tried not to gape at him as she took his hand.

"'Tis clean," he assured her with a wink and a grin. "I just washed up outside at the pump."

"I'm pleased to meet you," Katherine replied in awe. His resemblance to the daguerreotype of her father was incredible. She felt tears prickle behind her eyelids, though she didn't know why.

"Sit, Patrick, and I'll fetch you some tea," Eileen directed, starting to rise. "The food will be done shortly."

"You sit, darlin'," Patrick told Eileen, pressing a light kiss on the top of her head. "You don't need to wait on me hand and foot when my own hands will fetch the tea more easily." He poured a cup from the pot above the range and sat down on the bench across from Katherine. "Don't you see Garrett in her, Eileen?" he asked, gazing at his niece.

"That I do, Patrick."

Katherine sat forward. Finally she would learn the truth. "Tell me about my father."

"Where to begin?" Eileen said with a laugh. "Well, he had your hair color and your eyes, for one thing, and the build of my Patrick here, strong as a bull, and just as hardheaded."

"Hardheaded, you say?" Patrick cut in, pretending to be insulted. "When am I ever hardheaded?"

"When are you not?" Eileen replied, giving him a playful push. "A man of passionate beliefs your father was, Katie, and oh, how he could sing. 'Twould bring a tear to your eye to hear him."

"When your mother was in a room, no one else existed for him," Patrick told her. "Suzannah was his true love. And Garrett was just as devoted to you, too, lass. He wrote us after your birth telling us how beautiful you were, a true O'Rourke, he called you."

He couldn't have been too devoted, Katherine thought. "How did he meet my mother?"

Patrick shook his head, as if still bewildered by it. "He'd catch glimpses of her here and there, especially in the gardens at Lawthrop House, where she liked to read. One day

he announced to us that she was the loveliest creature ever
to inhabit this earth and that he was going to marry her."

"We didn't think it would ever happen," Eileen added.
"No two people could have been more different, nor their
families more at opposite ends."

"We told him it was pure folly to even try to court her,
that he'd bring disaster on all our heads, but once my brother
set his mind to something, there was no stopping him."

"How would he bring about disaster?"

"You must understand how it is here, lass," Patrick told
her. "Landlords don't consort with their tenants. If someone
crosses that line, it creates greater conflict for all of us.
There are even those who call it treason."

"Treason! That's a strong word," Katherine said.

"They're strong beliefs," Patrick replied.

"So even though he knew he might bring about disaster,"
Katherine mused, "he still pursued her."

"They were both very much in love," Eileen replied, as if
that were any excuse for taking such risks.

Katherine didn't understand how they could defend her
father when his actions had clearly put them all in jeopardy.
Horace had said her father was a hothead. She now believed
him.

"Your mother loved Garrett so much, in fact, that she de-
fied her parents," Eileen continued, "knowing she risked
being cast out of her home and publicly humiliated."

Katherine shook her head in astonishment. Was that what
love did? "Did you know they were planning to elope?"

"They didn't tell a soul, fearing what the Lawthrops
would do." Patrick's mouth thinned in anger. "But marriage
didn't protect them. Your grandfather turned Suzannah out
with not even a spare pair of shoes. Told her never to return
and not to write, either. Nearly broke your grandmother's
heart. We smuggled news in to her whenever we could."

Katherine pictured her parents returning to Lawthrop
House, young, happily married and deeply in love, having to
face a man whom Grainwe had said was stubborn and cold,
knowing the risks they were taking.

Eileen reached across to pat Katherine's hand. "It wasn't

so bad after all, their going to America. From your da's letters they seemed to be very happy there, especially after you were born."

Katherine felt her throat tighten in anguish. "Then why did he leave us?"

Twelve

Eileen came around the table and cupped Katherine's face in her small, work-roughened hands. "You have to believe this, Katie: he didn't leave you willingly, but only because he felt he had no choice. He never dreamed he wouldn't be back to care for you and your mother."

"Garrett knew we'd been turned out of our homes, you see," Patrick told her, "and that Colin's mother and sister had died because of it."

"What did he think he could do? Didn't you lose your homes because of crop failure?"

Eileen glanced at her husband, as though asking a silent question. He gave her an almost imperceptible nod of the head. She said, "Crop failure was only part of it. The loss of our homes was Garrett's biggest worry. There was talk up at Lawthrop House that he was coming back to take his revenge on your uncle Horace."

Katherine was stunned. "He was coming to *kill* Horace?"

"We don't know that. 'Twas only rumors we heard," Eileen cautioned.

"But why Horace? He was merely following his father's orders."

Again her aunt and uncle exchanged looks. This time, however, Patrick shook his head.

Eileen started to rise. "I'd better have a peek at the food."

"Please don't try to protect me by keeping secrets from me," Katherine beseeched. "I need to know the truth."

Eileen settled her bulk onto the chair beside her and gave her a sympathetic smile. "You must understand how difficult this is for us, Katie. You're family, but you're also a Lawthrop; we work for you."

"That's even more reason for you to be truthful." She turned to her uncle. "Please, Uncle Patrick. Tell me what happened."

"Go on, Patrick," Eileen urged at his silence. "She has a right to know."

He sighed heavily. "We didn't all lose our homes because of poor crops. Some, such as Colin's father, had enough money put away to keep paying the rent, and those like him that did could have taken in the rest of us—but for Horace Lawthrop's trickery." A look of bitterness swept across Patrick's broad face. "He cheated them, Katie. He took every bit of their savings, leaving us all homeless."

Katherine was flabbergasted. "Was this by my grandfather's orders?"

Patrick slowly shook his head. "'Twas Horace's own cruel revenge against us for Garrett marrying his sister."

"But that was six years before."

"Revenge hasn't a timetable," Patrick said.

"Couldn't someone have gone to my grandfather Lawthrop and told him what Horace did?"

"Would he have taken our word over his son's?" Patrick asked grimly.

"We have a saying, Katie," Eileen explained. "Don't bring your troubles to the person who hasn't got sympathy for your cause."

"Your father came back, you see," said Patrick, "because he was too good a man to stand by and do nothing to help us."

Eileen patted her hand. "Perhaps he thought he could

force Horace into giving us back the money, but we'll never know for certain."

"What happened when my father arrived in Ireland?"

"We don't know," Patrick replied. "Garrett wired that he was on his way, but he never showed up. The gardai—our police—helped us search, but there was no trace of him at all."

"Who received his wire?"

"My father did," Patrick answered.

Katherine sorted through the information, trying to complete the picture. But there were still pieces missing. "Do you think his death was an accident?"

" 'Tis . . . possible," Patrick answered with slight hesitation.

"Then it's also possible it wasn't." Katherine looked again to her uncle for answers. "Did Horace believe my father was coming back to get him?"

Patrick shifted uneasily. "That I wouldn't know."

Eileen pushed to her feet. "It's time to eat. Will you call the boys, Patrick?"

It was apparent that they didn't wish to discuss the subject any further, perhaps fearing they'd said more than they should have.

"Thank you for being truthful," Katherine said, and let the matter drop. But it wasn't gone from her thoughts. Foremost in her mind was the question of who would have wanted her father dead. If Horace had believed he was in danger, would he have taken steps to protect himself—steps that led to murder?

Colin headed home for a bite to eat after spending the early part of the morning helping one of the tenants repair his roof, and the latter part trying to find Mary Flynn. He'd managed to sneak around to the kitchen door at Tarkinton Manor without spotting old tar-n-feathers himself, and speak with a cook, who summoned the housekeeper, who sent for the upstairs maid, who'd said she'd never heard of Mary Flynn, and didn't he mean Mary Connelly? When he'd at last found someone who knew Mary Flynn, it was only to learn that she'd been fired for talking back to the master.

Wasn't that just like her? Colin thought, stewing. Now she'd taken herself off to Dublin to visit her mother and find a new job, which meant he'd have to go up there to look for her.

Ahead, Colin saw Patrick O'Rourke hailing him from the lane. He instantly reined in his horse, fearing bad news. "What is it? Is the baby on its way?"

"Nothing like that," Patrick said with a laugh. "We've got company. Come join us for a bowl of colcannon."

Colin dismounted and led his horse to the tethering post. "Who's the company?"

"A surprise. Come see for yourself."

"I'll wash up and be there directly."

A surprise it was, too: Katie—sitting at Patrick's table, talking with Eileen and her boys as if they were old friends. Didn't she look the very picture of a country lass, with a healthy flush on her cheeks and an arm around each of Pat's sons? He noticed with some surprise that she'd removed her gloves, but he had no doubt that they were somewhere close by.

She looked the complete opposite of how he normally pictured her in his mind—that is, how he'd pictured her before their meeting at the ball. Since that ill-fated eve, however, he'd had another vision of Katie entirely, a vision based on one chance encounter and any number of lusty dreams, a vision that haunted his every waking moment and quite a few sleeping ones, as well. His memories of their passionate embrace would not leave him—not the scent of her skin, nor the taste of her mouth, nor the feel of her breast.

There seemed no way to end his torture; he'd tried to scrub off her scent with harsh soap, he'd tried to drown her taste in bitter ale, he'd tried to erase every lustful thought of her by recalling his hatred for the Lawthrops. He'd even refrained from coming to see her, though he knew she was eager for him to arrange this very meeting.

Now, as he stood at the doorway, Colin's gut instinct told

him to turn around and leave quickly, before he was
seen. Yet he found himself not only unable to look away,
but also remembering everything he'd tried to forget, and
wanting more.

"Colin, how nice of you to stop by," Eileen exclaimed.

He saw Katie swivel around for a look, surprised by his
arrival. Colin watched for signs that she'd recognized him at
the ball, but she showed no embarrassment, so he knew he
was safe.

"I was just about to serve the food," Eileen said. "Come
sit down. You've met our Katie, haven't you?"

"I have. Afternoon to you," he said, with a brief nod in
Katie's direction.

Patrick laid a place at the table beside Katie, and the boys
scooted their chairs around to make room. Colin took his
seat, determined not only to drive out those erotic images of
her, but also to make sure that kiss never happened again.

To her amazement and to their credit, Katherine thoroughly enjoyed dining with her newfound relatives, and not
just because of the deliciously hearty Irish food. Freckle-
faced, red-headed Dermot and his younger, shyer brother
Cathal, miniature copies of their father, behaved as typical
boys with boundless energy and appetites. She watched
them elbow each other, squirm, giggle, and steal covert
glances at her when they thought she wasn't looking. Good-
natured Patrick, seated opposite his wife at the foot of the
table, kept her entertained with stories that amused even
him; and Eileen's warm, sweet nature made Katherine feel
instantly at home.

Sitting beside Colin, however, proved to be taxing. Every
nerve ending seemed to tingle at his nearness, bringing a hot
flush to her cheeks again and again. She tried to ignore her
discomfort, but there was no ignoring Colin. His presence
was like a beacon in the gloom, drawing her ever closer.

"What's America like?" Dermot asked her, as they finished their meal with cups of tea.

"I can't answer for the entire country," Katherine explained, "but I can tell you a bit about Chicago. It's a big city

with many, many stores and businesses at its center, and an elevated train that runs overhead. And there's a river that runs through it, and a large lake beside it, where one can see the sun rise."

"Speaking of big," Colin remarked, leaning back against his chair, "Kevin told me about a Texan he met up with in Dublin. The Texan boasted to him, 'It takes me two whole days to ride from one side of my ranch to another.' And what does Kevin reply? 'Ah sure, I know, sir. We have mules like that over here, too.' "

Katherine wasn't sure if he was poking fun at her or not, so she merely smiled. Patrick hooted with laughter, slapping his knee, and the boys giggled, while Eileen batted Colin's arm. "You're makin' it up."

"Would I make that up?" Colin asked, putting his hand to his heart.

"Tell us another," Dermot demanded.

"That'll be enough, thank you," Eileen said. "Boys, did you know that your cousin Katie is going to build an orphanage in Chicago?"

"You are?" a chorus of amazed voices asked.

Katherine felt herself blush as Eileen continued. "She works with a group of ladies that places orphaned children with families. They're hoping to build a big home for the ones no one wants."

"And is that your reason for selling Ballyrourke?" Colin asked.

Patrick and Eileen swivelled their heads to stare at her. "You're sellin' Ballyrourke?" they asked at the same time.

"She's had a listing agent come out from Dublin," Colin informed them. "So I told her of our wish to buy it back." He glanced at Katherine as he added," She's thinking about it."

Katherine felt her face grow even hotter as everyone looked at her. She didn't know what to say. She couldn't tell them flat out that Colin's proposal wouldn't work. Neither did she want to have them think badly of her.

As though she sensed Katherine's hesitation, Eileen got

to her feet. "Let's clean up, boys, so you can get back to your hoeing."

Her husband jumped up to give her a hand and the boys immediately began to clear the table.

"May I help?" Katherine asked, rising.

"And make a guest in my house work?" Eileen exclaimed. "Not while there's a breath left in my body. Now, a husband is an entirely different animal—born to work."

"Are you calling me an animal, darlin'?" Patrick cooed in her ear, his arms around her expanded girth.

Seeing their playfulness and obvious love for each other made Katherine wonder if her parents had ever behaved in such an affectionate manner with each other. She glanced at Colin and saw that he, too, was watching them. Was he envious? Did he wish for that kind of marriage? Did he wish for marriage at all?

Why did she care?

"Will you come back again before you leave for America?" the boys asked, as Katherine put on her gloves and hat.

"I'd love to."

Katherine was touched when her aunt and uncle hugged her warmly and pressed kisses on her cheek, and both boys presented their own for her to smooch. She kissed and hugged them all tightly, regretting that she wouldn't have more time to get to know them.

Colin left the cottage with Katie. He strode ahead to open the gate for her, passing by his tethered horse, though he should have leaped on the animal's back and ridden away from her as quickly as possible. Why hadn't he? Because he was an eejit.

Where was the man who had vowed not an hour ago to drive out all lusty images of her, to never kiss her again? Where was his mettle? Was he made of paper or iron?

At that moment he was neither, finding himself instead made of flesh and blood that was all too vulnerable to Katie's charms. "What do you think of your Irish kin?" he asked, groping for something to say other than telling her she had the most sensual mouth he'd ever kissed.

It took her a moment to reply, as though her thoughts had been far away. "Oh, I like them very much." As if suddenly realizing that they were on the lane, she glanced back at his horse, then gave him a questioning look.

Colin looked around, feigning surprise. "Well, what do you know about that? My horse came here all by herself to carry me home, and that's the thanks she gets."

Katie's ripple of laughter made his insides melt. "Would you like to meet more of your kin?" he asked her, leading his horse to the lane.

She threw him a sidelong glance that was nearly his undoing. "Are you offering to take me?"

"I might be." His horse nudged his shoulder from behind, as if to warn him of his folly.

Katie gave him a happy nod as they walked together toward Kilwick Road. "I'd love to meet more of my relatives. There's so much more I'd like to find out about my parents."

And there's so much more I'd like to find out about you, beauty. "Would you want to go tomorrow, then? I can make time in the afternoon."

Colin was surprised to see Katie's smile fade. "I'm supposed to attend a tea at Lady Tarkinton's house tomorrow afternoon."

"That's fine," he said, and when he glanced at her, it was her Lawthrop side he saw. He cursed himself for falling into her trap, where images of seducing her overpowered his good sense. Now he'd gone and made a fool of himself, a task that had come about much too easily.

"But I'd much rather go with you," she blurted, then blushed hotly, making her freckles stand out. "That is," she quickly amended, "I'd rather go with you in the morning to meet my relatives, and have tea with Lady Tarkinton in the afternoon."

Suddenly she was Irish again, and he wanted to kiss her.

Thirteen

Katherine's face burned with embarrassment. Her reply had been forward and impetuous, and had surely shocked Colin. If he now thought of her as the most presumptuous female he'd ever met, he'd be right! Where were the manners her mother had strived to teach her? Where was her gentile deportment? Where had this unrestrained behavior come from?

The sad truth was that when she was near him she behaved unpredictably, irrationally. Emotionally! Shocking thoughts popped into her head at the most awkward moments, and words came out of her mouth that stunned her by their boldness. Yet at the same time, she felt more alive than she'd ever felt in her life.

"MacCormack is dangerous, Katherine. You must keep your distance from him," her uncle had warned. She glanced at Colin covertly. He was most definitely a danger, but not in the way her uncle had meant. The danger was that the attraction between them was so overpowering, it jeopardized her ability to think logically. Katherine didn't ever want to make the same mistake her mother had made.

Preoccupied, she didn't notice the rock in the road until the toe of her shoe hit it. Katherine quickly regained her balance, but it didn't stop her from feeling like a complete idiot. Now he could add graceless to her list of faults.

Colin picked up the offending stone and hurled it into a field. "Dangerous things, these sneaky devils, always lurking alongside the road, hoping to catch the unwary. I nearly tripped on it myself. Now then, what time would you like to go?"

His gallantry made Katherine's heart swell with gratitude. If she let her emotions have free reign, she'd find a lot to like about Colin MacCormack. "I don't want to take you away from your duties."

"How would nine o clock be?"

"That would be perfect."

"Nine o clock in the morning it is." His horse nudged his shoulder again, causing Colin to look around at the animal with a laugh. "Are you jealous, Lizzie? Is that what these little pokes are about? Well, I haven't forgotten you." He pulled a carrot stub from his pants pocket and held it up to the horse's muzzle. "She's terribly jealous," Colin said in a low voice, as though the horse could understand him.

"Her name is Lizzie?"

"Elizabeth is her formal name, but it doesn't suit her, much as Katherine doesn't suit you. Would you like to ride her?"

Ride? No one had ever taught her to ride. "Perhaps another time."

"No time like the present," Colin said with a wink.

"There's always tomorrow," she replied cheerily.

He peered closely at her. "You're afraid, aren't you?"

"I am not!" she retorted, lifting her chin. "I just don't know how."

Colin's eyes widened in disbelief. "You don't ride? I've never heard of such a thing." He stopped in the road, interlaced his fingers and said, "Come on. Up you go. It's time you learned."

She took a step backward. "I don't have the proper clothing to sit astride."

Colin studied her for a moment, rubbing his chin, then he smiled. "That's easily remedied." Before Katherine knew what he was up to, he lifted her up and sat her on the saddle sideways.

She gasped as she nearly slipped off, trying to shift her skirt to a decent position. "This isn't a sidesaddle. I'll fall!"

"You won't fall if you hold on. I'll walk her slowly."

Katherine grabbed hold of the pommel with white-knuckled fingers and prayed silently.

"That's not so bad, is it?" Colin asked.

She took a steadying breath and tried not to think about how high up she was. "You don't think Katherine suits me?"

"At this moment, I'd have to say you're more suited to Katie."

"But not always?"

"No, not always."

"When am I more suited to Katherine?"

His expression grew solemn as he nodded toward Lawthrop House in the distance. "When you're up there."

She turned to gaze at the house with him. What he didn't seem to understand was that Katherine was who she really was. Katie was a girl she'd have to leave behind when she went back to America.

As quickly as Colin's mood had turned somber, it changed back. "So you're going to build an orphanage, are you? That's quite an undertaking."

"There are quite a lot of homeless children in Chicago."

"None of us here are strangers to homelessness," he said grimly.

"Yes, but you weren't abandoned by your parents. These children have no one to protect them."

Colin regarded her for a moment. "It's a fine thing you're doing, Katie."

"Thank you." She held her breath, praying he wouldn't bring up the subject of buying Ballyrourke.

"Were Patrick and Eileen helpful to you?"

The muscles in her shoulders relaxed. "Yes, quite helpful, although they were reluctant to talk about my father's death."

"You understand why they can't tell you everything."

"Because I own Ballyrourke."

"That's part of it." Colin held a low-hanging branch out of her way. "The other is their fear of Horace Lawthrop."

Katherine hadn't wanted to mention her uncle, knowing the bitter feelings between Colin and him, but since he'd brought it up, she pursued it. "I don't understand their fear. Horace can't hurt them. Ballyrourke isn't his."

Colin's blue eyes flashed angrily. "It wasn't his when he stole our savings. But he still did it, didn't he?"

"Are you certain he was the culprit?"

"He was the one, all right. Everyone knew it."

"I hardly think my uncle is that evil. He was angry about his sister marrying an O'Rourke, is all."

"Is that all?" Colin replied lightly. "So it's all right to cause a child's death because you're angry."

"That's not what I meant."

"It seems that what you see as evil is different than what I see," Colin said, keeping his eyes on the road ahead.

"My definition of evil," she explained, "is a moral corruption of character."

"What do you call stealing money from poor people?"

"How could he have stolen your father's savings? A bank wouldn't let him take someone else's money."

"A bank? Do you see a bank anywhere around here?" he asked, sweeping his hand in a wide arc around him.

"Then how did Horace get the money?"

"My father kept his money in a locked strongbox hidden in our root cellar. Your uncle Horace came to my father one day and accused him of cheating him on his rent payments. He demanded payment for the next two months in advance, on the spot, and when my father hurried to get the money, Horace saw where it was kept. The box was stolen the next morning while we were at church. We were quite relieved that we had paid up our rent in advance, or so we thought, until our house was set afire."

Katherine was so appalled that she couldn't think of anything to say. Could Horace have committed such an abominable deed? Would his hatred of the O'Rourkes push him to that extreme? She just couldn't fathom anyone being that cruel.

But if he had done it, why had it fallen to her father to settle the score?

"Eileen said it was rumored that my father was coming back to seek revenge on Horace. Do you think that's true?"

" 'Tis what I've heard," Colin replied. "To be truthful, I'd have done the same in his shoes. A man has to step forward to defend his land."

"You'd have abandoned your family in America and crossed an ocean to protect your land?" she asked indignantly.

"Some of us are born leaders."

"Or fools," she muttered under her breath.

"I have no argument with you there."

She wasn't about to let him wiggle out that easily. "Do you find it honorable to desert your wife and child?"

"Your father didn't know he was deserting you. He was simply doing his duty."

Katherine fumed silently at his single-mindedness. It was all so black and white to him. Clearly, Colin was cut from the same mold as her father. She pitied the woman he'd marry, for she'd never feel secure. "Why didn't Patrick, or any of the other O'Rourke men who lived here, do something about the situation?"

"They'd have to answer that for themselves. Tomorrow you'll meet Brigid, your grandfather O'Rourke's sister. Brigid's ancient, but her mind is as sharp as a needle. She'll have more to say about it."

Katherine sighed in frustration. "I hope so." There were so many different stories, she wondered if she'd ever learn the whole truth.

They rode along in silence until, while still a good distance away from the house, Colin pulled the horse to a stop and lifted Katie down, instantly setting her heart to pounding. All she could think of was the last time, when she thought he was going to kiss her.

Nonsense. He hadn't done it then. Why would he now?

"See there?" he asked, standing so close that she had to clasp her hat to her head and crane her neck up to see him. "You rode your first horse. Very bravely, too."

"I hardly think I was brave."

"Well, I think so, and that's what counts, doesn't it?"

What an egotistical remark! She started to tell him so, and then he smiled. Colin was teasing her.

She couldn't help but laugh. But as Katherine gazed up into those vivid eyes, her smile disappeared, as did Colin's. In the span of a heartbeat the world around her vanished, leaving only the two of them standing inches apart, the heat from their bodies mingling, his scent enveloping her, making her almost dizzy with desire. Her gaze moved to his mouth, and she felt at once that he was going to kiss her. Or perhaps it was just wishful thinking again.

Katherine's heart began to race as Colin lifted her chin and dipped his head toward her. Her wish was about to come true.

The sound of running feet caused them both to step apart. Colin, instantly on guard, moved in front of her, just as the stable boy came running out of a stand of trees and onto the road.

"What is it, Tommy?" Colin asked.

The youth swept off his tweed cap and gulped air. "Grainwe sent me," he said breathlessly. "She said mistress's uncle is askin' where she is, and that she should come at once."

Katherine stepped out from behind Colin. "Did Grainwe say why he was asking for me?"

The boy shook his head. "Maybe 'tis due to the English gentleman what came a bit ago."

"Oh, heavens," Katherine exclaimed. "I forgot that the listing agent was coming today. I should have been present to greet him." She said to the boy, "Tell Grainwe I'll be there directly."

As the youth rushed off, Colin said to Katherine, "Will you tell Horace where you've been?"

"If he asks." Katherine frowned as she imagined her uncle's unpleasant reaction to the news that she'd not only dined with her aunt and uncle, but had also walked home with Colin. There was sure to be a lengthy lecture.

"Are you certain you can get away in the morning?"

"I'm certain."

Colin thought he saw a slight wrinkle of worry on her brow. He lifted his hand to run his palm alongside her face, to reassure her that everything would be fine, but then he checked himself. He had come dangerously close to kissing her only moments before. He didn't want to tempt himself again. Besides, her worries were no business of his. "Nine o'clock," he reminded her, as he strode to his horse.

"I'll look forward to it."

"It would be best if you met me here," he told her as he swung up into the saddle, "so your uncle doesn't see us together."

Colin waited until Katie was out of sight, then he headed the horse through the trees, taking a back way to the stables. What was he to do? He certainly could never fall in love with Katie, yet now he found he couldn't hate her, either. The truth of it was, his lust for her was so potent that it blinded him to who she was.

His only saving grace was that she'd be gone soon. And if he could persuade her to sell them the estate, he'd have all he ever wanted anyway.

But now there was a new worry—the orphanage. Colin had a sinking feeling that she intended to build it with money from the sale of Ballyrourke. If that was her plan, then she'd want her money right away. It made selling those paintings all the more urgent.

He gave the horse to Tommy to be rubbed down. "Whose animals?" he asked, noticing two strange mares in the stalls.

"One belongs to Mr. Calloway," the youth answered. "He's the man I told you had come here from Dublin. The other is a younger fellow, Irish by the looks of him. Is Ballyrourke to be sold then, Colin? Will we lose our jobs?"

"Not if I can help it."

"Me mam says you're our only hope. She says if anyone can save us, it's you."

Colin ruffled his hair, more pleased by his compliment than Tommy knew. "Tell her I thank her for the kind praise and I'll do my best."

"If you need two more hands to help, I have them at the ready," the youth called.

"Did ye enjoy yer lunch with yer aunt and uncle?" Grainwe called, as Katherine changed into a fresh outfit in her dressing room.

She stepped out, hurriedly fastening buttons down the front of her bodice. "Very much. How did you know about it?"

"Word travels as fast as the foot at Ballyrourke." Grainwe poured water from the pitcher into the wide, porcelain bowl for Katherine's use.

"Does my uncle know?"

"None of us have breathed so much as a word to him, lass."

Katherine felt an instant relaxing of the tense muscles in her neck. "What does Ballyrourke mean, Grainwe?"

"A *baile* is a town. This is O'Rourke town."

"Is it true that the Lawthrops came in to save it from ruin?"

Grainwe's lips pinched slightly, as though to compress her words into something palatable. "Some would say that."

"If the Lawthrops hadn't taken over Ballyrourke, what would have happened to it?"

Grainwe sighed thoughtfully. "Hard to say, lass. If the Lawthrops had never come here, then it would have passed down from father to eldest son on the O'Rourke side."

"And right now, who would be living here?"

"As the eldest living male, it'd be Patrick."

Katherine dipped a cloth into the water, then wiped her forehead and cheeks. "How sad that the O'Rourkes weren't able to hold on to Ballyrourke."

"Not for ye, miss. T'was just that what brought yer mother and father together."

For an ill-fated romance, Katherine thought morosely. She thought back to what Colin had told her about Horace. Was her uncle truly responsible for the terrible deeds of which he was accused? Could his hatred of the O'Rourkes have been so strong that he would have stolen money and forced them out of their homes?

"The O'Rourkes are a deceitful lot," Horace had warned her. *"Never forget, they are not to be trusted."*

Who was she to believe?

Fourteen

When Katherine swept into the library, Horace was sitting at the massive walnut desk, a half-written letter in front of him. He looked up with a scowl. "Where have you been?"

"Out for a walk," she said hastily, which wasn't the entire truth, but also wasn't a fabrication. At least it would spare her his lecture.

He put the pen back into its holder. "You missed lunch and you missed Calloway's arrival. You should have been here to meet him."

His reproachful tone irked Katherine, but she bit back a sharp reply. "I'll go apologize to him at once. Where is he?"

"Making the rounds of the gardens. I should tell you that Calloway has brought along his young assistant, John Bloom. You'll meet him at dinner."

"I'll look forward to it."

Horace pushed back the chair and came toward her. "I've been thinking, Katherine. If you have no interest in meeting with Calloway over the next few days, I shall gladly assume that responsibility. I understand that such a task is bound to be tedious for you, when I'm sure you'd much rather be completing your inventory."

What Katherine found truly tedious was his insistence on

controlling her affairs. "Thank you," she said evenly, "but I believe I can handle both."

Katherine spent the remainder of the afternoon touring the house and grounds with the agent. Calloway agreed that the gardens were some of the most beautiful he'd ever seen and would increase the desirability of the property. But he cautioned again that the costly repairs on the house would have the opposite effect.

"Will I be able to realize a profit?" Katherine asked anxiously.

"I'm sure there will be some profit. I won't be able to say how much until I complete my report." The vagueness of his answer didn't do much to calm her worries.

"Just out of curiosity," Katherine asked, "what usually happens to a staff when someone new moves into a home such as this?"

"Sometimes they're kept on. Sometimes a new owner prefers his own people."

"What about the estate manager?"

"The owner usually hires his own man."

Katherine frowned at the thought of Grainwe and Doreen and the others at Lawthrop House losing their positions. And what about Colin? What would he do?

You're becoming too attached to Ballyrourke, her conscience warned. *The O'Rourkes would manage as they always have.*

At supper, she met Calloway's aide John Bloom, a thin, nervous sort with wiry brown hair that lay flat against his scalp from a heavy dose of hair oil, and eyes that darted constantly between her uncle and the listing agent as they talked politics. He made Katherine uncomfortable, though she didn't know exactly why.

While the men smoked their cigars and drank their whiskey, she slipped outside. With the Keats book in hand, she headed straight for the rose garden, a place where she felt immediately at peace.

The sun was setting as she walked along a path, stopping here and there to pick up brightly colored rose petals. She sat on a bench at the far side of the garden, opened the book, and sprinkled the delicate petals on the page to study them. At once, the little calico cat appeared at her feet. She jumped up on the bench and rubbed against her arm.

"You certainly pop up at the oddest times," Katherine said with a laugh, stroking the animal's soft head. "Where have you been? I haven't seen you in a while."

The cat sniffed the rose petals, then sneezed.

"*Sláinte chugat,* Cali," said a girl's voice behind her. Katherine looked around in surprise as Gersha reached over her shoulder. "That means good health to her. And here's another petal for your collection."

Gersha deposited a tiny wedge of bright orange on the book, then came around to sit beside her. "I knew I'd find Cali with you. She likes you as much as everyone else does, Eileen and Patrick especially."

"That's very kind of you to say so."

"Patrick says you're the perfect blend of your mother and father, as if they'd been rolled together into one person. They're something of a legend here, ye know. Me mam used to tell me how they fell wildly in love, the most unlikely pair. One a proper English lady and the other a brash Irishman. And just like in the fairy tales, the brave knight rode off with his fair maiden."

Except that it didn't have a fairy tale ending, Katherine thought.

Gersha swung her legs. "Have you ever seen a baby born?"

"No, I haven't."

The girl pursed her lips. "Sure, 'tis not good news. Eileen will need help when her time comes."

"There must be a doctor or midwife who can help her. Or your mother, perhaps. Do you live close to Eileen?"

Gersha shrugged as she leaned over to examine the petals in Katherine's hand. "This one reminds me of you," she said, pointing to a white one. She selected a dark red one and placed it beside the white. "This one is Colin."

"Quite different, aren't they?"

"In color. Aren't they both roses, though?"

Katherine had to laugh at her analogy. "True, but you'll never see a white rose and a red rose on the same bush." She tipped the book and let the petals fall to the ground, scattering softly in the evening breeze.

"It's nearly dark, Gersha," she said, rising. "You'd better take Cali home with you now."

The little girl obediently slid off the bench and started away, only to look back suddenly. "You won't sell Ballyrourke, will ye, Katie?" she asked, gazing at her expectantly.

"I have to, Gersha. I made a promise I have to keep."

Seeing the disappointment on Gersha's face, Katherine couldn't help but feel guilty. Yet she couldn't expect the child to understand her commitment. Gersha had a family and a home.

Cali meowed, and Katherine glanced down to find the cat reaching up to her with one little paw. "Gersha, you forgot Cali," Katherine called out, but the girl had already gone.

"Come on, Cali," she said, picking up the cat, "you can stay with me tonight. But this absolutely must be the last time."

It was well past midnight when Colin crept into the attic. At the top of the stairs he pushed down the hood on his black cloak and looked around for the three canvases he had set there and was baffled that they were missing. He hadn't dreamed it, had he? He took the nearest ones, three paintings in fancy frames, and lugged them down one by one, hoping the frame wouldn't slip from his hands and bang against the floor.

When he stepped into the kitchen for the third time, he nearly jumped out of his skin as a shadowy figure moved toward him. Quickly, he put the painting down and stepped forward with his fists up, ready for whatever happened.

"Colin?" Doreen whispered.

He sighed in relief. " 'Tis me."

"What are you doing here?"

He put his arms around her and pulled her close. "I've come to see you, what else?"

"Liar!" she said with a giggle, pushing on his chest. "I saw you put something behind you."

"Are you sure you want to know what it is?"

"Get out, then, before someone else awakens."

Colin gave her a quick kiss on the cheek. "Would you be kind enough to lock the door behind me?"

His friends were pressed against the side of the house, and stepped out of the shadows as he approached. "Who were you talking to?" Kevin asked softly, taking the heavy painting from him.

"Only Doreen. Don't worry."

A murmuring of voices woke Katherine. Was the noise coming from the hallway? She sat up in bed to listen, disturbing Cali. No, the voices were coming from the open window. She threw back the covers and hurried across to the window. Below, she could just make out three dark figures moving through the rose garden. She rubbed her eyes and looked again. They were each carrying a large object. Were they robbers?

She grabbed her wrapper and sped down the hall, shoving her hands through the sleeves and tying the belt at her waist as she hurried down the stairs, nearly tripping over a drip pot. She headed for the kitchen and almost collided with Doreen.

"Oh!" the startled girl cried, holding a hand to her heart.

Katherine, too, had to catch her breath from the surprise. "Doreen! Were you in the garden just now talking to someone?"

"Oh, no, miss! Whatever would make you think that?"

Katherine hurried toward the back door. "I saw people from my window."

"I didn't hear anything, miss," the maid said, running after her. "I would've heard them if they'd been out there. I have good ears."

Katherine opened the door and stepped outside to look around.

"Oh, do come in, miss, please!" Doreen cried from the doorway, as Katherine moved carefully along the path toward the garden. "You have no slippers on. You'll catch your death."

The girl's voice seemed to echo in the night. "Hush, Doreen," Katherine whispered. "You'll wake the household."

"Then let me go get me own shoes for you," the maid entreated. "Stay right there. I'll be back in a moment."

"That won't be necessary," Katherine replied. She glanced at the doorway, but it was empty. Doreen had already gone to fetch them. She looked back toward the rose garden, but the figures had vanished, as well. Had she imagined them?

Colin, Michael and Kevin lay flat on the grassy lawn, hidden behind the low wall of yews that encased the garden. As soon as Colin heard a door close, he slowly raised up and peered over the hedge. "She's gone," he whispered.

Cautiously, they rose, picked up their bounty and stole away from the house. They didn't breathe easy until they were well out of sight of the windows.

"That was close," Michael said as he handed a painting up to their leader, standing in the opening four feet above him.

Colin stashed the painting on the first floor of the tower, then reached down for another. "Sorry, boys. I guess we'll have to make it even later tomorrow night."

"I can't do it, Colin," Kevin said, handing his up. "My wife is already upset with me for being out again so late."

"If she's already upset, we may as well do another run tonight." Colin climbed down the ladder, jumping the last two feet to the ground.

"Tonight?" Kevin glanced at Michael in dismay. "We were nearly caught, and he wants to go back."

"I haven't any time to waste," Colin explained. "A listing agent is already preparing the sale papers."

"What if you go to all this trouble of taking the canvases, Col, and it doesn't pay off?" Michael asked.

"I've already made contact with an art dealer in Dublin who's eager to see them. He'll pay in cash for whatever he buys, and he won't ask questions. I'm taking a couple in my wagon tomorrow. I want to find out what he'll pay for them before I take more." Colin pulled up his hood. "Ready?"

"We're just as daft as he is," Kevin muttered, as the three men headed back to Lawthrop House.

While his friends lay low in the garden, Colin once again snuck up to the house. But the kitchen door was as far as he got. Through the glass he could see Katie sitting at the kitchen worktable, her long hair brushed out and laying on her shoulders. Doreen, he saw, was tending a kettle of water on the stove, no doubt making tea. He muttered a curse at his bad luck and started to turn away. But suddenly Katie rose, and he saw that she had on her nightclothes. At once, his loins tightened at the thought of what lay beneath.

He shook away his lustful thoughts. He hadn't come to ogle her. Quietly he crept back to the garden with the news. "Go home, boys. We'll not be taking anything more tonight."

He waited until they had slunk away, then he started back for the stables. But did he go there? Like the eejit he was, he veered off instead and went straight toward the kitchen, drawn to that room where Katie sat nearly naked—at least in his imagination.

He tapped lightly on the glass pane in the door and saw both women look around in surprise. Seeing him, Katie's face lit up, warming him all over. She hurried to open the door.

"What are you doing up at this late hour?" she whispered.

"I might ask you the same question." Colin let his gaze sweep down the thin green wrapper she wore, where her white nightdress was just visible at the neckline. The wrapper was tied snugly at her waist, showing off the nice curve of her hips. He felt his blood surge, thickening his shaft. Ah, wouldn't he like to make love to her right this very moment?

Watch yerself, Colin. Now's not the time.

Now wasn't the time? What was he thinking? There never would be a time.

"The mistress thought she saw someone in the garden," Doreen explained, giving him a pointed look as she poured tea into Katie's cup.

"I thought I heard voices myself," Colin told her. "I had a look around, but didn't see anyone."

"You were outside?" Katie asked.

"No. I live above the stables and heard it through my window."

"You live above the stables?" The news seemed to surprise her.

"When it suits me." He didn't say that since his father died he hadn't been able to return to the empty cottage.

"Will ye stay for tea?" Doreen asked, giving him another pointed look. Colin knew she wanted him to leave.

He winked at her when Katie wasn't looking. "No thanks. Don't care for it." Also no sense tempting himself by staying so close to Katie, where his thoughts had a will of their own, and no good could come of them.

"If there's nothing else, then, I'll bid ye good night," Doreen said, stifling a yawn.

"Good night," Colin and Katie both answered at once.

Colin waited until Doreen had left the room, then he looked down at Katie, standing there in her nightclothes, with her pretty hair falling about her shoulders, her lips looking so soft and ripe for kissing. At times like this he wished she was merely a maid, for then she wouldn't mind at all if he tossed her over one shoulder and carried her back to his bed.

An arousing image of her lying across his coverlet wearing nothing but a shy blush leaped into his mind. He felt himself begin to harden and decided he'd better leave quickly, before a certain member of his body convinced him she *was* a maid.

He strode to the door and opened it. But then Katie made the mistake of following. He tried not to think of that picture of her in his head, nor of the memory of those soft, sensual kisses, but Katie's standing so close to him made it very difficult.

"You needn't fear any robbers," he told her. "But if you'd feel safer, I can always sleep here in the kitchen at night." Giving him the added benefit, he thought, of having free roam of the house, including the attic. "All I'd need is a cot and a blanket."

"I couldn't ask you to do that."

"Sure you could," he said softly.

She gazed up at him with her big, guileless eyes, and Colin knew he wouldn't sleep that night unless he kissed her. And if he kissed her, he wouldn't sleep for dreamin' about her. He was doomed either way.

He took her hands and pulled her outside the door, standing there in the open doorway with the light from the kitchen shining on them, where anyone happening by could see. Did he give a thought to it? Not Colin. His thoughts were elsewhere.

Fifteen

Katherine gasped in surprise as Colin drew her outside the door. Before she could react, he cupped her chin, tilting it up as his mouth came down full upon hers, a wanton, arousing assault of his lips.

Her mind ceased to function, halted in mid-thought by a potent rush of desire. As Colin held her in the sheltered circle of his arms, her breasts snuggled against his powerful chest, her nipples tingling from the contact, she kissed him back, shamelessly, hungrily. His hands slid down to her derriere, pulling her firmly against his groin, where she could feel a hard bulge pressing against the vee of her thighs. Her body reacted at once, passion flowing like a current to a well deep inside her, coiling tighter and tighter, causing her body to throb with the pleasant, heavy ache of anticipation.

The spicy scent of his skin spiraled around her, reminding her of something vaguely familiar. Then his tongue edged between her lips, and as it slipped inside, stroking the roof of her mouth, a strong memory assailed her. She pushed away from him, staring at him in shock.

Colin was her Adonis!

* * *

Eejit! He'd done it again, let his lust override his common sense, or what was left of it. He wasn't sure anymore if he had any. And by the way she was gaping at him, she didn't think he did, either.

He tried to make light of it, glancing up at the sky, then pointing heavenward. "Aha! There's the culprit: a full moon. 'Tis known to have strange effects on some people. It seems I'm one of them."

He offered a smile. What was wrong with her? Hadn't he explained himself? Why did she keep staring at him as if he'd grown horns and a tail.

Katherine's heart thudded loud enough to wake the house, her blood so thick with desire that, for a moment, she couldn't speak. She stepped back into the doorway, pressing her fingers to her mouth. "It was you!" she whispered.

Colin glanced down at himself. "Last time I looked."

"In the library—at the Tarkinton's ball. It was *you* who kissed me!"

He stuck his hands into his pockets and looked down at his shoes, a posture of humility. "An honest mistake. It was dark."

A mistake? Then Colin had known all along it was her. Why hadn't he said something? Of course. He was meeting someone else there.

Katherine felt an unexpected surge of jealousy. Why? He was single, handsome. It should come as no surprise that he'd have a girl. Her jealousy changed to embarrassment. She had taken his kisses greedily, and they had been meant for someone else.

And his kiss tonight? He'd already explained it: the moon. Now how was she to explain her shameless behavior? How could she make a graceful retreat?

Colin solved the problem for her. "I won't let it happen again. From now on I'll ask before I kiss."

"Yes. P-please see that you do." Katherine backed inside and quickly shut the door, sagging weakly against it, still trembling from the shock. All those passionate fantasies she'd had after the ball hadn't been about a stranger. They'd been about Colin.

She shoved herself away from the door and hurried up to her bedroom, where she slid into the bed and pulled the sheet up over her head. She had to erase those lustful images, every single blasted one, before they did something strange to her, like cause her to use words such as "blasted," or make her believe she was falling in love. Her mother had made the fatal mistake of falling for an Irishman. She, Katherine Lawthrop O'Rourke, would not repeat history.

When Katherine came down to breakfast the next morning, she saw a letter addressed to her sitting in the salver on the hall table. Recognizing the handwriting as being one of her friends from the ladies' society in Chicago, she opened it and read it at once.

> *Dear Katherine,*
>   *I hope this letter finds you in good health. Everyone has been asking about you and sends good wishes.*
>   *We are all very busy as we have received twelve more children to place in the past two weeks and have only found homes for three. What a sad state of affairs it is. An orphanage is needed now more than ever.*
>   *Take care, my dear. I will continue to keep you posted.*
>
>   *Sincerely,*
>   *Edith*

With a sad sigh, Katherine tucked the letter in her pocket and went to the dining room. Twelve more children just in two weeks. She could well imagine the ladies' dismay. She had to get this estate matter resolved soon and get back home.

Yet as she sat at the table in that beautiful room, gazing out the windows at the lush, rolling carpet of green beyond the glass, she felt a deep sense of regret that she would be leaving Ballyrourke behind. And that wasn't all she would be leaving.

But she had made a promise to the children.

"Where are you off to so early this morning?" Horace called, just as Katherine was ready to let herself out the front door.

She steeled herself for his rebuke, just as she'd steeled herself for seeing Colin again after her shocking behavior. "I'm going to meet my great-aunt."

"And why is that?"

She suddenly noticed John Bloom standing just off to the side, his watchful eyes on her. Ignoring him, she took a breath and said, "I have some questions for her."

Horace lifted his eyebrows. "About your parents?"

At her nod, he said, "You realize that any answers will be completely biased."

"I'm aware of that."

"Are you having tea with Lady Tarkinton this afternoon?"

"Yes. I'll be back in plenty of time."

He gave her a nod, then turned and walked toward the dining room. With a sigh of relief, Katherine slipped outside and shut the door. At least he hadn't lectured her.

"John," Horace said to the young man hovering nearby, "I want you to follow my niece to see where she goes and with whom. And please be discreet."

"I'll take care of it for you," his assistant said, giving him a cocky nod of his head.

"I'll take care of it for you, *sir*," Horace corrected.

"Eh?"

"Not *eh,* John. I beg your pardon."

"For what?"

Horace shook his head in frustration. "Never mind. Just go."

He watched John scurry up the back hall toward the kitchen. He had been exceedingly leery about trusting an Irishman, but Calloway had assured him that this young man had been raised and educated in England, and would be completely loyal to him. Today would be his first test.

A light, gentle rain misted the air, bringing a sweet, grassy freshness to it. Katherine raised her umbrella and inhaled deeply. She'd never seen rain like this back home. It was so soft, one barely felt it. Weighed down by a sudden feeling of regret, she walked through the park, let herself out the gate and started up Kilwick Road.

In the distance, she saw Colin sitting on the stone wall, his arms folded, his keen gaze upon her. He had on a tan shirt this morning, and black pants, with a black tweed cap on his head. He looked so ruggedly handsome that he took her breath away.

She should have felt annoyed, for she'd slept very little, and what sleep she did have was full of sensuous dreams of Colin. But instead, she felt alive. Seeing his face again was enough to bring back all those delicious memories of his kisses.

She pressed her lips together in firm resolve. No matter how his presence affected her, she would have to ignore it.

"Mornin'," he called, hopping down from the wall. "A bit damp today, isn't it?"

"Yes, it is," she replied, peering at him from beneath the umbrella.

"Any problems with your uncle?"

"None."

Colin glanced at her as she walked primly along beside him. In her white blouse and narrow-waisted navy skirt, and her tidy bun tucked beneath her properly beribboned navy hat, holding her little ruffled parasol over her head, and wearing those ever-present white gloves, any stranger would think her an English schoolmistress. But didn't he know how deceiving those looks were.

Beneath that cool exterior lay a woman of great passion, though she had yet to tap that hidden well. And it wasn't only by her lusty kisses that he knew it. No, it was also the rosy blush in her cheeks, the sparkle in her eyes and that alluring sway of her hips, all of which she'd acquired since coming to Ballyrourke.

Ah, wouldn't he love to be the one to open Katie's eyes to that wanton side of her. Didn't he yearn to lay her down and spread her thighs, to peel away the layers of her prudish disguise and expose that lusty creature hidden beneath. Just thinking about the delights that awaited him made him feel that familiar ache, that swelling of his manhood, that overpowering urge that was so hard to ignore.

At that moment, what Colin wanted to do more than anything was to pull her into his arms and ravish her with kisses. And that would be only the beginning—with any other woman.

But Katie was not any other woman; she was a Lawthrop, which he seemed to be having a hard time remembering lately.

He summoned up the image of her uncle's hawkish face and instantly felt his enthusiasm wane—for the moment, at least. He wasn't fool enough to think he'd tamed his lusty side forever.

"Where does Brigid live?" Katie asked, gazing at him from beneath her parasol with those beguiling eyes.

Stay strong, his conscience whispered. "On Padraig Lane, just over the hill and down Kilwick a piece." He glanced at her as they walked along, this time noticing a certain strained look about her face. "Are you sure you're feelin' all right?"

Her answer was as forced as her smile. "Of course I'm sure."

"Out with it, Katie. You're irked about something, and now that I look at you, your face is a bit blotchy. Now I'm thinking that perhaps it was because of last night—"

"I'm fine," she said hastily, rubbing her cheeks.

"—and if you'd like me to apologize for kissing you, then I will," he said. "But if you want me to say I regret it, I won t."

"I'd like you to forget it ever happened," Katherine snapped, then immediately clapped her hand over her mouth. "I'm sorry. I didn't mean to be rude." But he did vex her no end. She didn't want to be reminded of what had happened and how forward she'd been, or of how she'd foolishly fantasized for days about him, believing him to be her Adonis.

"Aha! So that's the way it is."

She gave him a wary glance. "What do you mean?"

"It's comin' clear to me now. I should have thought of it before. Shame on me for being so dense."

"Will you please tell me what you're talking about?"

"It's not that I *kissed* you; it's that *I* kissed you. Me! An Irishman."

At once her cheeks grew warm. "Don't be silly."

"Tell me I'm a liar, then," Colin challenged.

"It's not that at all," she said, knowing it was she who was lying.

"Then what is it?"

"It's not something I can discuss."

"If it wasn't that, you'd discuss it."

Having no defense, she said, "This is the most ridiculous conversation I've ever had," and marched ahead of him, fuming at his perceptiveness.

"If it's not that, prove it," he called. "Kiss me now."

Katherine came to an abrupt stop and stared at him. "Here? In the middle of the road?"

"There's no better place."

Barbarian! She started walking again. "A public road is no place for a display of affection."

"Neither is standing outside your back door, but you had no problem with that. Besides, we can always slip off into the trees. My kisses are legendary, you know. And legends are best passed along."

"Fine," she said evenly. "Tell your grandchildren about them."

"You enjoyed those kisses, and you know it, even though I *am* an Irishman."

That was all too true, unfortunately. "You're arrogant, is what you are."

"I've been called worse things."

Oh yes, she was certain of that. She would have added a

few more to the list were it not for civility's sake. On the other side of the coin, she couldn't help but note a number of good things about him, such as his incredible handsomeness and his sense of gallantry and family loyalty. But why add to an overinflated self-esteem?

Katherine gazed down the long stretch of road, searching for signs of a cottage. But she saw only stone walls and fields as far as the eye could see. "How much farther does Brigid live?"

When Colin didn't answer, Katherine turned to look at him. His head was turned to the left, his eyes sweeping the fields, his head cocked as though listening intently. Katherine listened, too, but heard only the sound of sheep bleating.

"Rub your eyes," he said quietly.

"I can see just fine."

"Rub them; I'll explain in a moment."

Puzzled, she gently rubbed the fingertips and thumb of her left hand against her eyelids. "Is that good enough?"

"That'll do." He hooked his hand in the crook of her arm and pulled her to a stop. "Now let me have a look."

Katherine lowered the umbrella to her side and gave him a wary glance as he cupped her head between his hands. "This had better not be a ruse to kiss me."

"I don't need ruses." He bent close and squinted at her, as though examining her eyes. "In the first place, we should have turned at the lane back there. In the second, we're being followed."

"What?" She started to glance around but his hands on her head prevented her from moving.

In a louder voice he said, "Your right eye, you say? I don't see anything there."

His lips barely moving, he said, "Now when I let you go, we'll turn back and go up to the crossroad. Just smile and act like nothing's amiss. When we get to Brigid's, I'll take you inside, then I'll go out the back window and find out who it is. Don't leave there until I come for you."

"Are we in danger?" she whispered.

"It's not likely, but I never take chances." He released her and lifted her chin to look into her eyes. "There, now," he said loudly. "Is that better?"

"Yes," she said, raising her voice to match his. "Thank you."

He led her back to the junction in the road, where a small wooden sign on a post proclaimed in crude letters Padraig Lane, with an arrow beneath pointing to the left. "We'd better hurry along or Brigid will fear something has happened to us."

"How did you spot him?" she asked in a whisper.

"I always keep my eyes and ears open."

They walked up a lane of other thatched-roof cottages and finally came to a stop at the last one. "Here it is," he told her. "Remember to stay here until I come for you."

It took Katherine's eyes a few moments to adjust to the dimness of the small cottage. Then she saw a white-walled, sparsely furnished room with a tiny figure sitting in a rocking chair in front of a stone hearth. A low turf fire glowed pleasantly in it, though it was a warm day outside. Cross-stitched samplers hung on the walls in handmade frames, the brightly stitched words written in Gaelic. The crude wooden mantelpiece above the fireplace held an assortment of cups, candles and carved figurines.

"*Dia Dhuit,* Brigid," Colin said, his respect for the woman evident in the tone of his voice.

"*Dia is Muire dhuit,*" Brigid replied in a warbling voice, drawing her black wool shawl closer about her frail shoulders.

"'Tis an Irish greeting," Colin explained quietly to Katherine as they crossed the creaky wooden floor together.

"Is this our Katie, then?" Brigid asked, squinting up at her with eyes that had faded to a watery ice-blue. Her coarse gray hair was braided and coiled around the back of her head, and her neck was shriveled like a prune. Her cheekbones jutted from her sunken face, as did her nose, which seemed overly large in such a tiny face.

She was so fragile, Katherine was almost afraid to touch her. "I'm Katie, and I'm very pleased to meet you," she said, tentatively offering her hand.

"Have ye a chill, Katie? Colin, stoke up the fire. The lass is cold."

"No, I'm fine, really," Katherine replied hastily.

"Then why are ye wearin' gloves? I'm not the queen, am I?"

Feeling her cheeks redden, Katherine removed her gloves, casting Colin a quick glance only to find him trying hard not to laugh. The old woman reached out for her hand, but didn't shake it. Instead, she turned it over and studied the palm. Then she rubbed a wrinkled thumb across it and looked up with a squint. Katherine fully expected her to predict her future.

"Sit ye down, lass. I'll get a crick in me neck if I have to keep lookin' up at ye."

Colin brought over a rickety kitchen chair and placed it across from Brigid's. He bent down and kissed the woman's papery, liver-spotted cheek. "Take care of Katie for a while, Brigid. I'll be back soon."

"Would ye care for tea, Katie?" the woman asked, gesturing to a teakettle on the hearth. "Help yerself, lass. There's a clean cup on the mantel shelf."

"May I pour some for you, Brigid?" Katherine asked as she poured herself a cup.

"Tank ye, no. My, but yer the spittin' image of yer mother."

"Everyone else says I look like my father."

"Paugh! What does everyone else know?"

"You remember my mother, then?"

"Aye. She came to see me quite often in those last weeks before she left. Took her a while before she felt easy with us. She had those Lawthrop ways, ye know." Brigid studied her silently, as if deciding whether Katherine had them, too. "What is it I can do for ye?"

"Answer some questions, if possible."

"Ask, then, and I'll tell ye what I can."

"I'd like to find out what happened to my father when he came back to Ireland, and why he alone came to fight for the O'Rourkes."

Brigid clucked her tongue. "Yer da was a fearless fool is

why, though most people called him a hero. Did he think he could solve our problems by bullying the Lawthrop boy? Or killing him? He'd only have brought the gardai down on him, and us as well. The other men knew it, and so did nothin'. But Garrett O'Rourke was too full of himself to think it out reasonably."

Katherine was surprised at the woman's rancor, but relieved that someone at last shared her opinion. "What do you think happened to him?"

Brigid rocked silently in her chair, her lips pressed tightly together.

Katherine leaned forward. "You needn't fear telling me anything. I want to know for my own private reasons. I know there are some who believe my uncle Horace was responsible for his death. Is that what you think?"

With a heavy sigh, Brigid turned her misty gaze toward the window, as though returning in her mind to that distant time. "To his dyin' day, Horace Lawthrop will never forgive his sister for marryin' an O'Rourke. He made no bones about wantin' Ballyrourke for himself, but he was given only half, ye see. Even his own father didn't trust him to run it alone. And Suzannah, poor lass, feared what Horace would do to get her half once her parents were gone. When she got married, ye see, then Garrett stood to inherit should she die first. And do you think yer uncle would have stood for sharin' Ballyrourke with an Irishman?"

"But that wouldn't have happened. My mother was disowned."

"Aye, 'tis true her father disowned her, but he didn't disinherit her."

Katherine gazed at the old woman in surprise. She had assumed her mother had been cut from her grandfather's will, and had only been reinstated by her grandmother's. "Are you sure?"

"Didn't she sit right here and tell me so? 'Twas the very night that Garrett vowed to take her to America where he'd give her the grandest life of all."

A grand life. Katherine sighed, remembering their year in the orphanage, struggling to survive.

"Was it bad for ye, lass?"

"In truth, I don't remember what it was like before my father left us, only afterward. My father was wrong to leave us, Brigid, and I'll never forgive him for it."

"'Never' is a word usually regretted, lass." The old woman took her hand between her own, clasping it with her bone dry fingers. "'Twas a mistake that they married, that I'll agree. Yer mother and father were of two different worlds and two different minds. But ye've come through it fine. Aye, yer a strong woman, young Katie."

"Thank you for your kind words. What I don't understand is why my mother didn't appeal to her parents for help when we were in such desperate straits."

"Perhaps 'twas her pride." Brigid shook her head. "Poor gentle lass. She was like a wounded dove, so hurt by her father's rejection."

So hurt she'd rather be a charwoman in an orphanage? Or was there something else behind her mother's refusal to ask for help? "*Do* you believe Horace had something to do with my father's disappearance?" she asked again.

Brigid leaned back, the old chair creaking as she rocked slowly in it. "Well, now, if I answer yes, ye'll think it's the fanciful workings of an old woman's mind. If I answer no, ye'll think I'm protectin' ye. So I'll answer this way: we've all seen how he let nothing stand in his way to get rid of the likes of us. 'Twas only by the grace of the Lord and yer grandfather's favor that we were able to come back here.

"Now *you* have Ballyrourke," she said, stabbing a gnarled finger in Katherine's direction, "and once more yer uncle is denied what he wants. Think hard, lass, and if ye suspect he had anything at all to do with yer father's death, then watch out for yourself, for ye'll be in danger, too."

Sixteen

"Did you save me some tea?" Colin said from the door.

He came through the narrow, arched doorway, a large dark figure silhouetted against the light from outside, and instantly Katherine's heart leaped in joy. She pressed her palm against it to still the pounding, vexed by the way her body always responded to him. Hadn't Brigid just said what a mistake it had been for her mother to fall in love with an Irishman?

"There's always tea for me guests," Brigid replied. "Lass, will ye fetch another cup from the shelf?"

Katherine poured Colin tea from the kettle as he propped his foot on the raised stone hearth. She handed him the cup, watching his expression to see if he would give her any indication as to whether he had accomplished his mission. He accepted the tea with a nod of thanks, but otherwise gave no reply.

"So what do you think of Katie?" he asked Brigid.

The old woman gave her a long, scrutinizing stare. "She's got steel in her. A good woman is our Katie."

"That's high praise coming from Brigid," Colin said with a wink. To the elderly woman he said, "And how have you been faring? Do you have enough peat stored away for the coming winter?"

Katherine watched him as he conversed easily with Brigid, teasing and causing her to blush as though she were a girl again. Colin had such charm, such potent magnetism, that even an old woman wasn't immune to it.

As they chatted about family matters, Katherine thought over what Brigid had told her. "*. . . once more yer uncle is denied what he wants. Think hard, lass, and if ye suspect he had anything at all to do with yer father's death, then watch out for yourself, for ye'll be in danger, too.*"

If all the warnings were true, then was Horace even now scheming to get Ballyrourke from her? Was that why he wanted to handle her investments? And the agent Edward Calloway, was he in on it, too?

Once again Katherine felt as though she had no one she could trust.

They stayed only a short while longer, though Katherine would have liked to hear more of Brigid's stories. But Colin was in a hurry to leave. As soon as they had stepped outside into the misty rain, he said to Katherine, "What time is it?"

"She held her umbrella in one hand and opened the watch pinned to her white shirtwaist. "Ten o clock. Still early. Did you find out who was following us?"

"No sign of the bastard, pardon my language. If he follows us again, though, I'll nab him."

"Could it have been the police?"

"The police?" he said, throwing her a curious glance. "Why would the police be following us?"

"Perhaps because you're involved with a band of rebels?"

"A band of rebels! And I suppose I'm the leader of this band, as well? Where did you hear this silly rumor?"

Katherine squirmed inwardly, wishing she'd never brought it up. "I believe I heard it on the night of the ball," she replied vaguely. If she told him the whole truth, it would only create greater animosity between him and her uncle.

"Is that right? And might the someone you heard it from be your uncle Horace? Ha! I can see by the high color on your face that it was. Well, I'm not surprised. He doesn't like you hobnobbing with me because he's afraid of what I'll tell you, so he'll do whatever he can to make you believe the worst of me.

"I won't deny having faults, including a bit of arrogance now and then, but I'll tell you what I'm not, and that's a liar. I might give the truth a bit of a honey coating once in a while, so as not to hurt your feelings, but I'll never lie to you, either, which is what Horace is plainly doing. So believe me when I say I'm not the leader of a rebel band; I'm not even *in* a band. Now what do you have to say to that?"

That she was incredibly relieved. But all she could bring herself to say was, "I appreciate your honesty."

She could see in his eyes that she'd disappointed him. He'd wanted her to say something more personal. She just couldn't admit that she cared, not to him or to herself.

"Well then," Colin said solemnly, "I'd appreciate the same favor in return, which brings up my next question. Have you given serious thought to my offer?"

Katherine's stomach plummeted. This was the conversation she'd been dreading. "I've given it some thought, yes."

"Now before you say anything," he said, as they turned onto Kilwick Road, "I've been thinking about your wanting to build the orphanage and I've decided you'll probably need some money right away, so I'm working hard to get it for you."

She couldn't help but pity him. Colin was so set on buying the land that he couldn't see the problems. He and the others would never be able to get together the kind of money she'd need to build the orphanage. And even if they did manage to scrape enough together, what would they live on?

Katherine knew what it was like to be poor, to dream of a better life, but his plan was impractical if not impossible. She simply couldn't allow him to go on hoping in vain.

"Whatever it is you're thinking," Colin said, "it can't be good or you wouldn't be frowning."

Tell him. He asked that you be honest. But she couldn't hurt his feelings, either. Perhaps she could try some of that honey coating he had mentioned. "I was merely wondering if *you've* given serious thought to this matter."

His dark brows drew together. "Only for about three years."

"Have you considered how expensive it will be not only to make much-needed repairs to the house but also to maintain it, plus the stable, the barn, the tannery and all the other outbuildings?"

"Worth every cent, too," Colin said.

"Then there's the crucial matter of deciding who controls the land, who lives in the house, who manages the finances."

"Patrick would make those decisions. He's the head of the family."

"And with all the O'Rourke money put toward the house, there'd be none left over for emergencies, or even basic needs."

"Ah, but most worries never come true, you see."

"There are other problems: I don't have the figures yet for how much it will cost to repair Ballyrourke, or what its asking price will be."

"Isn't that what the listing agent is for?"

Colin's nonchalant attitude worried her. He brushed off concerns as if they were nothing but pesky flies. But she knew how those flies could bite. "You don't seem to realize that a major undertaking like this cannot be left to happenstance or luck. One must carefully think everything out ahead of time. An imprudent attitude is simply foolish."

The muscles in his jaw twitched. "So I'm foolish, am I? And imprudent, to top it off. Well, thank you very much, Katie, for your honest assessment of my character. I take it your answer is no."

"If you'll let me finish my explanation," she replied with growing frustration, "you'll see that my logic is sound."

Colin came to an abrupt halt and swung to face her, his eyes glittering dangerously. "Logic? Does your logic take into account our love of Ballyrourke? Is your heart made of stone, Katie O'Rourke?"

Is her heart made of stone, indeed! "You don't know anything about me!" she found herself blurting.

"Don't I, now?" he answered a little too snidely.

"Do you know why I want to build an orphanage? Because a long time ago I had friends who died in one, and I was helpless to do anything to save them." Her voice thickened with emotion as her shame rushed to the surface. "Well, I'm not helpless anymore. I have Ballyrourke."

"And what about us, your family?" Colin shot back. "This land is our lifeblood! We were born and raised here, and we'll die fighting for it, if we must."

"Colin, please understand, I'm not trying to hurt the family; I'm family, too. This is a debt I owe to those children who died. I *have* to pay it back. Besides, it doesn't have to be a fight to the death. If you want land, save up your money and look elsewhere for it. There must be good farmland somewhere nearby."

"There's good land to be found—right beneath our feet. It's called O'Rourke land, and it's our home. But you can't understand that, can you, Katie? As the well-fed never understand the lean, you Lawthrops will never understand our feelings for Ballyrourke."

You Lawthrops. Katherine dug her fingernails into her palms in an effort to control her temper. "I understand a lot more than you think."

"Sell Ballyrourke to a stranger, then," Colin sneered. "Put your own relatives out of their homes so you can build another for children you don't even know. Go back to your safe home in America where you can use all the logic you want, and your heart can stay frozen forever."

How could he be so cruel? She wanted to cry out that he knew nothing of her feelings. Instead, she hid her hurt behind a mask of indignation. "It's certainly clear that *you* never use logic or you'd know you're being ludicrous!"

She turned her back on him and started toward the house at a dignified, ladylike pace, determined to show him that he hadn't ruffled her feathers at all.

"'Tis a good thing those children have you, Miss Katherine Lawthrop O'Rourke," he called out, "for there's surely not another kind person in the whole big city of Chicago who would help them if you don't."

Katherine hummed tunelessly as she walked away from him, trying to block out his sharp gibes. But as she mounted the stone steps to Lawthrop House, she felt such anger welling inside that when she entered the hall, she shoved the heavy door with all her might, causing a loud slam that echoed down the hallway. Frozen heart, indeed!

"Good God," Horace said, coming out of the library, with John Bloom close behind. "What was that?"

Katherine didn't stop to reply. She marched straight up to her room, muttering every vile thing about Colin MacCormack she could think of. She removed her hatpin, tossed her hat on the bureau, caught sight of herself in the mirror, and stopped in surprise.

She moved closer, curious, until her full face came into view, and then she stared at the stranger with flames in her cheeks, with squinting eyes and scowling brows, and locks hanging loosely from the bun in the back. She didn't look dignified or ladylike. She didn't even look familiar.

"Miss, are ye ill?" Grainwe asked, bustling in, her brow furrowed with worry. "Yer uncle said ye were in a tizzy."

Katherine plunked down at the dressing table, shook the pins from her hair and began dragging the brush through her locks. "Colin MacCormack," she began, "is the most infuriating, most bull-headed, idiotic man I've ever met."

"That's on a good day," Grainwe added. "What did the scoundrel do this time?"

"It's what he won't do—use logic!"

"And never will. Colin always speaks from the heart." She took the brush from Katherine and ran it through her hair in long, soothing strokes.

"Well I speak from the head, which is how every sensible person should speak. It prevents one from saying hurtful things."

"Aye. Sensible people always speak from their head." Grainwe began to twist Katherine's hair into a chignon. "There's many people like yerself who think things out in a calm way, but then there are others, like Colin, who are driven by an inner fire. Both have their values. Meself, I've always thought a combination of the two is best. Then you have both good sense and strong convictions."

"I have strong convictions. It's just that I was taught that it's very unladylike to voice them."

"What's ladylike isn't always what's honest," Grainwe remarked.

"If being honest means hurting someone, then I'd rather be a lady and keep my thoughts to myself."

Grainwe finished pinning her hair in place and set the brush aside. "Tell me this, lass: what did yer mother tell ye about yer father?"

Katherine gazed at Grainwe's reflection in puzzlement. What did her mother have to do with Colin? "She said very little."

"Aye, that's right. Yer mother, being a lady, kept her thoughts to herself, and so ye knew nothing at all about the man who was yer father until ye came here. Now tell me which is best, being ladylike or being honest?"

"I don't see why I can't be both."

"Ye can, lass, but ye must listen here first," she said, tapping her chest, "*then* follow up here." She touched a finger to her temple. "Yer poor mother closed off her heart to everyone, even to ye, because it was easier than rememberin' how it felt to love someone deeply. Ye must guard against that happenin' to ye, lass. Ye don't want to end up a bitter old woman."

Katherine sighed. It was just so much easier to let her head govern. It didn't cause her the anguish she felt now. The problem with listening to her heart was that it was being tugged in two directions, with each side being an ocean apart. She was determined to build an orphanage. At the same time, she didn't want to put her own relatives out of their homes.

"There's surely not another kind person in the whole big city of Chicago who would help them if you don't," Colin had sneered. But that wasn't the point. She had made a pledge to those homeless children, and nothing in the world would cause her to break it.

There was a light rap at the door. "Mistress, luncheon is served," Doreen called.

Grainwe patted Katherine's shoulders. "Think about what I said, lass."

Colin swore under his breath as he strode to the stables. Find a new home? The daft woman didn't know the O'Rourke clan at all if she thought they'd walk away from their homeland. Then again, she cared more about strangers than she did her own family. What could he expect from her?

"It's certainly clear that you never use logic or you'd know you're being ludicrous!" she'd said in her haughty tone, as if losing Ballyrourke were nothing more than an issue in the newspaper to be discussed over tea.

Muttering angrily, Colin hitched up the wagon and headed for the round tower to load up three of the oil paintings. He'd show Miss Katherine O'Rourke. Wouldn't she be surprised when he handed her a sack of money and demanded the land back?

Seventeen

Horace watched Katherine covertly as she sat opposite him at the dining room table, devouring her chicken as if she hadn't eaten in days. Her face had too much color, and her eyes fairly gamboled with vivacity. He shuddered with distaste. The O'Rourke influence on her was becoming more apparent each day.

It didn't help that she sought out those peasants. Despite his warnings and his attempts to discourage any contact, it seemed Katherine was doing her utmost to disregard his wishes. He'd learned from John Bloom that she'd even gone with MacCormack to a ramshackle cottage where the old crone Brigid resided.

Horace knew the treacherous natures of those O'Rourkes. There was no doubt but that they were planting traitorous ideas in her mind.

"So, Katherine," he said, as their coffee was served, "how was your visit with your great-aunt?"

"Quite pleasant," she answered, looking steadily at him. "I was amazed at how well she remembered the past."

Horace's gaze never left her as he lifted his cup to his mouth. What did Katherine mean to imply? What had the old crone told her? He waited for her to expound on her answer, but she only stirred cream into her coffee.

"I suppose she was full of imaginative tales of her youth," he said. "The mind tends to revert at that age."

Katherine paused, her cup halfway to her mouth. "Actually, she was quite lucid."

"Or at least she appeared to be."

"I was satisfied that she was."

"I suppose she told you how cruel the Lawthrops were to her."

Katherine gave him an odd look, an unsettling, suspicious look.

"I hope you didn't believe her stories," he said.

"Why shouldn't I?"

"Because they are fabrications."

Katherine merely continued to sip her coffee. Horace's eyes narrowed. He didn't like the way she ignored him, as though she knew a secret. Her mother had been just like that, the termagant. But he'd taught her a lesson, hadn't he? He just might have to teach Katherine one, too. And he most definitely had to put an end to her association with Mac-Cormack.

The Lawthrop carriage conveyed Katherine to Tarkinton Manor, where she was ushered into a plush sitting room. Lady Tarkinton awaited her there, dressed in an afternoon gown of lightweight plum wool serge. She perched regally on a beautiful, white moiré sofa, a low, marble-topped cherry wood table laden with an elaborate silver tea service in front of her.

Katherine sat down and accepted the dainty porcelain cup from a maid. "Thank you for inviting me, Lady Tarkinton. I'm so happy to have this opportunity to become acquainted with one of my grandmother's dear friends."

"As I am you, dearest Katherine. How pleased your grandmother would be. You've become quite a lady. You do the Lawthrop name proud." She sighed loudly. "I only wish you could have known your grandmother. She was a noble woman and good friend. How I miss her."

Katherine took a sip from her cup, wondering how to approach the subject of her parents.

"How are you faring at Lawthrop House?" Lady Tarkinton asked. "I understand you've decided to sell it."

"Yes, that's true."

"Is it also true that Horace is buying it?"

Katherine looked at her in surprise. "No. Not at all. Had you heard he was?"

The woman waved the subject away. "I thought someone at the ball had mentioned he wanted to purchase it from you, but then my hearing isn't always what it should be." She signaled to the maid, who instantly refilled Katherine's cup.

"He's certainly never mentioned the idea to me," Katherine told her, although, as she thought about it, if her uncle was intent on having the estate, then he might very well make her an offer. It would be the most logical thing to do.

But what would she say if he did? Mr. Firth had made it quite clear that her grandmother had not wanted Horace to have Ballyrourke. She'd have no choice but to tell him that she couldn't in good conscience sell it to him. Katherine shuddered at the thought of his reaction, and hoped that her grandmother's friend had, indeed, heard wrong.

"Lady Tarkinton, I hope you won't mind, but I have some questions that I'd like to ask about my parents."

"Of course, dear. I shall do what I can."

"Do you remember when my mother and father eloped?"

The woman nodded her head. "It was a dreadful time. After your grandfather ordered Suzannah and Garrett to leave Ballyrourke, your grandmother came here and wept in my arms. Oh, how she pleaded with him to relent, but he believed dangerous precedents would be set unless he took stern measures.

"In my opinion, Katherine, what had really angered him was that he'd wanted better for his daughter than to wed a poor Irish farmer. I certainly didn't fault him for that. However, he went to extreme measures to make his point. When Suzannah left, I was afraid my dear friend would never recover from her grief."

"Were my mother and grandmother close?"

"Oh, yes. Very close."

"What puzzles me," Katherine said, setting aside her cup, "was that my mother stopped writing to my grandmother. I can't understand why she would do that if they were close."

"Especially considering that your grandmother sent her money to live on," Lady Tarkinton added, "a great deal of money, using her own inheritance, so your grandfather wouldn't find out."

"When was that?"

"Perhaps a year after Garrett's disappearance."

That was where her mother's sudden wealth had come from!

"You know, dear, it could have been Suzannah's pride that kept her from writing. She was a very sensitive girl." Lady Tarkinton sipped her tea, her brows wrinkled pensively. "Although," she said slowly, "I've sometimes wondered if she didn't fear for her life. Someone did away with her husband, after all."

"But there's no proof that my father was killed."

Lady Tarkinton leaned forward, as though to share a confidence. "I didn't know your father, Katherine, but I do know what was said about him at the time: he was a determined man, and nothing but death would stop him from returning to Ballyrourke to help his family. Perhaps your mother feared she was in danger, too, and went into hiding. I know she would have done whatever was necessary to protect you."

"How well do you know my uncle Horace?"

A look of disdain came over the woman's face. "As well as I ever want to."

"Do you think it's likely that he could have had something to do with my father's death?"

Lady Tarkinton pursed her lips as she pondered the question. "I know there was intense dislike between the two men, but as to whether Horace would actually commit murder against him, I wouldn't want to speculate."

"How did my mother and Horace get along?"

"Not well, from what your grandmother told me, but then

that's fairly common among siblings. I do know that Horace's mistreatment of their tenants was a continuing source of distress for your grandmother. I wasn't surprised to hear that she sent him away last year. In fact, it was just after your grandfather died that they had their big row."

Katherine was stunned. "She sent him away?"

Lady Tarkinton's eyes danced excitedly as she warmed to her topic. "Oh, my dear, it was a dreadful quarrel, from what my maids told me. You know how servants love to exchange gossip. In fact, your grandmother ordered him to leave very suddenly. He didn't tell you this?"

Katherine shook her head. Her uncle's story had been quite different. "Do you know what their argument was about?"

Lady Tarkinton sighed. "Unfortunately, I didn't see much of your grandmother after your grandfather passed on. Her health went into a rapid decline. But I can promise you, she wouldn't have sent him away without a strong reason."

Katherine sipped her tea in silence. What else had Horace lied to her about?

Although Lady Tarkinton offered a carriage to take her home, Katherine chose to walk instead, needing the time to organize her thoughts. There were so many bits of information to be sorted through from both Brigid and Lady Tarkinton that it would take her days to assimilate them. But one thing stood out: she could not trust Horace.

The rain had stopped and a balmy breeze carried the scent of heather on it, helping to soothe her troubled mind. Up ahead she spotted Gersha sitting in front of a hedgerow, playing with her cat.

As Katherine approached, a frown appeared on the girl's face. "You're troubled, Katie. It makes me sad to see you so."

Katherine crouched down beside her and held out her fingers for the cat to sniff. "It's nothing for you to worry about. I just have to figure something out."

She studied the child curiously as she played with the cat. It puzzled her that Gersha was never with other children, or helping out her mother with the crops as she'd seen Eileen's boys doing. *A fairy* is what Colin had called her, and she suspected Grainwe was of the same opinion. Yet here the child was, as real as the nose on Katherine's face. But how could she prove Gersha's existence? "Is your home near here, Gersha?"

The child heaved a sigh and climbed to her feet. "I suppose you'll never be satisfied unless I show ye. Follow me and I'll take you there."

Katherine followed her up Kilwick Road past several large wheat fields to a signpost marked Gerald Lane, a narrow road overgrown with weeds, as though it was rarely used.

"Close your eyes now and I'll lead ye along. It'll be a surprise."

Katherine scrunched her eyes shut and held out her hand. Guided by Gersha, she walked carefully down the rutted path, praying she didn't stumble, until the child announced proudly, "We're here."

Katherine blinked to accustom her eyes to the light. Ahead of her was a tidy cottage with dark brown shutters at the windows.

"I'd ask ye to step in for tea with me mam, but she's gone to market. Tuesday is our big market day, ye know."

So Gersha was a fairy, was she? With a mother who went to market on market day? Katherine couldn't wait to tell Grainwe and Colin that she'd actually seen her home. "Thank you for bringing me here, Gersha. It's very pretty. Perhaps I'll be able to come back another day."

"Ye'll be back," Gersha said, gazing at Katherine with her strange light eyes. "One day very soon. Shall I lead ye back to the road now?"

Colin sat grimly on the wagon seat as it bounced along on the long trip home. He should have had a sack full of money in his pocket as well as fresh hope in his heart. But all he had were three paintings hidden under horse blankets in the back of the wagon, the same three paintings he'd carried all the way to Dublin.

It wasn't the art dealer's fault. The man had offered to

pay him well, and couldn't wait to get his hands on more. Colin heaved a sigh of regret. It was no one's fault but his own. He'd stood there in that fancy art shop shifting guiltily from foot to foot as the dealer had blathered on about the paintings' value. Weren't they the most exquisite examples of their time? Wasn't it generous of the O'Rourkes to put them on the market? In fact, he already had a buyer, a fellow in England who collected rare paintings. Bring them all, the man had said, rubbing his mushy white hands together in anticipation of the money to be made.

Money to be made for Colin, as well. And what had he said to the prospect of all that money? "No, thank you, sir. I've changed my mind." And then he'd carried his paintings back to the wagon, one by one.

Wouldn't Kevin and Michael have something to talk about now? Kevin had been against his plan from the start, pricking his conscience as only Kevin could do. But he, Colin MacCormack, had self-righteously defended his decision.

"Is it criminal to walk into your own house to claim your own possessions? Those paintings belonged to O'Rourkes long before the Lawthrops arrived."

He'd made a good argument for it, too, even though he'd known deep down that those paintings weren't his to sell. He'd just refused to admit it until the very moment when he could have thrust out his palm and accepted payment.

Colin straightened his back. He might be quick-tempered at times, and even a bit stubborn, but the one thing he was *not* was a thief. He could no more sell those paintings than sell Ballyrourke itself. They were part and parcel of the O'Rourke heritage.

Still he felt the crushing weight of disappointment. His dream to buy the land was gone. The only hope left to him now was to find the will. But even there he'd failed in his search for Mary Flynn. He'd only found her mother who'd said Mary had gone that day to look for work. She had no idea how long her daughter would be out. So Colin did the only thing he could do—he left word for Mary to write and tell him a day they could meet.

Up ahead in the road he saw the slender figure of a woman, and as he drew closer he saw the navy hat and white gloves and knew it could only be Katie. He cursed his run of bad luck. There walked the very symbol of his anguish, the heiress of a land that should belong to the O'Rourkes, a woman who cared nothing for Ballyrourke, who didn't know what it meant to be loyal.

He wanted to urge the horse into a trot and ride straight past her, but she'd already glanced back and seen him. Colin pulled up alongside her and slowed the horse instead. "Want a ride?" he grumbled.

"No, thank you." She kept walking and didn't even bother to look at him.

So it was still Her Haughtiness, was it? Colin glowered at her proud, stiff back as she marched up Kilwick, then whistled to the horse to go on, but then he noticed Katie was favoring her left foot. "You're limping," he said, pulling even with her again.

"I happen to have a stone in my shoe."

"Are you too prideful to bend down and shake the blasted thing out?"

She threw him an icy glare and kept walking.

"You've a long way to go with only one good foot."

"I'll manage."

"Stubborn, haughty female," he muttered to himself. Did he care if her foot ended up a bloody mess? Ha!

Colin gritted his teeth in frustration. Damn it, he did care. He just might have to pick her up and toss her into the wagon.

Not likely, boy-o, with those paintings lying there under the blanket.

All right, then he'd put her on the bench beside him. She wouldn't like it, but he wasn't about to watch her limp home.

"Colin!" Young Dermot O'Rourke called, running across the meadow from the direction of his cottage, waving his arms. "Colin! The baby's comin'." He climbed over the low stone fence, breathing hard, his face red from exertion. "Me mam needs help."

"Slow down, Dermot. She'll be fine. Now who can we get for her?" From the corner of his eye Colin noticed that Katie had stopped and turned to listen.

The boy's eyes welled with tears. "It's market day, Colin. Everyone's gone to town. Cathal has gone to fetch da, but he's far out in the fields today."

"Aren't there any doctors nearby?" Katie asked. She had come up to the front of the wagon near the boy.

"We use midwives," Colin explained. "The nearest doctor wouldn't make it in time."

"You've got to come, Colin," Dermot cried in a panic. "Mam said to hurry."

"Climb up then and we're off." Colin glanced at Katie. "Do you want to come?"

"Yes," she said without hesitation.

As the boy scrambled up into the back of the wagon, Colin saw Katie start to follow. *Jaysus,* he thought. *Not in the back!* He glanced over his shoulder and saw the corner of one frame peeking from beneath its cover.

"Sit up here," he called to her. "You'll dirty your gloves back there."

She hesitated, as though the thought of sitting beside him didn't appeal to her, either.

"Come on, we've no time to waste," he ordered.

The gloves won out. She pressed her lips together and climbed up, perching primly on the bench. It was Katherine who sat beside him now.

Eighteen

Katherine knocked lightly on the cottage door, then glanced back to where Colin and Dermot waited anxiously beside the wagon. They had decided it would be best for her to go in unless more help was needed.

"Come," Eileen called in a voice that was strained and thin.

Katherine opened the door and stepped in, quickly shutting it behind her. Eileen was pacing the cottage floor, wearing a white cotton nightgown, holding her swollen abdomen with both hands.

"Katie! Saints be praised! I didn't expect the child this soon." Sweat poured down her brow as a contraction overtook her. She braced herself against the table until it passed. "Will you put water on to boil? I can't lift the bucket."

"I'll see to it." Katherine took off her hat and gloves and put them on the table. "Why don't you go lie down?"

"'Tis better to keep moving. Where are my boys?"

"Dermot is outside with Colin. Cathal went to find Patrick."

Eileen grabbed hold of the back of a chair as another contraction engulfed her. "You'll need a clean knife—and a piece of twine." She clenched her teeth together and waited until the worst had passed. "I've set out towels, and a blanket to wrap the baby in."

She would need a knife? Katherine poured water from a pail into a large pot on the stove and lit the fire beneath. The thought of the enormous responsibility of delivering a baby made her quake with fear. What if she did something wrong, and the baby died? She wasn't qualified to bring a child into the world. She'd never even been present at the birth of an animal.

She heard Eileen groan again and turned to find her as pale as a sheet.

"Perhaps . . . I should . . . lie down," she said, gasping for breath. "Something's different . . . this time. I hope there's not . . . a problem."

Katherine suddenly felt weak-kneed but steeled herself not to show it. Eileen needed her.

She put her arm around Eileen and helped her into the small bedroom off the kitchen. Eileen laid on her side on the thin mattress of the small, rope-slung bed and drew her knees up. "Do you see the towels on the bureau? Would you bring them here?"

Katherine followed her directions, making her as comfortable as possible, then went to the kitchen to check on the water. She heard a soft tap on the door and opened it to find Colin there, concern etched on the strong planes of his face.

"Is she all right?"

Katherine saw Dermot standing behind him, waiting for any word. "Eileen is fine," she said with a smile, nodding in the boy's direction.

"Are you all right?"

Seeing Colin standing there so solid and safe, she had the strongest urge to bury her head in his shoulder and tell him how frightened she was. Instead she said, "Yes. I'm fine, too."

Colin called over his shoulder," I'll be right out, Dermot." He stepped inside and shut the door behind him.

"You're not fine," he said, taking her hands in his. "You're shaking like a leaf."

"Is there anyone else who can come help her?"

Colin's grip tightened reassuringly, his gaze fierce and gentle at the same time. "You know there's not. You have to be strong, Katie. Eileen is depending on you. Do what comes naturally. Ease her pain. She'll guide you. She's gone through it twice before."

Katherine dropped her gaze. "I'm frightened."

He lifted her chin. " 'Tis nothing to be ashamed of, Katie. You'd have to be a fool not to be a bit scared. Just don't lose your nerve. Remember what Brigid told you. You've got steel in you."

Her stomach clenched as Eileen cried out in pain. She drew another breath and released it. "Will you call me when the water boils?"

Colin paced the kitchen, feeling as edgy as a caged fox. Why wouldn't the water heat faster? Would it never boil? Where the hell was Patrick?

He could hear Katie talking to Eileen in a soothing voice, telling her she would be fine, trying to make conversation to keep her mind off her pain. He could also hear the strain in Katie's voice, and knew it was taking a lot of courage to pretend to be calm. In spite of his resentment of who she was, he was proud of how she was handling herself. She had stepped forward to help and hadn't backed down. He admired her for that. There was a lot of O'Rourke in her.

Hearing Eileen cry out, Colin's hands balled into fists. If ever a man felt helpless, it was when a woman was giving birth. The water began to bubble noisily. He quickly ladled it into a big enamel bowl and called out, "The water's ready."

"Would you bring it in, please?" Katie asked.

Colin tried not to look at the woman curled up on the bed as he placed the bowl on the floor beside them. He glanced at Katie, instead, who was sponging Eileen's forehead, her own damp with sweat.

"I'll be just outside in the yard if you need anything

else," he said quietly. He strode out the front door and took in deep breaths of fresh air. The good Lord had known what he was about when he'd made Colin a man and not a woman.

"Is my mother all right?" Dermot asked him.

"She's fine. Katie is taking good care of her."

To pass the time and to keep the boy busy, Colin took out his pocketknife and taught Dermot how to throw it with perfect aim. He could hear Eileen's cries growing closer together, and said a silent prayer for her.

"Da!" Dermot shouted, and ran toward his father who was coming from the field as fast as he could, his youngest son close behind. Colin snapped his knife shut and stuck it in his pocket.

"Katie's in with her," he said, as Patrick loped past him.

Colin waited with the two boys for another hour while Katie and Patrick brought the new baby into the world.

"You sent for me?"

Horace put down his book and cast a contemptuous eye on the scrawny figure lounging indolently in his doorway. "You sent for me, *sir*. For God's sake, use some manners, John. And remove that filthy cap when you enter this house."

He waited until Bloom had stuffed the dirty tweed cap into a pocket. "That's better. Now I have a task for you. My niece was due back from Tarkinton Manor hours ago. I can't imagine what is holding her up. I want you to go there and look for her. If you find her, come directly back and tell me so."

"What if she's not there . . . sir?" he added with a sly glance.

"Then find her, wherever she is. You can start by looking for the land manager, Colin MacCormack. I shudder to say this, but she might be with him. And, as always, John, be discreet."

John Bloom grinned. "I'll find her. You can count on that . . . sir."

Standing just outside the library with her ear to the door,

Doreen's eyes widened in alarm. That slimy little man was a spy! "For your sake, I hope the mistress is not with ye, Colin," she whispered, and quickly crossed herself for good measure. She heard footsteps coming her way and, with a startled gasp, darted into the pantry, where Grainwe was taking stock of the canned jams.

"The elderly servant turned in surprise as Doreen slipped behind the door. "What are ye up to now, lass?"

"Shhh!" Doreen cautioned, holding her finger to her lips. "And don't stare at me or you'll give me away. Go back to your work."

As soon as Horace and John had passed by, Doreen stepped out from behind the door and cupped her hand over Grainwe's ear. "Master is sending John Bloom to spy on the mistress 'cause he thinks she's with Colin, and ye know how the master hates Colin. Do ye know where Colin is? I've got to warn him."

Grainwe pulled back and glared at her. "What I know is that it's none of our business. Go about yer work and forget what ye heard."

"But Colin—"

"Colin is a grown man. He'll take care of himself."

Doreen hung her head. "Yes, Grainwe." She went back to her duties and tried to remember what Grainwe had said. Still, Colin ought to know about that nasty little John Bloom being a spy. The next time she saw Colin she'd warn him, no matter what.

When Colin and the two boys were finally called into the house, Patrick was beaming broadly, holding a tiny bundle in his arms. "It's a girl!" he said proudly, his voice husky with emotion. He bent down to show his sons their new sister.

"How's Eileen?" Colin asked, peering at the tiny wrinkled face buried in the blanket.

Patrick said near his ear, "She's had a very rough time of it. Katie's just finishing with her now. I think she'll sleep for a while."

With a hearty sigh of relief, Colin went back outside to

his wagon. He could leave now, his mind at ease. The baby was safely delivered, and Katie could find her own way home. In fact, she'd probably insist on it, sore foot and all.

So why didn't he leave?

He heard a slight sound and turned. There stood Katie, just outside the house, looking at him with huge eyes. Her face was pale and strained. Her hat and gloves were gone. Her white blouse and navy skirt had dark smears of blood.

Colin stood there gazing at her like an eejit, not sure what to do. She started walking toward him, and then he toward her. When they met, she fell into his arms and clung to him.

There was his answer.

Nineteen

"It's all right," Colin crooned into her ear. "You did it, Katie. The baby and the mother are doing fine, all thanks to you."

She looked up at him through tears of joy, her emotions running so high, she was at a loss for words. "I can't begin to describe what an experience it was."

"You needn't describe it. Just say how you feel. Wasn't it the most frightening and the most incredible event you've ever witnessed?"

"Yes! It was all that and more. That tiny baby, so fragile and helpless—for a few moments she was blue, and I thought she was dead, but then she started to wail." Katherine laughed through her tears. "It was the most beautiful sound I've ever heard."

"You witnessed a miracle today, Katie."

His arms held her close and his voice soothed her. Katherine closed her eyes and laid her head against his chest, surrendering herself to the comfort as exhaustion set in.

"Come. I'll take you home."

She relinquished the warmth of his arms reluctantly and glanced down at her bloodied clothes. "I can't go back like this."

"Then I'll take you to a place where you can wash and change. Climb into the wagon."

Katherine was too drained to ask him where he was taking her. She sat silently on the bench, going over in her mind the wonder of that birth.

They stopped before a whitewashed cottage on Padraig Lane, near Brigid's house. Colin opened the door and stepped back for Katherine to enter.

She knew the home hadn't been used in a long time by the telltale layer of dust on the kitchen table, as well as the black range standing against an outside wall. On the other side of the room, two chairs covered with sheets flanked a stone hearth. The wooden floor was bare except for a braided rug in front of the hearth, and the ecru curtains at the window were simple muslin. There were no decorations on the walls or mantelpiece. It was clearly a house that lacked a woman's touch.

"This was my father's house," Colin told her as he uncovered the chairs, revealing dark green upholstery beneath.

"Why don't you live here?"

He took out a cloth of lamb's wool and dusted off the table and chairs. "I do, on the rare occasion. Usually I've got enough work to do that being near Lawthrop House is handier."

"Was this the cottage that was set on fire?"

Colin's jaw tensed. "No. We never went back there." He moved aside a curtain and peered out a small window, where, in the distance, a row of thatched-roof cottages were visible. "That house sits empty still. A reminder of the evil done to us."

Katherine could hear the fierce anguish in his voice. She pictured him as a boy with only a father to look after him, and imagined the emptiness he felt from the loss of his mother and sister. It was no wonder they never went back to their home. It would have been a painful reminder of a happier life. She felt fortunate, in a way. She couldn't remember her life when her father had lived with them.

Katherine wished she could wrap her arms around Colin and tell him how sorry she was, offering him comfort as he had her. But that wouldn't be proper. Besides, Colin was a proud man. He would take her comfort as pity.

He turned away from the window and went into one of the bedrooms, where she could hear him rummaging about. She peeked in the doorway and was surprised at the cheerfulness of the small room, a sharp contrast to the drabness of the main room. A colorful quilt covered an iron bedstead, with woven rugs on either side of it, and checked curtains at the window.

"Very cozy," she remarked, as he dug through a cedar chest beneath the window. "Was it your room?"

"Yes, and I promise I won't tell a soul if you step inside."

Katherine felt her cheeks grow warm.

"Out with it, Katie," he said, coming toward her, a garment slung over his shoulder. "Are you afraid to be in this room with me?"

He stood inches away, close enough that his scent wrapped around her, bringing all sorts of arousing thoughts to mind. She wet her lips and took a tiny step back. "No."

Colin's mouth quirked devilishly, making her think she should be. He held up a pale yellow dress with white embroidery around the neck and hem. "It's a bit old-fashioned, but it's clean." He handed it to her and said, "Let's get some water heated for your bath. I'll hunt up some tea leaves so you can have a cup while we wait."

She laid the dress on the bed and followed him to the kitchen part of the room. The thought of Colin being nearby while she bathed gave her a fluttery feeling. She had a sudden image of him kneeling beside the tub, taking up a sponge and running it slowly over every curve of her wet body as she lay back with her eyes closed, sighing in pleasure.

Where did she come up with these shocking thoughts?

To keep her mind away from such matters, Katherine hunted through a cupboard and found cups and saucers, then took the canister of tea leaves Colin had set out and laid them in an old china teapot. Colin put water on to heat, then opened curtains and lifted windows for fresh air, found a towel for her, dragged out a wooden washtub from the second bedroom, then poured buckets of cool water into it.

Katherine watched him, fascinated by his quick, efficient movements. Colin was always so confident, and so extraordinarily handsome. She sighed regretfully. If only his beliefs weren't miles apart from her own.

"Aren't you having tea?" she asked as he poured hot water over the leaves.

"A day such as this calls for something stronger." He hunted through the cupboard and found a bottle of whiskey. He poured himself a small glass, then held up the bottle. "It'd do you good to add some to your tea. Steady your nerves."

Katherine declined with a shake of her head and a polite smile. *"A lady never imbibes in the afternoon,"* her mother had admonished her.

Colin shrugged and set the bottle on the table, then took a sip from his glass and sighed with pleasure. He gave her a sidelong glance. "I suppose it wouldn't be proper and lady-like, would it?"

Katherine ignored his attempt to poke fun at her. She watched his throat move smoothly as he swallowed more. He put down the glass and leaned back against the chair, running his tongue over his lips as though the whiskey were a sweet nectar. She knew he was goading her.

Katherine glanced at the bottle sitting between them and suddenly had a rebellious thought: who would know if she had a taste? Without saying a word, she pushed her cup toward him.

Colin grinned as he added a measure of whiskey. "Go easy with it now," he cautioned, as she took a drink.

She swallowed the warm mixture, gasping as the liquor seared its way down her throat and into her stomach. She put down the cup and wiped her watering eyes. "It's strong," she rasped.

"Have you never had Irish whiskey before?"

She shook her head.

" 'Tis the best in the whole world, bar none."

"Perhaps it's an acquired taste," she croaked.

He tipped back his head and laughed. "Give it a moment to settle, then take another sip."

She did, this time swallowing a much smaller amount. Although it still burned on the way down, a few moments later a soothing warmth spread upward from her stomach, reaching all the way across her shoulders. She sipped more as Colin rose to pour the heated water into the tub. She was starting to feel the whiskey's effects.

"Your bath, my lady," he said, bowing formally as he indicated the tub. "I'll even be a gentleman and wait outside."

Katherine finished the tea and stood up, swaying slightly. "I think the whiskey might have been a little too strong."

"It'll wear off," Colin said from the doorway. "Toss your clothes through the window by the kitchen sink, and I'll rinse them at the pump."

As soon as he'd shut the door behind him, Katherine moved around the room closing the curtains he'd opened, then she undressed. Holding the cotton towel in front of her with one hand, she carried her soiled blouse, corset cover, petticoat, and navy skirt to the window by the kitchen and tossed them out. Colin, standing just outside, caught them, his eyes darkening as his gaze swept over her from neck to waist.

Katherine glanced down to find that the towel wasn't covering as much of her as she thought. With an indignant gasp, she jumped back, letting the curtain fall into place. Hearing Colin's hearty laugh, Katherine couldn't help but giggle. Giggle? She wasn't a giggler.

She hiccuped as she stepped into the tub and sank down into the soothing water, resting her head against the back and letting the mellowness of the whiskey relax her. Through the window she could hear Colin singing and the sound of water running. He had a clear, resonant bass voice that was as pleasant to the ear as his speaking voice was.

She smiled wistfully, remembering his words of encouragement before the birth of Eileen's baby, and his comfort afterward. Just the thought of his strong arms around her made her insides tingle. And oh, those kisses! They were nearly enough to make her forget all about their disagreements.

A tap on the door brought her forward with a start. Katherine noticed suddenly that the water was growing cold. Had she dozed off?

"Katie, have you fallen in?" Colin called.

"No, I'm fine. Don't come in! I'll be done shortly." She scrubbed her skin clean and called out, "I'm getting out now."

Her teeth were chattering as she stepped out of the cool water and dried herself. She put on her corset and drawers and pulled the dress over her head, fastening the buttons down the front to the waist, and tying the sash in the back. She opened the door, smiled up at him and promptly hiccuped.

Colin tried not to laugh as she clapped a hand over her mouth and muttered an apology, a blush coloring her face. There were wisps of long hair clinging to her neck, and her feet were bare. She looked so innocent and vulnerable that his heart swelled up as big as a melon. He could have picked her up and carried her to his bed then and there. But he tempered his lust. He'd know when she was ready; she wasn't ready yet.

"The dress is a bit short," she said, glancing down at the hem, "but . . . oh, good heavens! I forgot to put on my stockings and shoes." Her cheeks flaming with embarrassment, she ran to get her stockings in the bedroom, where he could hear her muttering, "It must be the whiskey. I've never forgotten to put on my stockings and shoes before."

Colin couldn't help but feel for her, stuck in her proper English ways. She was so busy being a lady that she'd never learned how to be a woman. He stood in the doorway, shaking his head, as she sat on the bed and rolled a stocking over her fingers. "Your feet are nothing to be ashamed of. How long has it been since you've walked barefoot through the grass?"

She looked up, aghast. "Never! It wouldn't be seemly. Now would you turn around, please?"

He came to her and knelt down instead, causing her eyes to widen in surprise. "You're in the heart of Ireland now,

Katie. It's not a sin here to go without shoes. Let loose of Katherine for a while."

She seemed shocked at the very idea of going barefoot. Her attitude called for strong measures. She'd been mired too long in those suffocating manners. Colin tugged the stockings from her grasp, tossed them over his shoulder and stood up. "Come with me."

"Where are we going?"

He raised her to her feet. "For a walk. I promise nothing bad will happen. No one will scorn you. No eggs will fly at your head."

Colin saw the wariness in her eyes as he led her outside. He took her around to the back of the cottage, past the privy and through a gate in the low hedge surrounding the yard, into a meadow where sheep grazed. The grass was still damp from the rain and slightly slippery. He looked at her as they walked and saw a childlike smile of delight spread slowly across her face.

"Well? How does it feel?" he asked.

Katherine lifted the hem of the dress to glance down at her bare feet. She hated to admit Colin was right, but he was. The grass felt cool and moist and the blades tickled her soles. "It feels good."

"Sure, it's more than just good," Colin said as he sat down and removed his own shoes. "Isn't it the best feeling your feet have ever had?"

"All right," she said with a laugh, "it's the best feeling my feet have ever had."

"Now you're learning," he said, jumping up. "And now we're equal." He held out a bare foot.

"No, we're not," Katherine cried, darting away. "I'm quicker than you." She looked back and squealed when she found him fast on her heels. Her pins came loose and she didn't care. She pulled them out and tossed them into the air as her hair fell free. Yes, free! That's how she felt. Light and free as a butterfly.

Suddenly Colin swept her up in his arms and tumbled to the ground with her. Katherine shrieked as he rolled her on top of him. They both laughed until their eyes watered, then slowly Katherine's laughter stopped as she became aware of the man beneath her—his smiling blue eyes; his firm, sensuous mouth; his muscular chest and rock-hard thighs. She gazed down at his face, suddenly serious, and his eyes, darkening with passion, and her body responded with a slow, steady throb of desire.

Colin cupped her head with his hands and drew her down, his lips gently meeting hers. He took his time, tasting, nibbling, letting her get used to the idea of it. Then, when he felt her body relax, he rolled her to the grass and leaned over to kiss her again.

Her hair fanned out, spilling onto the green like burgundy wine. Her eyes, heavy-lidded, watched him expectantly, and her lips trembled, waiting eagerly for more. He kissed her with more passion this time, letting his tongue coax her lips open, sliding inside, teasing her, tantalizing her, until she groaned with pleasure.

She was ready.

Colin's body reacted instantly, his shaft thickening, pulsing, demanding satisfaction. This was what he'd fantasized about during those long, tortuous nights since he'd first kissed her at the ball. But he couldn't make love to her here, on the soggy grass, with the threat of more rain hanging over them. He wanted to lay her down on a soft, clean bed and undress her slowly, then make love to her until the sun set.

Colin gazed down at her lovely face and tenderly brushed wisps of hair away from her eyes. "Come, let's go back before it rains again, and I'll make a fire to warm you."

Twenty

Colin stood and gave her a hand. Katie seemed embarrassed as she brushed off the skirt of her borrowed dress, then shook the grass from her hair. He watched with some amusement as she tried to twist it into a semblance of a bun.

"I look a mess."

He put his arms around her and drew her close, smiling down at her and thinking she was the loveliest female he'd ever laid eyes on. "You look like a little girl again, happy and free of worries."

A furrow creased her brow. "I don't ever remember being free of worries."

Colin's own joy dimmed as her elation slipped away. He tilted her head up and gazed into her eyes. "You are right now, at this moment, free of worries, aren't you?"

"Only if I don't think of—"

He put his finger against her lips. "Then don't. Think only of this moment."

"But sensible people—"

"You don't have to be sensible all the time, Katie." He dipped his head down and kissed her—a slow, tender kiss that was meant to soothe her.

He didn't trust himself to get any more excited than he already was—they'd never make it back to the house if he did—so he reluctantly broke the kiss. "So you think you're quicker than me, do you?" he teased, and started off for the cottage at a trot, hoping she would join in.

She watched him for a moment, as though trying to decide whether to play the game again, then she gathered her skirt and dashed after him, laughing once more as they raced back over the meadow.

"I win!" Colin called breathlessly, tagging the white wall of the cottage.

Katherine stopped beside him to catch her breath. "If you won—it was by only a nose."

"Depends on whose nose you're talking about. Now a horse has quite a long nose." He stopped suddenly and looked back toward the meadow, then at the row of trees separating the cottages.

"What is it?" she asked breathlessly.

"Why don't you go inside while I have a look at your clothes?"

"Are we being followed again?"

"I don't know."

Katherine stood at the kitchen window, cautiously peering out. Colin had laid her clothes over a line, and now stood in front of them, checking for dampness. But she could see his eyes scanning the cottages on the lane and the trees behind them.

He came inside a few moments later. "They're almost dry. I'll make a fire and hang them in front of it. Another cup of tea and they'll be ready."

"Did you see anyone out there?"

"No."

While Colin started a fire and hung her clothes on the screen, Katherine put on a small kettle to heat, then braided her hair and wound it into a bun. This time Colin poured himself a cup of tea, too, and added whiskey to both. He raised his cup and waited for her to do the same.

"Here's to Eileen and Patrick and the newest O'Rourke,"

he said, clinking the rim against hers, "and to the county's newest midwife."

Katherine laughed. "I'll second the first part, but I'm afraid I'd never make a good midwife."

"Don't belittle yourself, Katie. It's not the Irish way. You should be saying instead, 'Wasn't I the best midwife ever seen this day?'"

"But it's not true."

"Who's to say it's not true? Do you know of any other?"

"No."

"Neither do I." He took a drink of his tea, watching her over the rim, his blue eyes crinkling at the corners.

"I wonder what they'll name the baby."

"Moira, after Eileen's grandmother, is my guess. You were named after yours, you know. Her name was Caitlin, which is the Irish form of Katherine."

Caitlin. The same as Gersha's. A tiny shiver of premonition darted up her spine, which she forcefully pushed aside. "I wish I could have met my grandmother."

"I hear she was a bit on the wild side in her youth."

It felt so natural to be sitting across the table from Colin in this cozy room, sipping tea and having a conversation. Katherine tried to imprint the moment in her mind to take back with her when she returned to Chicago.

How far away her home seemed at that moment. The thought of it made her slightly homesick. And she still had so much to do before she could return. There was the estate to be sold, donations to be made, and those last few ends to be tied. Plus, she still hadn't learned what had happened to her father. And then there was this handsome man sitting across from her, an infuriating, arrogant, hotheaded, loyal, tender Irishman with whom she could easily fall in love. But the thought of following in her mother's footsteps frightened her.

"I don't like that," Colin said. "You were smiling a moment ago, and now you look as gloomy as the sky outside."

"I was thinking about going home."

"To Lawthrop House?"

She shook her head. "America."

"You miss it, then."

Katherine took a slow sip of tea. She'd felt a bit homesick only a moment ago, but in truth, *did* she miss it? Did she miss the banging pipes and noisy radiator, and the dreariness of living alone? "I miss my work with the children. I made a difference there."

A heaviness settled on Colin as he gazed at Katie. He had grown used to her being at Ballyrourke and suddenly felt the shortness of time until she left. He absorbed every detail of her face, the soft spray of freckles across her nose, the play of her mouth as it formed a sigh, even the tiny scar below her lower lip, wanting to carry it all with him. But he wanted more than that. He wanted to make love to her, he wanted to know her as only a lover can. That was something he would carry in his heart forever.

The image of lying between those glorious thighs made his lust flare, hard and demanding. Katie gave him a cautious glance as he took her hand and wordlessly tugged her to her feet.

"What are you doing?" she asked nervously.

"Just this." He uncoiled her braid and loosened her hair with his fingers, enjoying the luxurious feel of it, lifting a silken lock from her shoulder to draw it across his face, inhaling the lavender scent that clung there. "Such lovely hair you have, Katie," he murmured near her ear, pressing light kisses there.

He could feel her tremble as he lifted her hair away from her neck and bent to nibble the tender skin of her nape. He was so aroused he could think of nothing but his need to make love to her.

"But when he cupped his hand over her breast, her body went rigid. Colin looked at her and saw fear in her eyes. At once, he took his hand from her breast and stepped back. Had he been wrong about her being ready? He'd certainly never meant to frighten her. Embarrassed, he turned away. "Your clothes should be dry now. I'll fetch them for you."

Shaken by the desire rampaging through her body, Katherine went immediately to the bedroom to remove the borrowed dress. She knew what Colin wanted, but she

couldn't allow it to happen, no matter how much she wanted
it, too. His lips on hers, his hands touching her body, ignited
passions she felt nearly powerless to control. She had felt
that same powerlessness when he'd kissed her at the ball, in
the darkened room, and again in the meadow, when she'd
laid beneath him, wanting him so much she couldn't
breathe.

Her fingers trembled as she loosened the sash at her waist
and unbuttoned the blouse. Making love to Colin was im-
proper, not to mention illogical. She tugged the dress down
over her shoulders. She couldn't give her most sacred possession to a man and then leave him. Nor could she stay and
marry him. Not Colin. Not a man who would abandon her
for a piece of land.

There was only one thing she could do: return to
Lawthrop House and finish her business, then sail back to
Chicago, where she could concentrate on the children.

"Here they are," Colin called from the doorway. "Dry
and mostly clean."

Startled, she swung around as he strode into the room.
Colin stopped abruptly, his gaze sweeping down her nearly
nude body. Katherine quickly pulled the loose material up
around her breasts, clutching it nervously as a heated blush
spread up her neck. "J-just leave them on the bed."

Colin knew he looked like an eejit as he stood there gaping at her, but he couldn't seem to get his brain to work. Seeing her with her dress hanging around her waist, with only
the corset covering the lower part of her bosom, all he could
do was stare. The only thing that was functioning fully was
his shaft, which was turning harder than a shepard's crook.
All he could think of was how it felt to kiss her, and how
much he wanted to see her lying naked beneath him.

He swallowed hard and forced his gaze to her face. Her
eyes were huge and her cheeks were flushed. She held the
top of the dress before her like a shield, as though she
needed protection. That struck him hard. No woman ever
needed to fear Colin MacCormack.

He glanced down at the clothes still clutched against his
chest. Moving woodenly, he placed them on the bed, then

walked toward the door, a painful task in his aroused condition.

Katherine swung away, appalled by the fierce desire caused by just the sight of him. How she wanted to call him back, to tell him how desperately she wanted him to kiss her, to hold her in his arms and make love to her, but she couldn't bring herself to do it. Her mother had taught her too well.

Now the moment was lost. He wouldn't touch her again unless she asked. She knew it was for the best, yet it didn't halt her anguish as the door closed softly behind her.

Suddenly she heard his footsteps, and then she felt his hands on her bare shoulders, and his lips touch the nape of her neck.

"Katie," he said huskily, running his hands down her bare arms. "I want to make love to you."

Twenty-one

Katherine melted against Colin's hard body as he pressed hot kisses below her ear and down the back of her neck. She wanted to turn and wrap her arms tightly around him, surrendering to her desires, to Colin. But something inside still resisted, a voice—her mother's—whispering, *"Be sensible."* How could she not follow a rule she'd lived under her entire life?

Then other voices sounded in her ear, louder and stronger than her mother's: Grainwe's voice saying, *"Listen to your heart,"* and Colin's, *"Think only of this moment."*

But one had to think of the ramifications.

"You don't have to be sensible all the time, Katie."

She swallowed hard as Colin put his hands over her fingers and gently loosened them, letting the dress fall around her waist. He turned her to face him and lifted her hands to his lips. "You're the loveliest woman I've ever seen, lovelier than any flower in the garden."

He kissed her knuckles one by one, then turned her hands over and pressed his lips into each palm. She shuddered when his tongue tickled the center of the left one and then the right. He pressed more kisses up one wrist, up the delicate skin of her forearm and back down again, making her shiver with anticipation.

Listen to your heart.

"Your skin is softer than the finest satin," Colin whispered as his lips nibbled a path up to her shoulder. Her stomach fluttered as he moved across her collarbone, then to the hollow below her throat.

"As fair as the most exquisite pearl in the ocean." He straightened and tilted her chin up. "And your lips are"—he pressed his mouth to hers, whispering against them—"as ripe as the dewiest peach."

Katherine's knees grew rubbery as Colin held one hand to the back of her head to hold her steady as he kissed her passionately, invading her mouth with a probing tongue that caressed and tantalized, stoking a furnace of desire, until it seemed every bone in her body had melted from it. He kissed her eyelids and her temples and her mouth once again, as if he couldn't get enough of her. He kissed her lips again, longer and more passionately, until she could only cling to him helplessly, overwhelmed by a fierce need she couldn't begin to understand.

Then he broke the kiss and led her by the hand to the oval mirror hanging above the chest of drawers. Standing behind her, he combed his fingers through her hair, setting it tumbling around her shoulders in wild abandon.

"My sweet Katie," he whispered against her ear. His hands glided down her shoulders and around to her breasts. His fingers slid beneath the edge of the corset to cup them, lift them, fondle them gently. "You're the loveliest woman I've ever seen."

Katherine gazed at her reflection, amazed at the woman who stared back at her, a woman with untamed hair, sparkling eyes and pink cheeks, her bosom bared daringly. Was that really her? Could she be that desirable? That lovely?

She wanted to be, just for Colin.

He kissed the top of her shoulder as he tugged the dress down over her hips, until it puddled on the floor around her bare feet. He turned her around and reached for the hooks that held her corset together, nimbly unfastening them and tossing the stiff garment to the side. He unfastened the tape that held up her drawers and inched them down over her hips, his hands gliding down the outside of her thighs and calves, his cheek pressed against her hip as she lifted one foot and then the other to step out of them.

He turned her to face him, his hot gaze raking upward, pausing on the mound of curly hair, lifting to her bosom and then to her face. He ran his hands up the front of her legs, then leaned to press a kiss at the top of each thigh, drawing his tongue toward the center while she watched in breathless anticipation and gasped as his tongue found its mark.

Before she'd even managed to catch her breath, he lifted her in his arms and carried her to the bed. Katherine lay with her head on the pillow, feeling as though she were in a wondrously exciting dream as Colin stripped off his shirt and pants, and then his underwear, until his entire, beautiful, male body was exposed to her. His muscles glistened sleekly as he moved toward the bed, his male organ jutting proudly from a mat of black, curly hair, making her own body throb in response.

Colin lay down beside her and leaned over to kiss her, letting his tongue slide sensuously between her lips, encouraging her to do the same. Katherine followed his example, exploring his mouth with her tongue. Feeling suddenly bold and wanton, she slid her hand between their bodies and curled her fingers around his shaft, surprised and aroused by the steeliness of it, amazed by the contrast of its velvety tip.

Colin instantly broke the kiss and grabbed her hand, bringing it up to kiss it. "We have to take it a bit slower, beauty, or I'll never last."

"I don't understand."

Smiling, he kissed the tip of her nose. "You will soon enough. Relax now." Then he drew his hand gently down to caress her breasts.

"Your heart is beating as fast as a bird's," he said softly. He lowered his head and covered one breast with his mouth, circling the delicate nipple with his tongue, suckling until it shriveled to a tight bud, sending sweet rushes of pleasure deep inside her.

Sitting back on his heels, Colin let his gaze travel slowly up her body. Instead of feeling shy and embarrassed by his bold appraisal, Katherine was amazed at how brazen she felt.

"You're so lovely you take my breath away, Katie. Pure and soft, the way a woman's body should be." Colin ran his hands down her stomach to the mound of curls, cupping her for a moment, then moving down one leg and up the other, as if he couldn't believe she was real. He separated her legs and knelt between them, running his hands up over the insides of her calves, knees and thighs as he gazed at her body. "Do you know how lovely you are?"

Katherine could only shake her head.

"Then you'll have to take my word for it." He lifted one of her legs and leaned over to run his tongue from her ankle to the inside of her thigh, stopping just short of the juncture. Then he lifted the other leg and repeated the procedure, making her insides quiver and quicken in anticipation.

Then he was leaning over her, kissing her mouth as his fingers slid into the folds of her womanhood, probing gently, finding the tiny nub that throbbed with desire. As he stroked and kissed her, Katherine moaned and arched against his hand, as a growing tension deep in those folds kept winding tighter and tighter. And still he stroked, his fingers drawing forth a slickness that only made the delicate area more aroused.

And then her world exploded, sending such spasms of pleasure radiating from that core that she wrapped her arms around Colin and gasped as her body bucked from the force of her release.

Suddenly, she felt his body on hers and felt his shaft slide between the folds, into the slickness and deeper, probing, until she felt a sharp pain and cried out.

"It'll be all right in a moment, Katie," he crooned in her ear as he eased his shaft out, then gently back in, letting her accustom herself to the thickness. It was all Colin could do to hold back, but he wanted to enjoy this moment as long as he could, knowing there might never be another.

But her body was too inviting, and he was too aroused to hold back much longer. Not wanting to hurt her further, he pushed in as far as he could and let his release come, groaning in ecstasy as he emptied himself into her, slowly letting the spasms subside. Then, sated and drained, he lowered himself to the bed beside her and took her in his arms, stroking her hair.

Katie had taken a great stride forward, pushing aside those stiff manners, allowing herself to be a real woman for the first time in her sheltered life. But she was too quiet, too still; he prayed she wasn't having regrets.

John Bloom crouched beneath the open window, his hand clapped over his mouth to muffle his snickers. He knew what had just happened inside the cottage, but he couldn't resist listening a bit longer. His cock was stiff as a board from picturing what Colin was doing to the Lawthrop woman, and now he'd have to find a willing girl in town to help him relieve it. But first he'd take care of business.

With a smug grin, he crept away and headed back for Lawthrop House. What a story he had to tell. It would certainly earn him a nice fat coin purse.

Katherine felt completely sapped of energy, yet more alive than she'd ever been in her life. It was as if she'd never tasted, or saw, or touched before. The colors in the quilt beneath her seemed more vivid, the chirps of the birds in the trees outside more crystalline. Even her thoughts felt different—unfettered and untroubled for the first time in her life.

She lifted her head and found Colin watching her, his eyebrow raised questioningly. "Katie?"

She rested her head on his chest and ran her fingers across the hard muscles of his torso, savoring the texture of the springy, coarse hair against the sensitive skin of her palm. "Mmmm?"

"How do you feel?"

She drew in a slow breath and let it out on a sigh. "Serene."

"Not just serene, Katie. Aren't you the most serene woman in the entire world?"

Katherine smiled at his exaggeration. "All right. I'm the most serene woman in the entire world."

Colin sighed and stretched out on his back, arms folded behind his head. "And I'm the happiest man alive at this moment."

At this moment. His words fell like cold water on her skin, bringing her back to the cruel reality of her situation. She had no future with Colin. This precious, fleeting moment they'd shared was all she could give him. Perhaps even that had been too much, for she could feel her heart begin to shrivel at the thought of leaving him, a feeling that couldn't be explained by simple passion alone. It was love.

Colin felt a change come over her. She was staring at the ceiling, her mouth curved into a troubled frown. Was it the thought of returning to Lawthrop House and facing Horace that worried her?

"Will you tell me why you're frowning?"

She sighed deeply and turned her head to look at him. He was dismayed to see tears glistening in her eyes. "I have to leave, you know."

Just as he thought. She didn't want to go back and face her uncle. Colin could feel his jaw tighten at the thought of the bastard waiting there for her return. "Will Horace question you about where you've been?"

She seemed momentarily confused. "My uncle? Yes, I'm sure he will." She nibbled her lip for a moment, as though his words had reminded her of something else that worried her. Finally she sat up and turned to face him, pulling the quilt up to cover her nakedness.

"Colin," she said, giving him a cautious glance, "I know you hate my uncle, but I need to talk to someone about him. I can't burden Eileen with it; Grainwe is no help; and there's no one else I trust."

Colin's gaze softened at that. "All right. You can tell me."

"Horace told me he and my mother had been very close. But both Brigid and Lady Tarkinton said just the opposite was true. In fact, my mother was concerned about what he'd do to get her inheritance. He also told me he had been in England for several years before he came back here with me. But, according to Lady Tarkinton, Horace was here until my grandfather died last year, when he and my grandmother had a huge row, at which time she ordered him to leave Ballyrourke for good. Horace has lied to me so many times, Colin, that I don't feel I can trust him anymore."

"How well do you really know him, Katie?"

"I only met him in England, before sailing here. But I've never felt in any danger."

"Listen to me well, Katie," Colin said, sitting up. "Horace Lawthrop is a cunning, evil man. He'll stop at nothing to get what he wants, and what he wants is Ballyrourke."

"That's what Brigid told me."

"Can you tell me, if something happened to you, who would inherit Ballyrourke?"

Katie stared at him for a long moment, as though trying to recall what she'd been told. "I don't know," she finally admitted, twisting her fingers together. "I'll have to ask my solicitor when he returns next week."

"You'd better wire him tomorrow instead. 'Twould be faster."

She nodded, staring at him with huge eyes. Colin ran his finger gently beneath her lower lip, tracing the tiny, curving scar there. "No frowning now. You've too beautiful a mouth to spoil it with a frown."

A blush instantly colored her cheeks. "I can't help it. It isn't very pleasant to be frightened of one's own uncle."

She suddenly seemed so fragile that Colin felt all his protective urges rise up inside him. He reached for her hand and held it tightly in his, vowing fervently, "I won't let him harm you, Katie."

Her eyes widened, as though shocked by his impassioned vow, but she wasn't nearly as shocked as Colin was. How could he protect her? He didn't live in the house with her. He couldn't guard her twenty-four hours a day. He was a fool to have promised her anything.

He wouldn't take it back, though. Not after he'd given his word. There was only one thing to do.

"Marry me, Katie."

Twenty-two

Colin wanted to marry her! Even in her astonishment, Katherine felt her heart fill with tenderness as she gazed at his earnest face. She wanted to throw her arms around his neck and hug him and kiss him and promise to be his forever.

Then her practical mind took over.

Marry Colin so he could protect her from her uncle? Illogical. *He didn't even say he loved you.* But it wouldn't make any difference if he had. She couldn't marry him. She had to go back home. Even so, her heart ached at the thought of leaving him.

"Now don't say you'll think about it," Colin warned, lifting her hand to his lips and kissing her palm. "I'm too impatient for that."

She stroked the side of his face, wondering how she could keep from hurting his feelings. "Colin, I thank you more than I can say for your gallant offer, but I have to go back to America. I can't break my promise to those children. Building the orphanage is as important to me as Ballyrourke is to you. I'm sorry."

Colin couldn't help but breathe a sigh of relief. He wasn't ready to marry, though it did cross his mind that marrying her would be one way to get Ballyrourke. But it wouldn't be right. He couldn't lie to her and say he loved her, not even for Ballyrourke.

You were a bit hasty there, boy-o. What would you have done if she'd said yes?

His heart gave a hard lurch as he gazed at her, this woman with two identities. If she'd said yes, he would have made good his offer, is all. Now he had to find another way to keep her safe.

He pulled her against his chest and stroked her hair. "I'll kill anyone that tries to harm you, Katie."

Horace sat behind the desk, his eyes closed and his hands folded, listening to John Bloom's report. Outwardly calm, inside he was an inferno of indignant rage. How dare Katherine consort with that Irishman like a common trollop! Indeed, like her mother. And Colin MacCormack—how he loathed the bastard.

He slowly opened his eyes and fixed them on John Bloom. "That was quite a report. You did fine work, John. Now I think it's time we taught Mr. MacCormack a lesson. I'd like for you to hire some men to help me do that."

"I know just the crew," the little man bragged, puffing out his pigeon chest.

"How soon can you round them up?"

"If all goes well, I should have 'em by tonight."

"I'll leave it to you to set it up, John. I want you to make sure Mr. MacCormack understands the rules. Do you know what rules I mean?"

"Sure I do." Bloom sauntered up to the desk and leaned his hands on it, smiling ferretlike, displaying a set of badly decayed teeth. "Thing is, these blokes will want to be paid up front, you see, and I'm a little light in the pockets these days."

Horace contemplated the matter for a moment, then unlocked a drawer, opened a steel box and removed a leather pouch. "Will that do?" he asked, sliding it across the desk.

John held the sack in his open palm and tested the weight, then grinned. "That'll do just fine for starters—sir."

Horace locked the strongbox and put it away. Yes, it would do for starters. At least it would take care of Mac-Cormack. Then he would have to find a way to discredit the bastard in Katherine's eyes. But how best to go about it? Perhaps if he knew more about the man's habits, he could come up with a plan.

Horace ushered John Bloom to the door, then took a rare journey outside, wandering casually across the wide green yard and across a dirt lane to the stables, his hands in his pockets as if he hadn't a care in the world. He found the stable boy mucking out stalls and asked him if he'd seen Mac-Cormack.

"No, sir, I haven't," the boy said, ducking his head like the simpleton he was.

"Then I suppose you'll have to go in his place," Horace said, and sent him on a meaningless errand. As soon as he was out of sight, Horace climbed the stairs to the first apartment over the long fieldstone building.

The room was disgustingly crude, Horace noted as he peered inside, but good enough for someone of MacCormack's ilk. There was a narrow bed in one corner, a pine washstand and metal basin in another, a small table and one chair in the center, and wooden hooks on the wall for clothing. He noticed nothing at all that would be of any help.

Then he saw something peculiar dangling from one of the hooks and walked closer to take a look. It was a long white ladies' glove edged with tiny seed pearls.

So you lost it at the Tarkinton's, did you, Katherine? Horace's upper lip curled back in a sneer as he imagined how the glove came to be in MacCormack's room. He snatched the garment from the hook, folded it neatly in fourths and slid it into his vest pocket. Stepping out of the room, he hurried down the wooden steps and along the long side of the building, then walked toward the house as if he'd just been on the most delightful stroll.

How he relished the idea of confronting Katherine with the missing glove and watching her squirm in humiliation. But, no, it wouldn't be prudent to humiliate her, not when he wanted her trust. His goal was to discredit MacCormack, and the glove certainly wouldn't do it. Neither would suggesting he was a troublemaker, as that plan had so obviously failed. He had to find some way that would prove beyond a shadow of a doubt that the man had a criminal bent.

Horace entered through the loggia and passed by the room that contained the collection of gold artifacts. He came to a sudden stop and turned sharply. There was an idea!

He glanced both ways to be sure there weren't any nosy servants loitering about, then he slipped into the room and quietly opened the back of the glass display cabinet. He stuck his hand inside and removed one of a set of beautifully etched goblets. Glancing over his shoulder, he tucked it beneath his jacket, then quietly returned to the hallway.

He'd have to come back later that night for the rest. For now, however, the goblet would do perfectly. He had only to plant it in MacCormack's room, then call the police and say someone had broken into the house. A search of the estate would turn up the piece, and the blackguard would be hauled off to prison.

What a brilliant idea.

It was dark when Colin drove the wagon into the big barn behind the stables and unhitched the horse. He had let Katie off some distance from the house, then he'd kissed her one last time, and hugged her tightly against him. He'd stood there with his heart in his throat as she'd hurried up the road. If Horace so much as touched a single hair on Katie's head, he'd tear the devil apart with his bare hands.

Colin had already come up with a plan to protect her. All he needed to do was use his key to slip into the house at night, then set up watch in the bedroom next to hers. He hadn't told her about his plan, fearing the temptation would be so great he'd end up in her bed every night and risk being discovered by a servant in the morning.

"Let me do that for you," Tommy called, breaking into his thoughts.

"No need. I've already got a start on it. It's late anyway and you should be off duty now."

"Thanks, Colin," the boy called, and headed off to his own room.

Colin whistled as he rubbed down the mare and tied on a feed bag. How glorious it had been making love to Katie. She was all he thought she'd be—passionate, tender, and, when she let herself go, just a little wild. He smiled, thinking about how he'd like to bring out more of that wild side. But as he imagined it he felt himself getting hard. *No time for dreamin' now, boy-o. There's work to be done.*

Colin walked to the window and checked to see that the light was on in Tommy's room above the stables, then he took the paintings one by one across the yard between the buildings and up the outside stairs. He'd have to get them back into the big house soon, but for now they'd be safe enough propped against a wall in his own room with a blanket covering them.

As he lit a lamp, a shiver ran up his spine. He glanced around, feeling something menacing in the shadows that danced on the wall in the flickering light. He fixed himself a supper of hard cheese and bread and sat down at his table, facing the door. Then his gaze fell on the row of hooks, and he scraped back his chair in alarm. Katie's glove was gone.

He strode over to the row of hooks, staring at them as though, if he tried hard enough, the glove would somehow reappear. He searched the room, which took only a few minutes, and finally had to accept that it was missing. That meant someone had come into his room and left with the glove. Who? And most troubling of all, why?

Katherine quietly let herself into the house, shut the door oh so carefully, and moved straight to the staircase, hurrying up the steps as rapidly as possible. She had almost reached the top when she heard her uncle's voice.

"Katherine?" he called from the lower hall. "Is that you?"

Drat, drat, drat! "Yes, Uncle?" she called with forced cheer, turning to see him standing at the bottom of the stairs.

He started up the steps toward her, his face a bland mask, his eyes unreadable. Her stomach knotted in sudden apprehension. She'd never been afraid of him before and she didn't like the feeling.

"I've been worried about you, Katherine. You didn't appear for supper."

Fearing he'd notice her anxiety, she began to chatter. "I do apologize for that. I stayed much too long at Lady Tarkinton's, and then the most extraordinary thing happened as I walked home. My cousin—"

"Why didn't you take a carriage home?" he interrupted.

"Because I enjoy walking."

"Katherine, there are felons out on the road in the evenings. I shudder to think of the harm that could befall you if they were to come upon you walking alone."

"I'm sorry if I upset you. It's just that my young cousin came running up the road toward me calling for help." Katherine was careful to avoid any mention of Colin's role. "His mother—the aunt I met just the other day—was about to give birth, and since all the other women were at market, I volunteered my services."

Katherine paused for a quick breath. "It was the most amazing thing, Uncle. I actually witnessed the birth of a baby!"

Horace's eyes were flat and cold as he stood on the step below her. "All well and good, Katherine, but a message letting me know as to your whereabouts would have been appreciated. You are the only family I have, my dear, and I have made it my sworn duty to keep watch over you, as my dear sister wished."

More lies, she thought. She gave him a forced smile. "I'm sure my mother is looking down from heaven even now and thanking you for your concern." Then she turned and walked away.

"Don't forget that Lord Guthry is coming to dinner tomorrow night," he called.

Guthry! Katherine stopped with her back to her uncle and made a face. "I won't forget," she called back pleasantly.

"One more thing, Katherine. Edward Calloway finished his appraisal this afternoon. In your absence, I went over the figures with him." He paused, as though preparing to deliver dire news. "They weren't as high as I'd hoped, what with the extensive repairs needed."

She swung around. "What was the final amount?"

"I don't recall offhand, but I believe there'll be enough to build an orphanage in some form."

"I'd like to go over the figures with Mr. Calloway myself in the morning." Then she continued down the hall to her bedroom, shut her door and pulled the cord for Doreen. An orphanage in some form? She didn't like the sound of that at all.

Both Grainwe and Doreen appeared moments later. "Are ye all right, lass?" Grainwe asked as Doreen stood behind her, gaping curiously. "We were worried something happened to ye."

"Yes, I'm fine, but a little hungry."

"Doreen will fetch ye some supper," Grainwe assured her, shooing the young maid off. "I'll draw yer bath."

Katherine sat down at the desk and took out paper and pen to write a telegram to her solicitor, as Colin had suggested. "Was my uncle very upset when I didn't show up for supper?" she asked Grainwe.

"He didn't say a word," she called from the bathing chamber, "but I could see in his eyes that he wasn't pleased."

Katherine shivered, remembering his chilly gaze. She sealed her letter and took it to Grainwe. "I need to have this telegram wired first thing in the morning. It's very important."

"I'll see to it, lass." Grainwe tucked the envelope in her skirt pocket, then squinted at Katherine's blouse. "Is that blood on yer clothing?"

Katherine glanced down at the faint red stain that Colin hadn't been able to scrub out. "I'm afraid so. I helped Eileen deliver her baby girl today."

"Aye, we heard the news this evening, and weren't you there at the right time, lucky for them?"

"Yes, it was a fortunate coincidence." Katherine stepped into the dressing room to change into a wrapper. "I had just come from visiting Gersha when Dermot came running for help."

"*Girseach* again?"

Katherine was tempted to reveal Gersha's true name, but a promise was a promise. "I found out where she lives, Grainwe. She showed me her house today."

Grainwe appeared at the doorway, a curious look on her wrinkled face. "Did she, now? And where might it be?"

"On Gerald Lane, at the very end of the road. A pretty tan cottage with brown shutters. Gersha would have taken me inside to meet her mother, but she was gone to market."

Grainwe shook her head. "Ye must've dreamed it, lass."

"I didn't dream it. I saw it with my own eyes."

"Listen to me, lass. The house at the end of Gerald Lane belonged to the MacCormacks; it was where Colin was raised. It's been empty for over ten years."

Katherine sat down on the bed, unable to accept what the old woman was telling her. The house she saw hadn't looked abandoned. It was clean and well kept, as though a family lived there.

"No one has lived in that house since the house was set afire and Colin's mother and sister died," Grainwe explained. "Colin, Kane, and his father moved to a smaller cottage afterward."

"Why would Gersha take me there and tell me it was hers?"

"There's no tellin' her purpose. You'll have to wait and see."

Katherine stared at her dumbly. "Her purpose?"

"She's a fairy, lass."

Katherine shook her head as gooseflesh covered her arms. "There are no such things as fairies or ghosts or leprechauns. That little girl was as real as you are."

Grainwe sighed resignedly. "Ye'll only know it's true when her purpose is revealed."

Katherine heard a sound at the window and turned to see the little calico climbing through the opening. "Here's proof for you," she said, hurrying over to pick up the animal. "This is Gersha's pet. I've seen her playing with it. As you can see, she's real."

"Aye, she's real," Grainwe agreed with a gentle smile. "Animals can see what we're afraid to, just as they can sense

evil. They're not bound by our sensibilities. As for this animal, she's a stray. Haven't I seen her around for weeks, beggin' food at the kitchen door? Now why don't ye hand over
that mangy creature so you can go take yer bath before it
cools."

Katherine handed her the cat. Grainwe was determined
that she had seen a fairy and there was no talking her out of
it. Perhaps she *had* dreamed her meeting with Gersha. Perhaps she was just overcome by everything that had happened that day.

She sank down into the soothing waters and closed her
eyes, remembering Colin's kisses, and how wonderful it had
felt to lie in his arms. She remembered how sweetly and tenderly he'd made love to her, and how he'd vowed so passionately afterward to protect her, even to the point of
marrying her.

She sighed regretfully. She had made a dreadful mistake
in letting Colin make love to her, for it had forced her to rec-
ognize her true feelings. Her only saving grace was that she
would be leaving for America soon, preventing her from
making the mistake her mother had made. But the thought
of leaving him and going back to Chicago made her heart
ache so hard she feared it would shatter.

Think, she told herself, don't feel. Once she was home
again—planning the orphanage, helping the children—the
pain of leaving Colin would eventually diminish. She
hoped.

She was suddenly reminded of her mother's similar
plight. Was that how Suzannah had felt when she realized
Garrett wasn't coming home? Had she buried her emotions
in her work so she wouldn't feel any pain? Katherine
couldn't remember a time when her mother had ever
laughed, or sang, or even cried. She vowed not to let it happen to her.

Katherine toweled off, slipped on her wrapper and went
into the bedroom, where Grainwe was turning down the bed,
carrying the cat on her shoulder.

"I wish I knew more about my mother—what she was
like when she met my father."

"Have ye forgot she kept journals?" Grainwe asked, handing her the cat. "Ye could always read them. I'll go fetch one of the crates from the attic if ye'd like."

Katherine was tempted to say yes, but she couldn't put Grainwe to any more bother. "It's late tonight. Perhaps tomorrow."

"I'll do it first thing," Grainwe promised.

"Here's supper, miss," Doreen called as she carried a tray into the room. "I'll set it here on the table for you." She put it down and turned, spying the calico. "Ohhh! Aren't you pretty?" she cooed, taking the cat from Katherine to cuddle her. "Is she yours, miss?"

"Not really, although she seems to think she is."

"She's found a home here, hasn't she? Just like you, miss."

Too keyed up to sit and wait for midnight to come, Colin headed out to Teach O Malley, hoping to find a little solace with his friends.

Michael O'Malley was serving a tray of Guinness to a table of rowdies when Colin ambled in. As Colin took a seat in the corner, Michael gave him a nod in greeting, and came over as soon as he'd finished with them.

"Noisy bunch," Colin remarked, tipping his head toward the five loud men.

"From Dublin, I suspect," Michael said with a grimace. "How did it go today?"

"Bring me a pint first, then I'll tell you."

Michael shook his head as he turned and headed for the bar. "I know what that means. Didn't go well."

Colin watched the group of men as he waited for his ale. They were burly and belligerent, and made rude comments about the other patrons. One of them glanced his way, and Colin thought he recognized him. He saw the man say something to his companions, then they all looked around at him. The first one said something in a low voice, and the others guffawed.

"Here's your pint." Michael placed the mug in front of him, then sat down. "Tell me what happened with the paintings."

"I couldn't do it, Michael. The dealer was all set to pay me, and I couldn't do it."

Michael clucked his tongue. "All that work for nothing. Now you're back where you started. Well, my friend, I can't say as I blame you."

"I'm no thief, Michael."

"That you're not. So is it back to finding the will?"

"I have to find Mary first." Colin took a long, thirsty gulp and set the mug down. "By the way, Eileen and Patrick have a new baby girl, thanks to Katie."

"A girl, is it? Well, saints be pr— Did you say thanks to Katie?"

"I did. We were just going along the road when Patrick's oldest came running up the road to fetch me. 'You've got to help, Colin,' says he. 'Everyone's gone to market,' and didn't Katie roll up her sleeves and step forward? She and Patrick delivered that baby single-handedly." Colin shook his head, still unable to believe it, or what had happened afterward.

"That's a pretty wide smile, Colin. Is that all that went on?"

Colin looked up and saw the five strangers staring at him. He glared back. "Those men seem to have a problem with me, Michael."

"Leave them be, Col. They're itching for a brawl."

"I don't like the looks of them."

"Nor do I." Michael jumped up. "I'd better get back to the bar before the customers start pouring their own pints. I'm glad you didn't sell the paintings, Col."

Colin ignored the men's stares as he finished his pint. He sipped slowly, thinking about all that had happened that day. He'd seen his great plan to buy Ballyrourke crumble, and he'd seen his wildest fantasy come true. Where did that leave him? With no chance at all of keeping Katie and only a slim chance of getting Ballyrourke. He prayed that Mary would be able to tell him where the will was. She was his last hope.

Twenty-three

"It's all taken care of, sir," John Bloom reported, emphasizing the word *sir,* as though to impress his boss with his newfound manners. He came across the parlor to where Horace sat reading in an overstuffed chair. "MacCormack will learn a sound lesson tonight, that's for certain."

Horace nodded in satisfaction. "Good work, John."

"Anything else I can do for you? Sir?"

"Yes. There's a large crate in my room that I want delivered to an art dealer in Dublin in the morning." He removed a slip of paper from his coat pocket. "Here are the directions. He'll be expecting you."

Horace read until late in the evening, waiting until the house was quiet, then he retrieved the goblet he'd hidden in the library and let himself out through the loggia, stealing through the darkness to the stable stairs.

He opened the door to MacCormack's room and found a lamp. As soon as it was lit, he shut the door and looked around for a place to hide the gold cup. He saw a large, square object covered by a hideous wool blanket leaning against the wall behind the bed and crossed to have a look.

"Well, what do you know about that?" Horace said,

holding up a corner of the blanket. What marvelous irony. The bastard had incriminated himself.

Colin left the pub much later and walked back to Ballyrourke. As he came up Kilwick Road near a stand of pines, he was suddenly surrounded by a band of assailants who'd been hiding among the trees. As he raised his fists and braced his legs to defend himself, he recognized the strangers from O'Malleys. "If it's money you're after, you've got the wrong man."

"We don't want your money," the biggest oaf of the lot replied, grinning with malicious intent as he circled round him. "We're just deliverin' a message."

"If it takes five of you to deliver one message, then it's either colossal in size or you have brains the size of a pea."

When they jumped him, Colin managed to land a few punches to the face of one and the jaw of another before they pinned his arms back.

"Here's the message," the giant oaf said, breathing beer-soaked breath in his face as he punched him in the gut. "Tenants don't mix with landlords." He punched Colin in the stomach, taking the wind from his lungs. "And if they do, they get this." He punched Colin again, making him double over in pain, unable to draw a breath. Then he stepped back to let another take a turn.

They left him curled on the ground, bleeding from a gash in his forehead, battered in the ribs and gut, and bruised all over. Colin lay immobile for a long time, waiting for the pain and light-headedness to subside before he was able to stagger to his feet. Supporting himself against tree trunks, he concentrated on putting one foot in front of the other, until he reached the stables, where he collapsed just inside the door. His last thought before the darkness engulfed him was that he had to protect Katie.

"Colin, you're bleeding! Are you dead?"

Colin managed to open one eye and squint up into the morning light to see Tommy kneeling beside him. What did he mean, was he dead? And how had he come to be on the floor of the stable? Had he drank too much at O'Malley's?

Colin attempted to sit up, then fell back with a groan as pain stabbed him with lightning sharpness, bringing with it the memories of the previous night. "I think I am dead."

"What happened to you?"

"I met up with some men who didn't like me." Gingerly, he felt his jaw and nose and decided they were only bruised, not broken. His right eye was swollen shut and when he touched his forehead, he felt a crust of dried blood. He pressed his ribs and sucked in his breath at the burst of bright lights in his head.

"You'd better fetch Grainwe," he said grimly.

As he lay there waiting for help, Colin suddenly remembered his promise to protect Katie. Rattling off a string of swear words, he struggled again to get up. Nearly faint from the pain, he fell back in frustration. Some protector he was.

"Blessed angels in heaven," Grainwe whispered, crossing herself, as she stared down at Colin. "What did ye do to yerself, lad?"

"Got in the way of more fists than I care to remember. I might have broken a rib or two. Will you check for me?"

Grainwe knelt at his side and lifted his shirt. She pressed gently, causing Colin to clench his teeth and curse under his breath. She checked his face and eye. "As far as I can see, ye're bruised but not broken. But ye'd best let me put cold meat on that eye. Want me to call the gardai?"

"No. I want to do some checking myself first."

Grainwe clucked her tongue. "Don't get yerself in trouble, now."

"I'll be good as gold."

"That's what you always say. I'll be back shortly with some bandages and then we'll get ye fixed up. Stay put."

"As if I had a choice." Colin tried to grin, but his face wouldn't move. He touched a hand to the corner of his mouth and found that it was cut, too.

As soon as Grainwe had gone, Tommy crouched down. "Do you know who did it, Colin?"

"Some rowdies from up Dublin way. I've seen one of them before, when I went up to buy seed."

"They had it in for you, did they?"

"It seems that way." Colin didn't tell him about the message they'd delivered, yet there wasn't a doubt in his mind but that it had come from Horace Lawthrop.

He looked up as Doreen hurried over. "Oh, Colin! Poor boy," she cried, sinking down beside him. "Grainwe said ye were attacked."

"Some rowdies from London," Tommy chimed in helpfully.

"Colin, I have to tell you something I heard. Tommy, go away for a moment, will you? There's a good boy." Doreen glanced over her shoulder to make sure no one else was within earshot, then she leaned close to say, "Master Lawthrop has set that nasty little John Bloom to spyin' on you and the mistress. I heard them talkin' just yesterday."

She glanced around again and saw Grainwe coming. Instantly she hopped up and backed toward the doors. "And if there's anything I can do, Colin, just let me know."

"Thanks, Doreen," he called, as Grainwe knelt down and opened a jar of strong-smelling balm.

So Ratty Lawthrop had a spy, did he? No doubt that slimy bugger Bloom had been the one to follow them to Brigid's. Maybe he'd even been there when Colin had made love to Katie. Could he also have set the thugs on him?

Colin's hands tightened into fists. He'd find out who was responsible for his condition, and if it was John Bloom, he'd teach him a lesson, wouldn't he? And send a message back to Horace, as well. First, he'd have to get back to Teach O'Malley and do some investigating. Someone there was bound to have overheard the men talking.

Colin sucked in his breath as Grainwe pulled the first bandage around his rib cage. "Easy does it," he said through clenched teeth. "I'd like to be able to breathe once in a while."

"Ye'll have to take it slow," Grainwe instructed. "No heavy liftin' or horseback ridin' for a week."

"I don't want Katie knowing about this."

Grainwe paused to study him for a moment, then continued on with her task. "Ye'd best stay away from her, for both yer sakes."

"I can't do that, Grainwe. She isn't safe in that house with her uncle."

She handed him a piece of cold, raw beef for his eye, then gathered her strips of cloth and stood up. "And what would you do to protect her in yer condition?"

"What is it you always say, Grainwe? A person who isn't strong must be clever?"

"Aye, ye'd best be clever, lad. Use yer head for a change."

She gave Colin a hand and he slowly got to his feet. His glorious afternoon with Katie now seemed like a dream.

Katherine came awake with a smile. She stretched luxuriously and turned on her side to face the window, gazing out at the faint purplish outline of the Wicklow Mountains in the distance. She'd been dreaming of Colin, of lying in his arms again, of feeling his warm body next to hers, of making love all night.

She sighed regretfully and sat up, waking the calico cat curled by her feet. Katherine reached down to pet her. "I'm going to miss you, Cali." She blinked back a sudden mist of tears. She was going to miss Colin, too. How would she ever forget him?

Sniffling, she threw back the covers and slid to the floor, then padded barefoot to the window seat and sat with one leg tucked beneath her. Beyond her window, the skies were gloomy and a mist hung in the air. The melancholy sight only made her feel sadder.

What was Colin doing at that moment? Was he thinking of her, too?

With a heavy heart, Katherine washed and dressed and scooped up Cali for the trip downstairs for breakfast. The house seemed unusually quiet as she headed up the hallway to the kitchen, as though it was holding its breath, waiting for something to happen.

"Will someone pour a saucer of milk for this hungry little cat, please?" she asked the kitchen staff. "And she'd appreciate some leftover meat scraps, too."

"Aye, miss," a cook's assistant said, and took the cat from her.

Katherine again felt that tension in the air as she made her way to the dining room, where a steaming hot breakfast of sliced ham, oatmeal stirabout, honey, and toasted oaten bread awaited her. She had decided the best way to keep thoughts of Colin at bay was to spend the morning reading her mother's journals, and ate quickly so she could get started.

She was just finishing a cup of honeyed tea when she saw Doreen scurry past the dining room doorway heading toward the kitchen. It dawned on Katherine suddenly that she hadn't seen Grainwe around all morning.

"Doreen?" she called, stepping out into the hallway.

"Yes, miss?" the maid replied breathlessly.

"Where's Grainwe?"

Doreen stared toward the ceiling and tapped her chin thoughtfully. "Well now, let me think. Seems like she had to go outside on an errand."

"Outside? For what?"

"But then she came back," Doreen added hastily.

"And where is she now?"

"I seem to remember her going upstairs."

Katherine watched the girl curiously. Why was she stalling? Why wouldn't she want Grainwe's whereabouts known? "Never mind. I don't need Grainwe right now if you'll give me your keys to the attic."

"My keys?" she repeated blankly.

Katherine held out her hand. "Your keys."

"Ye see, miss, the thing about that is—" She glanced toward the kitchen and her face brightened. "Oh, there's Grainwe! And I thought I'd seen her going upstairs. Grainwe! Mistress needs you," she called, and fled into the addition of the house.

"Did ye send for me, lass?" Grainwe called, huffing as though she'd been running.

"Are you all right?" Katherine asked in concern.

"As right as rain. What do ye need, lass? The books, is it?"

"Yes, if you have time." Katherine glanced back up the hallway. "Is there something wrong with Doreen?"

"Why do ye think so?"

"She's acting very peculiar."

"That's our Doreen." Grainwe started up the staircase. "I'll get those books for ye now."

Katherine pursed her lips as she followed her up to the attic. Something was definitely amiss.

"Here's one set," Grainwe said, crouching before a small wooden crate. She hoisted it to her shoulders. "It'll do for a start. If ye want the second, I'll come back."

Grainwe took the crate back to Katherine's room and set it on the floor beside the desk. Katherine took out one of the leather-bound journals and flipped through the pages.

"Is there anything else I can do for ye, lass?"

"No, thank you, Grainwe," Katherine replied. She knelt down beside the crate and pulled out a second, then a third, each one detailing a year in her mother's life. She searched through the box until she found one dated 1871, the year before Katherine was born.

She curled up in the window seat and began to read, surprised by how sensitive and amusing her mother's insights had been, nothing like the somber woman she had known.

A third of the way through the book she found the first mention of her father.

There he stood, tall, proud and handsome, with the bearing of a lord, his feet braced apart, his hands clasped behind his back, his azure eyes holding me spellbound as I sat on the garden bench holding a book I had instantly forgotten the name of. How rude of him, I thought to myself. He's a mere laborer. How dare he stare so! I knew I should send him away immediately, yet I felt helpless to do so.

He took his hands from behind his back and handed me a rose—a white rose with red edges, and told me I'd want to keep it to remind me of our first meeting—as if there would be others! What arrogance! At that I stood up, thrust the rose back at him, lifted up my chin, and marched straight into the house. I hope that shall be the last I see of Mr. Garrett O'Rourke!

Stunned, Katherine read the first paragraph again. It almost sounded like her mother had been describing Katherine's first meeting with Colin.

She turned the page and three rose petals fell out. One was brown with age, yet still showed a darker tint on the edge and smelled faintly of roses. The other two looked freshly plucked. One was deep red, the other white. A chill ran down her spine as she remembered the evening Gersha had singled out two petals lying on her open book.

"This one reminds me of you," she'd said, pointing to a white one. She'd selected a dark red one and placed it beside the white. *"This one is Colin."*

"Quite different, aren't they?"

"In color. Aren't they both roses, though?"

It wasn't possible. The journals had been in the attic for years. No one could have put fresh petals inside.

She turned the page and read on:

I met the oddest child in the garden today. She came up to me as I was reading and handed me the same rose Garrett O'Rourke had tried to give me yesterday. She said I shouldn't lose it, and to hold on to it for good luck. A perfect blend of colors, she told me, white for purity and red for passion, white for myself and red for my true love. I asked what her name was, for I'd never seen her there before. "Gersha," she told me, and walked away, carrying a white cat over her shoulder.

Goose bumps rose on Katherine's skin. It couldn't be the same child. Impossible. She refused to even consider it. The girl her mother had met would be older than herself now.

She heard a commotion outside her window and looked down to see the yard swarming with blue-coated policemen. Alarmed, she put the book aside and hurried downstairs.

"What happened?" she called, spotting Grainwe standing near the kitchen, looking flustered. "Why are the police here?"

"Yer uncle has summoned them. Someone got into the house last night. Ye were robbed, lass."

Twenty-four

"Robbed!" Katherine hurried through the house to the back addition, where she found her uncle in the room that housed the gold artifacts. He was talking to two policemen, and glanced up when he saw Katherine.

"What was taken?" she asked, giving a nod to the policemen, who had doffed their hats at her entrance.

"Everything in this case," Horace said, turning to indicate the tall glass cabinet behind him. He shook his head in dismay. "The entire collection is gone—a priceless gold wrist cuff, a gold collar, an etched ring, a set of twelve rare goblets, bowls—I can't remember what else. Did you happen to make a list of them, Katherine?"

She stared at the bare shelves, sickened by the sight. "No. I was going to donate them."

"What a pity."

"There's no sign of broken windows or locks," an older officer announced, striding into the room.

"Katherine, this is Captain Beattie."

"Miss O'Rourke," the officer said, nodding politely. He was of stocky build, with a red-veined bulb of a nose, stark white hair and a white handlebar mustache. He glanced from

Katherine to Horace. "My guess is that someone had a key or was let in."

"You can't mean someone who works here might have done this?" Horace asked, his voice thick with indignation.

"At first glance it would appear so, sir."

Horace gave a frown of displeasure. "I suppose that means you'll have to search the entire grounds."

"That would be a logical step, sir."

"If we must, we must." Horace glanced at Katherine. "But then it's your decision, Katherine."

She looked from her uncle to the three policemen, who stood waiting for her answer. She wanted to assure them that none of her employees would do such a thing. They were her relatives, for heaven's sake. Honest as the day is long, as Colin had said. But would any of these men believe her? Certainly not Horace. Perhaps the only way to prove it was to allow a search.

"All right," she said reluctantly.

She went back to her room and sat in the window seat, trying to read the journal, but she found herself reading the same entry over and over, lifting her head every few moments to listen, as the police streamed through the house, opening cupboards, closets and drawers in each room. She prayed hard that they would find nothing.

When the noise subsided, Katherine went downstairs to investigate and learned that the search had moved to the outbuildings, which she assumed to mean that nothing had been found inside the house. She slipped out to the rose garden and anxiously walked the paths while the police checked each structure. *Please let it be someone outside Ballyrourke.*

Suddenly she heard a man call, "We found something!"

With her heart in her throat, Katherine hurried around the side of the house. A policeman stood in front of the stables gesturing to the others. "Up those stairs," he said, and led his captain and Horace up the wooden steps to the rooms above the stables. One of the rooms belonged to Colin.

Katherine stood at the bottom of the steps, her fingers clasped together. *It can't be Colin,* she assured herself. *He wouldn't steal.*

"Katherine," her uncle said, stepping onto the landing," I think you should come up here."

Taking a deep breath, she lifted her skirts and started up.

The room was stark, with bare white walls and plain wood floors—nothing to identify its owner. She stood in the doorway and stared across the room to where the men had gathered around a narrow bed. They turned as she approached.

"Show her," Horace commanded.

One of the policemen held up a slender gold goblet. "Found it under the mattress."

"Look at this, Katherine." Her uncle lifted a blanket covering a thick, square object leaning against the wall. Underneath were three large oil paintings. They appeared to have been taken from the attic; she recognized them by their distinctive Sunderland frames.

"Whose room is this?" she asked the police captain, with a knot in her stomach the size of an orange.

He lifted his chin and announced victoriously, "Colin MacCormack's."

Her heart plummeted. "There must be some mistake. I know this man; he wouldn't steal. Perhaps someone else put those things here in his absence."

Horace said in a consoling voice, "Katherine, I know you don't want to believe you've been duped, but this was found wrapped around the goblet's stem." He held up a long white glove edged with pearls.

Katherine felt as though she'd been stabbed through the heart. Colin had picked up that glove from the library floor the night he'd kissed her.

"We interviewed your stable boy and two of your gardeners," the police captain informed her, "and all three saw MacCormack here at the stable earlier this morning. It wouldn't be likely anyone else would get up to this room in broad daylight without being seen."

"I hate to say so, Katherine, but I warned you about Mac-Cormack," Horace admonished. "Now you're finally seeing the true man."

She turned to stare at the paintings, remembering when

she had heard a noise in the drawing room one night and had seen three canvases behind the door. Had she caught Colin in the act? Had he been standing in the shadows waiting for her to leave so he could sneak the paintings outside?

"And did you know, too, that this was O'Rourke land for over seven hundred years before the Lawthrops came? And that all the old treasures in the house belonged to the O'Rourkes, as well?" he'd once told her.

Did he think he had a right to take them?

Logic would have her believe Colin was guilty, but her heart didn't want to accept it. She'd made love with Colin. She'd confided her fears to him. She'd trusted in his honesty. Was this how he would repay her? By this terrible betrayal?

"Where is he now?" she asked her uncle, fearing Colin was even then being hauled away in chains.

"He could be anywhere about the estate."

She looked at the police captain. "What will you do to him when you find him?"

"We'll arrest him, of course."

Horace took her arm. "Let's go back to the house. You don't want to be here when MacCormack returns."

She walked woodenly down the steps and across the yard to the house, remembering to keep her face emotionless. It wouldn't do to let the servants see her in a state. When she reached the staircase, she thanked her uncle for his assistance and went straight up to her room.

For a while she simply paced, too shocked to think clearly, then she sat in the window seat and waited for the tears to come. What came instead was anger.

Colin had deceived her. All the while that she lay in his arms, he must have been plotting how to get into her house and steal the gold. Had his vow to protect her and his proposal of marriage been a ruse so he could keep stealing from her?

She pressed her hand to her breast, feeling as though her insides were shattering. Was this her reward for listening to her heart?

* * *

"Colin, what are you doing here so early?" Michael O'Malley called as Colin stepped into the empty pub. He took a better look at his friend's face, and immediately put aside his broom. "Good God, Col, what happened?"

"Remember those thugs who came in last night?"

"Those dirty bastards did this?" Michael quickly took down an overturned chair from on top of one of the tables. "Sit down, my friend, and let me get you some strong coffee."

Colin eased his bruised body onto the wooden seat and gratefully accepted the hot brew. Michael took down another chair and sat facing him while Colin filled him in on the story.

"I recognized one of the men," Colin said at the finish, "but what I need to know is who set them on me. Did you hear anything at all, Michael?"

"They were jabberin' away all night, Colin. I heard bits and pieces is all."

"Did you hear any names in particular?"

Michael wrinkled his forehead, thinking. "None that stand out in my mind."

"Horace Lawthrop?"

Michael shook his head.

"Bloom? John Bloom?"

Michael's eyes widened. "Yes, Colin! I did hear that name. They were making fun of him, calling him a bloomin' bogtrotter. Wait now, it's coming to me. Aha! I remember the rest. The biggest lout in the bunch said Bloom had overpaid them for the privilege of what they were to do. That set them all to laughing."

"The privilege of knocking me senseless." Colin banged his fist on the table. "I knew they were up to something."

Both men turned as Tommy dashed in, breathing hard. "Colin, I came to warn you. The gardai are waiting back at the house to arrest you."

"For what?"

"Someone broke into the house and stole some valuables. They searched all the buildings." The boy looked down, as though mortified by what he had to report. "They found 'em in your room, Colin."

Colin swore silently, imagining Katie's shock and Horace's triumph. Even Tommy thought the worst of him now. "Tommy, I swear to you I was going to put those paintings back in the attic. I wanted to sell them for money to buy Ballyrourke from the Lawthrops, but I couldn't do it."

"I believe you, Colin," Tommy said. "But what about the goblet?"

"What goblet?"

"Someone stole all the gold pieces from inside a case in the house. One of the goblets was found under your mattress."

Colin and Michael stared at each other in astonishment.

"Someone must have planted that goblet, Colin," Michael said. "Someone wanted you to get caught thieving. That's why the police were called."

Colin felt his body stiffen in silent rage. There was only one person who would do such a thing. 'Twas the devil himself. He finished his coffee and got to his feet, wincing at the pain. "I'd better go back."

"You can't turn yourself in, Colin," Michael warned. "You'll be tossed in jail."

"I won't be on the lam like a criminal, Michael."

"And how will you protect Katie from behind bars? Will you answer me that?"

Colin dug his fingers through his scalp. What could he do? All the evidence pointed to his guilt. No judge would believe his story about returning the paintings, or about being set up by Horace Lawthrop. Not unless he could prove otherwise. And how would he protect Katie behind bars? He'd be as useless as a lighthouse on a bog.

"Michael is right, Colin," Tommy chimed in. "You've got to lay low until we can find the real culprit."

"I know who the real culprit is," Colin said through clenched teeth. "It's Ratty Lawthrop, himself."

Tommy let out a low whistle. "It'll be a tough one to prove, Colin."

"That it will, boys. And I'll need your help to do it."

* * *

"Won't ye come down to eat a bite, lass?" Grainwe said, moving quietly across the bedroom to where Katherine sat in the window seat, staring vacantly through the glass. "It's long past the noon hour; 'tis not good to go so long without food."

"I don't have much of an appetite."

"A cup of tea and some cheesecake, then?"

"Perhaps in a bit."

"I'll tell yer uncle ye don't feel well. He wanted me to remind ye that Lord Guthry will be comin' to dine this evening."

Katherine closed her eyes and sighed. The last thing she felt like doing was entertaining that mumbling bag of pomposity. "Tell my uncle I'll be there."

"Have ye read any of yer mother's book?" Grainwe nodded toward the journal lying open on her lap.

Katherine picked it up and turned it over. "I've just started it."

"Then I'll let ye be. Ring if ye need me."

"Grainwe?" Katherine called suddenly. "Has he come back yet?"

The elderly servant didn't need to ask who Katherine was asking about. "No, lass. Not yet."

"You were right about Colin, you know. You warned me he wasn't above breaking hearts or laws to get what he wanted."

"Aye, that's true. He's brash and headstrong when he wants something, but one thing he'll never do is lie to ye. Before ye set yer mind against him, speak with him. And let yer heart hear what he has to say."

Katherine said nothing, but this time she knew Grainwe was wrong. She *had* listened to her heart, and had paid for it dearly. Even now, just the thought of Colin caused it to constrict in anguish. She wouldn't make the same mistake twice.

She returned to the journal, hoping to divert her thoughts. She read for over an hour, then found an entry dated a month before her parents' elopement.

I love him! There, I've said it. There's no use denying it any longer. I've tried to make myself believe it was pure infatuation, but now I know the truth. I love him as I've never loved anyone. I celebrate life, feeling as though I've been dead all these years.

What shall I do? I cannot think of marrying Garrett. My mother would be horrified; my father would disown me. And Horace already loathes him. I shudder to think what my brother might do if he learned that I've been seeing Garrett on the sly. What shall I do? What shall I do?

And a few days later:

I cannot believe what has happened. I am carrying Garrett's child! Dear, faithful Grainwe has verified it. I am both delirious with joy and paralyzed with fear, for I surely cannot tell my mother or father. Garrett says we must marry soon, but my father will never stand for it.

What shall I do? What shall I do?

The next entry had been written the day before her mother's wedding.

I have never been as happy as I am now. We are to be wed! Tonight! In secret! Garrett has made all the arrangements, and the dress I sewed late into the night all this past week is safely hidden in the barn. I dare not take the gown my mother had intended for my wedding. How shall I pass the hours until he comes for me?

The next time I write, it shall be as Mrs. Garrett O'Rourke. Surely once I am wed, my parents will accept him. It is only Horace who continues to worry me. He still hasn't forgiven Father for endowing half the estate on me. What will he do when he must acknowledge my new husband as family?

Garrett assures me that I'm worrying for naught, that Horace is a coward who hides behind big words. He promises that he will always be there to protect me.

I do love him so. I cannot imagine living without him.

It had been her mother's last entry; the rest of the journal was blank.

Katherine shut the book and put it aside. How was it possible that her life was following so closely to her mother's? Why had she ever let herself fall in love with Colin?

Even worse, what if she, too, found herself with child?

Katherine pressed a hand against her stomach, praying there was no life there. She wanted better for any child of hers than to have a thief for a father. If Colin was sent to prison, then for all practical purposes he might as well be dead, because she'd never burden her child with such a terrible history.

She had been foolish to follow her heart, but at least she hadn't been foolish enough to fall for his plea to buy Ballyrourke. No doubt Colin had planned to use the money from the stolen treasures as payment.

She hoped Colin *had* been arrested. She wanted to see him put behind bars for his crime; she wanted to visit him there, and hear him tell her how honest he was, and how he would protect her from Horace. At least she knew now who the real threat to her safety was.

Katherine glanced at the clock and saw that it was time to dress for supper. Rising stiffly, she went to the dressing room to change into a dinner gown, but stopped when she caught a glimpse of her reflection in the mirror. Her insides knotted as she moved closer. The face that looked back at her was pale, pinched and unfeeling, with a bitter downward curve at the mouth.

It was her mother's face.

Katherine recoiled in horror, and at once turned her back on the mirror. She took deep breaths, her fists balled at her sides and her eyes tightly closed until she felt a measure of sanity return. She began to undress, her fingers moving slowly down the row of buttons, but even the familiar actions weren't enough to keep the old wounds at bay. Angry tears welled in her eyes as memories of the past crossed that invisible shield she'd built in her mind.

How many times had she sat across the table from her mother, waiting in vain for a tender smile or a word of praise? How many nights had she crawled under the blankets of a cold bed, hoping her mother would come in to kiss her on the forehead and whisper, "Good night, darling. Sweet dreams." How many prayers had she uttered, asking only that her mother tell her she loved her.

Katherine had always believed it was her own fault, that somehow she had disappointed her mother, that she hadn't acted ladylike enough or sensibly enough to satisfy her. She was always mindful of her manners, always respectful of her mother, but nothing she did made any difference. They lived as distant relatives in that tiny house, and though Katherine had dutifully loved her, the awful truth was that she had felt a sense of relief at her passing. Then there'd been no one to please but herself.

Grainwe's words rang in her head: *"Yer poor mother closed off her heart to everyone, even to ye, because it was easier than rememberin' how it felt to love someone deeply. Ye must guard against that happenin' to ye, lass. Ye don't want to end up a bitter old woman."*

Katherine swiped the tears from her cheeks with the back of her hand. Setting her mouth in a determined line, she turned to face the mirror once more. "You," she said in a trembling voice, pointing to her reflection, "will *not* become your mother."

But what could she do to prevent it? How could she keep herself from feeling bitter over Colin's betrayal?

"Before ye set yer mind against him, speak with him," Grainwe had told her. *"And let yer heart hear what he has to say."*

Perhaps she should listen to Grainwe one more time.

Twenty-five

At suppertime that evening, Michael was standing behind the bar, filling a mug for a customer, when three policemen sauntered in. Michael recognized one as Captain
Jack Beattie, a blustery little man with short, stubby legs and
a red blob of a nose.

"We're looking for Colin MacCormack," Beattie announced to the room. "Anyone here seen him?"

The other customers, most of them of the O'Rourke clan,
ignored his question. Beattie gave the order to the other two
officers to search the back room, then he marched up to the
bar, puffing out his blue chest, full of himself.

"O'Malley, I know you're a friend of his. Where is he?"

Michael drummed his fingers on the counter and pre-
tended to give thought to the matter. "To tell you the truth, I
saw him a few nights ago, was it Monday or Tuesday?"

Beattie looked doubtful. "Not today?"

Michael wrinkled his forehead, as a man deep in serious
thought. "If he was here today, then my memory must be
getting poor, for I sure don't recall seeing him."

"I saw him," one of the patrons offered grumpily. "He
walked past my place late this afternoon."

"Couldn't have," his companion said. "He was past mine

about then, and he couldn't be in both places on opposite ends of the county."

"Yer both full of beans," said another. "I saw him at the gristmill unloading a wagon."

Beattie scowled, undoubtedly realizing he was getting nowhere. "If anyone sees MacCormack," he announced, "tell him I want to talk to him down at the station."

"I'll do that, sir," Michael said with a broad smile. "Mind if I ask what for?"

"Yes, I do mind." Throwing Michael a scowl, Beattie strode out.

Katherine sat across the dining table from Lord Guthry listening to the insufferable man brag of his racehorses, or at least she presumed that was the subject under discussion. Since most of his words sounded as though they were puffed through a mouthful of marbles, she couldn't be sure. It was either racehorses or Rafe's hoses.

Horace had taken the chair at the head of the table, claimed as if he had a right to it. Edward Calloway sat beside Guthry, to her uncle's right. She sat at Horace's left. They had made small talk during the first two courses of the meal, and now, as a roast pig and a roast goose and all the accompanying dishes were placed before them, the men turned to the subject of the estate.

"Like th'looks of th'place, even though it does need quite a bit o' work done on it," Guthry mumbled, his jowly cheeks ballooning like a bellows as he cast an appraising eye around the dining room. "Farms seem t'be productive, too."

"Quite productive," Horace said evenly, "as Mr. Calloway's fine appraisal so efficiently demonstrated." As if for Katherine's benefit, he added, "Although I'm sure they could be even more so with a little pressure on the tenants." He lowered his eyebrows at her, signaling that he wanted her to encourage Guthry, too.

"Have you seen the gardens?" she asked, forcing a smile. "They add so much to the beauty of Lawthrop House."

Guthry's eyes disappeared in the folds of his face as he leered at her. "P'raps you'd show 'em t'me after dinner."

Her smile weakened at the thought of spending time alone with him. Still, it was better than being in her uncle's company. She glanced at Horace and couldn't help but puzzle over the gleam of satisfaction in his shrewd gaze. If he wanted Ballyrourke, as the O'Rourkes claimed, why was he encouraging Guthry to buy it? What benefit would it be to him?

Her gaze shifted to Edward Calloway, who immediately looked away from her, almost as though he was afraid to meet her eye.

As the conversation swirled around her, Katherine tried to keep her attention on it, but her thoughts kept returning to Colin, causing her heart to shrivel a little more each time. And when she attempted to convince herself of his innocense, all she could think of was Grainwe's warning: *"He's not above breakin' hearts or the law to get what he wants."*

"Shall we, my dear?" Guthry muttered, offering her his arm, when the meal was over.

As he escorted her out of the dining room, Guthry put his other hand over hers and rubbed it, causing a shudder to ripple through Katherine's body.

"Been looking forward t'this," he told her.

Wish I could say the same. If you'll come this way, please," Katherine said, and led him out the front door and across the drive to the park, where she began to rattle off a detailed list of its features. Talking a mile a minute, she managed to slip her hand from his arm and still keep him moving right along, though he huffed at every third step as though the exertion was too great.

She took him next on a tour of the rose garden, and was well ahead of him on a path, extolling the virtues of the colorful blooms, when he suddenly blurted gruffly, "What d'ya think, gel? Should I buy th'place or not?"

Katherine turned around in surprise. "Lord Guthry, I wouldn't presume to make that decision for you."

Guthry came up to her, slightly winded, but with an astute gaze. "What's your opinion of it? And don't give me drivel about value pound for pound."

Katherine glanced back at Lawthrop House and the splendid grounds surrounding it. "I think Ballyrourke is magnificent. I can't imagine anyone not being happy here."

"Then why aren't *you*?" His small eyes bored into her, making Katherine squirm inside.

"But, my lord, I didn't say I wasn't happy," she replied tactfully.

"Don't hear you say you are, either."

"Then let me assure you that I love Ballyrourke."

"Odd way to show it," he harrumphed, "by selling th'place."

Katherine opened her mouth to argue, then realized he had a point. With a glum sigh, she sat down on the bench behind her. "The truth is, I can't keep it. I need the money."

Guthry studied her for a moment, as though pondering her remark. Then he looked around at the flowering shrubs, plucked a bright yellow rose from its stem and tucked it behind her ear.

Katherine glanced up at him in surprise as he ran his hand gently down her cheek. "Beautiful flower for a beautiful lady."

A sudden flash of memory crossed her mind: Colin, standing in that exact spot, handing her a dark red rose. *"Here you go, beauty. Not a stinger on it."*

A mist of tears blurred her vision. Katherine dropped her gaze. "Thank you. You're very kind."

Guthry's thick fingers lifted her chin. "Don't have to give it up and go back to America, y'know," he said, not as gruffly this time. "Place here for you—with me, if you understand my meaning."

Katherine blinked quickly to clear her gaze. Gadsbodikins! He was proposing! What could she say? She cast about for a polite answer, but her mind wouldn't cooperate. Instead, it rushed her back to Colin's little cottage, when he'd held her in his arms and said passionately, *"Marry me, Katie."*

She pressed her lips together, wishing she could rub out

that memory. "I'm truly flattered, Lord Guthry, but you see I must return to America. I have work to do there."

"Tut tut, gel. What kind of lady works?"

"I do. I help orphans find homes. In fact, I'm planning to build an orphanage with the money I receive from the sale of Ballyrourke."

He huffed indignantly. "Plenty of orphans hereabouts. No need to cross an ocean t'find 'em. Have 'em in your own backyard, y'know. Just have to open your eyes."

Katherine didn't know what to say next. She couldn't bring herself to argue with him.

Guthry cleared his throat, obviously embarrassed now by his impetuous proposal. "Think about my offer. Won't be sorry, y'know. You'll have the best of everything. I'll see t'that. Get rid of that sponge of an uncle of yours while I'm at it."

Katherine's eyes grew wide.

"Don't look at me like that, gel. I know a bad egg when I see one." He glanced back toward the house in the direction of the dining room. "In cahoots with that agent, I'd say. The two of 'em have their heads together right now. If I buy th'place, won't be through either one of 'em." He winked. "That'll rattle their roofs, eh?"

She stared up at him, amazed, and saw suddenly not the jowly, leering, self-important boaster, but a lonely old man who was not only brave enough to risk her rejection in the hopes of winning her favor, but who also was forthright and honorable.

Katherine stood up and faced him squarely. "You are a good man, Sir Guthry. I thank you for your most generous offer and honest advice."

He studied her for a long moment, then, realizing that she was letting him down gently, he heaved a quick sigh and straightened his shoulders. "Suppose you should get back. Wouldn't want 'em putting the hounds after you."

"Aren't you coming to the house with me?"

He shook his head with a frown. "Had enough of Lawthrop. M'carriage is around front."

"Then I'll walk you there." This time Katherine proudly took his arm.

Hidden deep in a stand of trees, Colin cursed silently as Katie paraded around the gardens on Guthry's arm. Sure, she was selling Ballyrourke to him. Why else would Guthry be there but to make her an offer? Hadn't he been buying up property all over the county? This would make a plum holding for him.

What was this, now? Colin's eyes narrowed as Guthry plucked a flower and placed it behind Katie's ear. Well, well. Maybe Ballyrourke wasn't the only plum the man was after.

Colin's stomach clenched as Katie gazed up at Guthry in that wide-eyed, innocent way of hers, just as she'd gazed at Colin only the day before. But what right did he have to be jealous? He had no claim on her; she'd turned down his marriage offer. He'd never told her he loved her, either, which was a lucky move on his part, for he'd only have looked like a fool when she returned to America.

He watched as Katie delivered Guthry to his carriage, expecting that she'd return to the house afterward. Instead, she moved swiftly along the front of the house and stopped beside a window, where she slowly peered around the frame, as though spying on the people inside.

Suddenly, she gave a little gasp and dropped down. Alarmed, Colin was ready to charge out and defend her, sure she was in mortal danger, when she suddenly rose, holding a bundle in her arms. She moved swiftly away from the house and headed back to the rose garden, whispering to the thing she held against her.

Colin backed farther into the shadows as she parked herself on a bench nearby. 'Twas only the calico cat, he realized as she held the creature up.

"Cali, you're supposed to protect me, not frighten me to death." She suddenly turned to look behind her, as though searching for someone. Had she heard him?

"I suppose Gersha will be popping up any moment, too," she commented.

She was so close that he could smell the lavender scent in

her hair. Two long strides and he'd be at the bench, holding her in his arms, bending her backward to kiss her deeply and tell her—what? That he loved her? Fat lot of good that would do.

What else? That he was innocent? How could she believe him when she'd seen evidence against him?

That she was in danger from Horace? She'd laugh at that. Her uncle hadn't been the one caught with the goods in his room.

"Oh, little cat," Katie sighed, causing Colin to grow still, "I wish you could tell me who to trust. I wish Colin— "

"Katherine?" he heard her uncle call from the house.

Finish your thought, Katie. What do you wish?

Katie's head jerked around, and even from where Colin crouched, he could see her jaw tense. "Yes?"

The devil himself appeared then, striding from the loggia, causing the cat to hiss and leap from her lap, fleeing into the bushes.

"Are you here alone? What happened to Guthry?"

Katie rose and brushed off her skirts. "He had to leave. He said to tell you good night and thank you."

Horace lifted a thick eyebrow, as though slyly suggesting she had something to do with it. "That was a rather sudden departure."

"He seemed tired."

"Did he give you any indication of his intentions?"

She started back toward the house with him. "I think he'll make an offer soon."

"Splendid. The sooner you sell Ballyrourke, the sooner you'll be able to build that orphanage."

Colin melted back into the trees. He had to find that will before Ballyrourke was sold.

Twenty-six

"I'd like to see Mr. Calloway's appraisal," Katherine told her uncle as they entered the house.

"There's really no need at this point, Katherine. Calloway will handle the negotiations."

"I am still the owner, Uncle," she reminded him. "I should know what my land is worth."

"I believe he has retired for the night. I shall schedule a meeting with him tomorrow morning so he can explain his figures to you."

"In the meantime," she said evenly, "I can be looking them over myself. Where are they?"

Horace heaved a sigh that indicated she was stretching his tolerance. "I don't have them. Calloway does."

She gave him a dubious look. "You don't have a copy?"

"No," he said tersely, "I don't."

Katherine had a strong hunch he was lying. "You met with Mr. Calloway all evening. Surely you know what the final figure was."

He turned on her with a cold glare. "Katherine, why are you questioning me? If you were truly that interested, you would have been here the last few days while Calloway was doing his calculations, instead of traipsing all over the county with that Irish burglar."

She blinked in surprise. How had Horace known she'd been with Colin? "Never mind, then," she said with a stiff smile. "I'll see Mr. Calloway in the morning. Good night, Uncle."

She could feel his icy gaze on her back as she marched to the staircase. Let him glare all he wanted. She was still the owner. Any decision about Ballyrourke would be hers.

Horace strode to the library, cursing under his breath. He was certain Katherine had caught his slip of the tongue. Now he'd roused her suspicions. Damn! Nothing was proceeding as he'd planned.

"Trouble, Horace?" Edward Calloway asked, looking up from his newspaper.

"Where is that appraisal?"

"On your desk, in the envelope."

"Is this what you showed Guthry?"

"Yes. Is something wrong?"

"Katherine wants to examine it in the morning. Have a seat at the desk, Edward. You'll need to make a new report especially for her."

Calloway put aside his paper and rose. "I don't know about this, Horace. I do have a reputation to maintain."

"No one will ever be the wiser, Edward. Just keep in mind all the money you'll make."

Throwing him a wary glance, Calloway took a seat while Horace produced fresh paper and a pen.

"Now, let's see how creative you are, Edward."

Kevin pushed open the creaking door and peered inside the old cottage. "Seems safe enough," he whispered. "Let me light a candle and have a better look."

Colin crouched down behind the overgrown hedges near the door and waited, alert to any sounds or movements around him.

"It's clear," Kevin called softly from the doorway. "Still smells of burnt wood, though."

Colin rose cautiously and slipped inside, dropping his knapsack at his feet as he gazed around at the charred walls and crumbling roof. Though he hadn't seen the place in years, it was no less painful for him.

"I set your blankets there," Kevin said, pointing to the stack he'd laid in the far corner. "Are you sure you wouldn't rather stay at my house?"

"This'll do just fine, Kev, and I thank you for your hospitality, but I don't want to put your family in jeopardy."

"What are you going to do first, Colin?"

"What I'd like to do is get my hands on John Bloom. But that'll have to wait. First I need to find Mary Flynn. She was supposed to write and tell me a meeting place, but I don't have time to wait for her letter."

"What can I do to help?"

Colin spread out the blankets. "I'll need to get to Dublin tomorrow. Can you help me get there?"

"I'll hitch up the wagon before dawn, and we'll leave before anyone knows we're about."

Colin clapped Kevin on the back. "You're a good friend, Kev."

He waited until Kevin had gone, then he propped a chair against the door to keep it shut, blew out the candle and lay down on his back, arms folded behind his head. He could see the stars through the gaps in the thatch overhead and found himself wishing upon one.

"Aren't you the sentimental eejit?" he said aloud. Wishing on a star was nearly as silly as Katie talking to the cat. He rolled onto his side with a regretful sigh. What had she been about to wish before her uncle interrupted? *Ah, Katie, what you must be thinkin' of me now.*

He wanted so badly to see her, to explain what he'd done. He was tempted to sneak back over to Lawthrop House and pay her a midnight visit, but his body was still too sore to be climbing trees and roofs.

Colin closed his eyes and pictured her sweet face looking up at him as he made love to her. He remembered how soft her lips were and how smooth her flesh was as his mouth skimmed over it, and how inviting she looked, spreading her legs for him, welcoming him into her. Hadn't it been the sweetest thing he'd ever known? Like he'd come home at last.

Sorrow filled his heart at the thought of losing her. For she was surely lost to him, if not from this incident, then when she left to go back to America. But he wouldn't let her go still believing him to be a robber and a thief. Somehow he'd clear his good name.

Katherine sat at the dining room table the next morning, reading with growing dismay the appraisal her uncle had put beside her plate. The report was extensive, one column covering all the leased farms as well as Lawthrop House and surrounding structures; another column listing all the needed repairs to Lawthrop House, including labor and costs of materials, the sum nearly rivaling the worth of the house itself. But the amounts were given in British pounds, and being unfamiliar with that money, she wasn't sure what it meant to her in terms of gain. Perhaps her uncle had intended it that way.

Katherine felt certain that Edward Calloway was helping Horace in whatever scheme he had devised. She'd seen them through the window last night, poring over documents, deep in discussion. Even Guthry suspected the two men of plotting against her. What she didn't know was what they intended to do.

"Any questions?" Horace asked.

Katherine glanced up at Edward Calloway, who waited quietly at her uncle's side. "I hadn't realized how extensive the repairs would be."

"It is an old house, Katherine," Horace answered for him. Old houses always need repair, this one even more so from neglect."

"And the farmland seems so—well—I don't know how else to put it—cheap," she remarked.

Again Horace answered. "It's not the best soil for farming, unfortunately."

"It doesn't appear there will be as much profit as I had hoped," she commented, studying the report, "but it's hard for me to tell exactly how much since it's calculated in pounds." She held it out to the agent. "Will you translate it into dollars for me, please?"

Calloway glanced quickly at Horace, as if to get his approval. When Horace didn't do so much as blink, Calloway gave Katherine a nod of assent, took the papers and retired to another room.

Horace filled his plate from the sideboard and sat down to eat. "There's been no word on MacCormack's capture. You haven't heard anything from him, have you?" He cast her a dubious glance.

"I haven't seen or heard from him." She finished her tea and rose. It was becoming increasingly difficult to be in the same room as her uncle.

"I hope we'll hear from Guthry today," he said.

"So do I."

"Have you selected the companies in which you'd like me to invest the profit you *do* realize?"

"I've decided to handle the money myself."

Horace turned in his chair to look at her. "You're being quite churlish, Katherine. I do hope you'll tell me if I've offended you somehow. I wouldn't want to be the cause of any distress."

His pretense of concern vexed her. "Since you asked," she said, turning to face him, "there *is* something that offends me, and that is being spied upon."

"Where the devil did you get such an absurd idea?"

"From you."

"You must have misunderstood something I said. Why would I need to spy on you?"

"That's what I'd like to know."

"What exactly did you hear me say?"

"That I'd been going around the county with Colin the past few days."

"Rest assured, dear niece," he said blandly, turning back to his breakfast, "that I know all I need to know about you."

She glared at his back. He'd given her no answer at all.

Fuming, Katherine marched out of the room, put on her hat and gloves and went outside, unable to bear another moment with him. There was a light mist in the air, but not enough to warrant an umbrella. As she walked down the steps, a messenger rode up and dismounted.

"Telegram for Mistress Katherine O'Rourke," he announced.

"I'm she," she said, and took the paper. It was a reply from Firth. She smiled at the delivery boy. "Please go around to the side door and ask for Grainwe. She'll give you a tip."

Katherine read the message as she cut through the park. If she were to die, the solicitor wrote, then her inheritance would be extinguished, and Ballyrourke would escheat to the government. "In other words," Firth explained, "Ballyrourke would become government property, and they could do with it as they pleased."

Colin's question had been answered: Horace would not inherit the estate. And in that case, Katherine decided, she needn't fear for her life. Obviously, her uncle was merely intending to swindle her. Or at least try.

She had to outsmart him at his own game. She wished she could discuss the problem with Colin, but even if she knew where he was, she wasn't sure she could trust him.

"Before ye set yer mind against him, speak with him," Grainwe had said. She'd also said Colin would never lie to her. Katherine searched her heart, wanting desperately to believe it, and suddenly knew the truth. Whatever Colin had done, he hadn't done it to hurt her, only to attain his dream. She couldn't blame him for it when she had done the same thing herself.

She stuffed the telegram in her pocket and hurried up Kilwick Road, turning at the sign that read Padraig Lane. Colin's father's house was just up the lane. Perhaps he was staying there.

She turned onto the narrow road and went straight to the little white cottage where she and Colin had made love. Her heart thudded anxiously as she knocked, then tried to open the door, only to find it locked. She cupped her hands around her eyes and peered through a window but saw no sign of anyone staying there. Everything seemed just as it had when she'd been there last.

The bittersweet memory of that afternoon flooded back. How happy she'd been for those precious few hours—happy and blessedly naive. Saddened, she started back to Lawthrop House.

On the road ahead she caught a glimpse of Gersha and called out to her, but the child was too far away to hear. She hurried after her, but no matter how fast she walked, she couldn't seem to catch up. Then Gersha disappeared around a bend in the road, and she lost sight of her altogether. But there in front of her was the signpost that said Gerald Lane. This was the road Gersha had taken her down to see her house.

She remembered what Grainwe had said: *"The house at the end of Gerald Lane belonged to the MacCormacks; it was where Colin was raised. It's been empty for over ten years."*

We'll see, Katherine thought, as she picked her way along the rutted, weedy road. She spotted a solitary cottage far ahead, but as she drew near, she saw not the cozy cottage with brown shutters that Gersha had showed her but a house scorched from fire, especially around the windows. Katherine stood in front of it, goose bumps covering her arms. This had to be where Gersha had brought her; there were no other houses nearby.

"You'll be back," Gersha had told her. *"One day very soon."*

Why had the child brought her here?

"She's a fairy. There's no tellin' her purpose. You'll have to wait and see."

As though someone whispered it in her ear, the reason came to her: Colin was there.

Her heart raced as she hurried to a window and peered in. A shaft of sunlight cut across the room, revealing shoe prints in the ash that covered the floor. In one corner she saw a pile of blankets that looked like it had been put there recently. She didn't see Colin, but she knew he'd been there.

She tried the door latch and found it unlocked. She

opened the door slowly, then stepped onto the threshold and looked around. The damage from the fire was quite evident, with charred walls and holes burned in the roof. How painful it must have been for Colin to see it again. He must have been desperate.

Katherine looked around for something on which to write, then searched her skirt pocket but found only the telegram from Firth. Placing it on top of the blankets, she left the cottage and hurried away, hoping that Colin would see it and come to her—hoping he would come back at all.

Twenty-seven

A Letter from home awaited her when she returned to
Lawthrop House. She took it upstairs to open it, glad for
some news.

> *Dear Katherine,*
>   *You will be thrilled to know that the ladies' society
> has found the perfect site for the orphanage and is
> currently looking at several plans. Of course, we are
> eager for your return so the final decisions can be
> made. Let us know your arrival date.*
>   *I hope this letter finds you healthy and happy.*
>   *Yours truly,*
>   *Edith*

Katherine immediately sat down at the desk and wrote
her a reply. She wrote that she was delighted to hear that the
ladies were moving forward with plans. It would make
things so much easier for her when she returned home.
Katherine paused to count up the days until Firth was due to
return for her.

Three days! So soon? Why, she felt as if she'd only just
arrived. What if Colin didn't return before she left? The

thought of never seeing him again, of not even being able to say good-bye, made her eyes sting with tears.

She could always stay.

Katherine shook that thought away immediately. Building the orphanage meant too much to her. She'd just have to plan to come back one day.

But even as she thought it, she saw the problems. Lawthrop House would belong to someone else then. The O'Rourkes might not even be there. And Colin, being the handsome man that he was, would no doubt have taken a wife. The thought of him married to someone else saddened her more.

She finished the letter and sealed it, then looked for something to do that would take her mind off leaving. She eyed the box of journals sitting beside her desk. She had read the last journal her mother had written, yet Grainwe had said there was another one in the attic. Whose books were in the second box?

Grainwe took her up to the attic, returning the first crate of books and opening the second.

"These are my grandmother's journals," Katherine said in surprise.

"Sure, I'd forgotten she kept journals. Do ye want to read them, lass?"

"Most definitely." Perhaps now she would find out the whole story of her father's disappearance.

Colin hid in the back of Kevin's wagon until they were near Dublin, then he threw off the blanket, moved aside the empty crates and joined his friend up front on the bench.

"I may be here all day, Kevin, so you might as well go back. There's no use waiting around doing nothing when you've got work to do at home."

"How will you get back?"

"Don't worry about me. I'll find a ride. Look, there's Mary's mother's house." He pointed to a brown brick four-story squeezed into a row of similar buildings.

Kevin pulled the wagon to a stop in front of the house. "Listen, Colin, everyone thinks I've come on a buying trip, and I've got lists of things to get longer than my arm, so there's no need for me to rush back. I'll do my shopping, then stop in at that friendly-looking pub on the corner there for a pint afterward."

"Thanks, Kevin. I'll pay you back somehow." Colin hopped down from the wagon, entered the building and walked up the stairs to the top floor. Mary's mother answered the door, pleasantly surprised to have a visitor from back home.

"Mary has taken a job at the Shelbourne Hotel," she told Colin proudly, over tea. "Quite a swanky place, too. 'Tis on Kildare. You won't be able to miss it."

Colin felt excited for the first time in days as he made his way through the crowds shopping on Grafton Street. He passed by the beautiful gardens on St. Stephen's Green North and not long after, spotted the hotel on the corner of Kildare.

Locating Mary, however, proved to be a bit more difficult. He learned she was working as a second-floor maid, and then he had to slip past a sharp-eyed bell captain to gain access to the staircase. He nearly laughed out loud as he came up a long, carpeted hallway and heard her slightly off-key soprano voice wafting through an open doorway.

"Mary Flynn, as I live and breathe!"

She turned around and gaped at him. "Colin MacCormack? Is it really you?"

"In the flesh."

She tossed aside her dusting rag and hurried to give him a hug. "Did you get my letter already? I only posted it yesterday."

"No, I took my chances and came anyway." Colin clasped her shoulders. "Mary, you don't know how glad I am to see you. I'm desperate for your help."

Mary glanced up and down the hall, then pulled him inside the room and shut the door. "I can't let them see me slacking on the job or I'll be fired. Now tell me what this is about."

"Ballyrourke is about to be sold, Mary, and I've got to

stop it. Is it true that Lady Lawthrop wrote a new will with the O'Rourkes as heirs?"

"Aye, Colin. 'Tis true. But I'd supposed she'd sent it on to her solicitor. She did fall ill right after that, so maybe it never got sent."

"Where could it be, then?"

"Let me think." Mary sat down on the bed, her forehead wrinkled in thought. "Last time I saw her working on it, I seem to remember her tucking it in the back of a book."

"What book, Mary? There's a thousand in that library."

She shook her head. "It wasn't a library book. This one she kept in her room, beside her bed. I think 'twas her journal." Mary's face brightened. "That's it. I remember now. She always kept private papers in her journal to be dealt with later. The will should be there, too."

"Are you absolutely sure you saw her write a will?"

"I witnessed it, Colin."

"I need to find her journal, then."

"You'd have to find the most recent one, of course. She kept it on her bedside table, and the rest on a bookshelf in her room, but they were all boxed up and taken to the attic when she died."

"Then that's where I'll look." Colin pulled Mary to her feet and kissed her on the forehead. "Thank you, Mary. We'll name a holiday for you once we have Ballyrourke back."

Colin was so eager to find Kevin that he nearly ran, but the crowded streets slowed him down. People strolled along, gazing in windows, chatting together, mindless of those that wanted to move past them. He finally skirted a large group and was about to turn the corner onto Mary's block when a man stepped out of an art shop directly into his path.

Colin lifted his cap, ready to apologize, when suddenly he recognized the man.

"Bloom!" he bellowed.

John Bloom's eyes widened in alarm. He spun around and darted off, with Colin in hot pursuit. He collared Bloom at the next corner, when the man nearly got hit by a passing coach.

"Afraid of something, are you, Mr. Bloom?" Colin asked, pulling him up by his lapels.

"I'm not afraid. I'm just in a hurry. So if you'll kindly let me go. . . ."

"Isn't that a coincidence. I'm in a hurry, too. What do you say we hurry together?" He set Bloom on his feet, got a firm grip on his coat sleeve and dragged him along, ignoring his squeals of protest.

Colin took him into the corner pub, where Kevin sat in a booth drinking Guinness. "Will you look who I ran into, Kevin?"

"Well, if it isn't Mr. Bloom!"

Colin plopped the little man down on a bench, then scooted in beside him. A barmaid sashayed over, and Colin smiled up at her. "Two more pints, please."

"What do you want with me?" Bloom asked them warily.

Colin leaned into his face and gave him a piercing glare. "Information."

"I don't know anything."

"I think you do, John." Colin waited while the barmaid set down their mugs, then he paid her and gave her a wink. She threw him a coy smile over her shoulder, a clear invitation that she wouldn't mind a little flirtation with him later.

A few weeks ago, Colin would have pursued her, but he had no inclination to do so now and knew the reason why: Katie. She'd spoiled him for any other female.

You'd best get over that, boy-o, for she'll be on her way home soon.

Colin shoved one of the mugs over to Bloom. "Here you go, Johnny. Have a drink and think about what you might know about those thugs who set upon me the other night."

"I don't know about any thugs," Bloom blurted nervously, reaching for the cool mug with trembling hands."

Colin jerked the glass away, sloshing the brew on the table. "Don't lie to me, John. I can see through a lie faster than you can blink. How much did Ratty Lawthrop pay you to set me up?"

Bloom pressed his lips together and stared at the glass.

"Come on, John," Kevin coaxed. "You're Irish just like we are. You'd help out one of your own, wouldn't you?"

Bloom thrust up his chin defiantly. "I'm an Englishman now."

"Is that so?" Colin said. "Where's your family home?"

"Don't have a family. They died, and I was sent to an orphanage in London."

"Donegal is my guess," Kevin said to Colin, "judging by his accent."

"I think you're right, Kev."

"You're both wrong," Bloom muttered. "It's Sligo."

"So you came back to Ireland to act as lackey for Horace Lawthrop," Colin sneered. "Want to know what kind of man your boss is, John? A murderer, is what. He murdered my mother and sister and set fire to our house. Now tell me why we should be kind to you when you work for a man of that sort?"

Bloom stared at him, sweat beading his nose. Colin shoved the mug back toward him, and Bloom grabbed it, gulping thirstily. He wiped the foam off his mouth with his sleeve and said, "What's the information worth to you?"

"Ah, so that's the way it's to be, is it?" Colin reached into his pocket and took out some coins. He tossed them on the table. "That's all I have with me, but there's more where that came from."

"Here," Kevin said, digging into his own pocket. "I have more."

"Hold on to it, Kev. We don't know what kind of information our friend has. What were you doing in Dublin today, anyway, John?"

"I was on an errand for Mr. Lawthrop, is all," Bloom said defiantly.

Colin rubbed his jaw, wincing when he touched a bruise. "You were coming out of an art shop, but I don't see that you bought anything. What does that say to you, Kevin?"

"If he wasn't buying, then he must have been selling."

"I was only looking," the little man squawked nervously. "I had some time to kill."

"John doesn't seem the type to browse those fancy art shops to me, does he to you, Kevin?"

"No, not to me either, Col."

"What were you selling, John?" Colin asked, peering into his eyes.

Bloom took another long swallow of ale, as if needing a boost to his courage. "It'll cost you."

Colin shoved the coins directly in front of him. "Let's start with those thugs," he said, and sat back with his arms folded as John Bloom bared his soul.

Twenty-eight

Katherine was interrupted in her reading by a knock on the door. "Miss?" Doreen said, poking her head in. "Master says he needs to see you at once."

"I'll be down directly." She marked her spot in the journal and laid it on the desk, irritated by her uncle's summons. She didn't like being ordered about.

Downstairs, she found Horace at the desk in the library. He stood up at once and came toward her, holding a thick envelope. "This came for you."

The seal on the envelope had been broken. She took it from him and saw that it was from Lord Guthry. "Who opened it?"

"I did. I assumed it was an offer for the estate, and I thought Calloway should see it." He glanced over her shoulder. "Ah, here he is now."

Katherine's temper flared. "No matter what you assumed, this letter was addressed to me. You should not have opened it." She turned toward the listing agent, standing behind her. "Mr. Calloway, do you have those new figures for me yet?"

"Yes, I do," he said sheepishly. He reached into his coat pocket and removed a folded sheet of paper.

"Thank you." She left the room, calling back, "I will be sure to tell the staff to bring everything directly to me from now on."

"Horace returned to his desk and sat down, careful to arrange his coattails neatly beneath him, his outrage well concealed beneath his stiff features. "This is untenable, Edward. Katherine is dealing with Guthry behind my back. He made her an offer directly. She's purposely cutting me out."

Calloway sighed. "I hate to say so, Horace, but she has every right to handle the sale herself."

Horace's lips thinned. "Her rights are of no concern to me. My only concern is getting my rightful due." He drummed his fingers on the desk, his eyes narrowing. "Katherine has become a liability. Something must be done about her."

Doreen stood in the doorway of the pink parlor, twisting an apron string around her finger as Grainwe polished a pair of brass candlesticks. "Grainwe, what does 'liability' mean?"

"Liability?" The elderly woman puckered her lips, thinking.

"Could it be like saying, 'She's liable to be in trouble'?" Doreen asked.

"I couldn't say." Grainwe peered at her suspiciously. "Why do ye ask?"

Doreen gave an innocent shrug. "I heard the master say it, and I was just wondering."

"Ye weren't listenin' at the keyhole again, were ye?"

"Grainwe, you told me not to!" Doreen proclaimed innocently. "I was just wonderin'."

Grainwe gave her a scowl and turned back to her candlesticks. "Wonder yer way upstairs and get those bed linens aired."

Doreen trudged upstairs, muttering to herself. She knew she wasn't supposed to eavesdrop, but she couldn't seem to help herself when it came to the master. She had a strong feeling about him being up to no good. What she'd heard him say just now only confirmed her suspicions. Whatever liability meant, it didn't bode well for the mistress.

Grainwe always told her to mind her own business, but sometimes she just couldn't.

Katherine opened the envelope as soon as she got to her room. Inside was a smaller envelope and on it had been written: PRIVATE AND CONFIDENTIAL: FOR THE EYES OF MISTRESS KATHERINE O'ROURKE ONLY.

How dare her uncle read her private correspondence! She opened the second envelope and found a letter inside from Lord Guthry with an offer for Ballyrourke that doubled the amount calculated by Calloway. Katherine quickly compared it to the new figures, now in dollars, a figure that was shockingly low. After making an adjustment for the difference in amounts, she sat down on the bed, stunned.

Lord Guthry wasn't a fool; he'd seen the appraisal and knew what the land was worth. Had Calloway made an error when he transferred pounds to dollars for her? Or had he purposely given her a false report? She knew the answer; it wasn't an error.

But it made little difference now. She had Guthry's offer. Her worries were over. She could sell the estate and return to Chicago to carry on with her work. And she could finally rid herself of her uncle.

She glanced around the room that had come to feel like home and felt a blanket of despondency settle over her. She was going to be able to fulfill her life's dream at last. Why did she feel such sadness?

You're leaving behind the one you love, a voice whispered in her head.

A soft meow made her look down. "Cali, I didn't see you come in."

Cali sat back on her haunches and leaped onto the desk, knocking the journal to the floor. Folded papers fell out of the back of the book and slid beneath the desk. As Katherine stooped to pick them up, she heard a light rap on her door.

"Miss?" Doreen called softly.

Katherine stuck the papers back in the journal and closed the book. "Come in."

Doreen glanced up the hallway, stepped inside the room and quietly shut the door. She said in a low voice, "Miss, I have to ask you something important. What is a liability?"

"Usually it's a debt or monetary obligation."

The maid dropped her gaze and twisted an apron string around her finger, looking very ill at ease. "What would it mean if a person was called a liability?"

"Did someone call you that? Are you in trouble?"

Doreen shook her head. "No, miss. He called you that."

Katherine felt her stomach roll over. "Who?"

"The master." She glanced up sheepishly. "I was just passing by the library, ye see, and I heard him talking to that other fellow about you. I didn't like the sound of it, so I asked Grainwe, but she didn't know. So I thought I should tell you in case it was bad. I wouldn't want anything to happen to you, miss."

"Thank you, Doreen. I appreciate your concern. Is that all he said about me?"

"He said you were dealing with Guthry behind his back and cutting him out, and that his only concern was getting his due. That's when he said you were a liability, and something had to be done about you."

A prickle of apprehension crawled up Katherine's spine. For the first time, she feared for her safety.

She would have to accept Guthry's offer immediately before Horace took action to stop her. "Doreen, come back in a quarter of an hour and I'll have a letter for you. In the meantime, please see that I'm not disturbed. If anyone asks, I have a headache."

"Yes, miss," Doreen said, and scurried from the room.

Katherine paced to the window and looked out, suddenly feeling like a prisoner trapped in her own room. She heard a meow and turned to find Cali sitting on the desk, waiting for some attention. Katherine picked her up and held her close. "Did you come to protect me tonight?"

The cat responded by rubbing her head against Katherine's chin.

* * *

Kevin stopped the wagon some distance away from Ballyrourke so Colin could get out. "Are you certain you trust John Bloom enough not to give us away?" he asked.

"You know what they say, Kevin. The best way to keep loyalty in a man's heart is to keep coins in his purse."

"Then be careful, Col, and good luck to you tonight."

"Thanks, Kevin." Colin turned up his collar, pulled his cap low on his face and ducked off the main road to make his way to Lawthrop House. At last he knew what Ratty Lawthrop was up to. Katie hadn't a clue as to Ballyrourke's true worth. How easy it would be for that devil to dupe her. And hadn't he suspected it all along?

Everything now hinged on finding that will. He'd have to sneak into the house as soon as everyone was fast asleep so he could search the attic. Once he had the will in hand, he'd have Patrick take it into town to be published, ensuring that the O'Rourkes would get their land back and Horace's scheme would fail.

Then Colin would confront the devil himself. The time had come for Horace to pay for his sins.

Colin snuck around to the side of the house to hide in the shadows of the rose garden. Once all the lights were out in the kitchen, he'd know the servants had retired for the night. He checked to be sure he still had the keys Doreen had given him, then looked up at Katie's window, surprised to see her sitting there, resting her chin in her hand, gazing up at the heavens.

Colin's heart swelled at the sight of her, but just as quickly deflated. He cursed the gods that he should be burdened with a love he couldn't have. For to have Katie, he'd have to give up Ballyrourke and follow her to America, and that he could never do. He'd fought too hard for this land.

But as he gazed up at her, he had the strongest urge to see her one last time, to let her know that he would never have stolen what wasn't his. Colin eyed the sprawling oak tree next to the house, hoping he was fit enough to climb it. Then he waited for the house to go dark.

"Miss?" Doreen said, knocking softly on the bedroom door. "Are you ready?"

Katherine left the window seat and went to the door. "Here," she said, handing the maid the envelope. "I want you to deliver this to Lord Guthry's house yourself and wait for his reply. It's very important."

"I'll go straightaway, miss. Grainwe wants to know if she should bring up a pot of willowbark tea for your head."

"No, I'm fine. Hurry, please, Doreen."

Katherine closed the door and put a chair beneath the door handle. Once Guthry had received her letter she would feel much better. As added insurance, she'd asked him to come over after breakfast so they could discuss details of the sale. Horace would be furious that she hadn't consulted him, but with Guthry there, he wouldn't dare do anything foolish.

"What do you have there?" Horace asked, seeing Katherine's maid return from the upstairs carrying an envelope.

"Just a letter, master," she replied, tucking it behind her. "Nothing important."

"I have some other things to post. I'll have that put with mine." He held out his hand.

The maid stared at his palm, then looked up at him with wide eyes. "It-it's not for posting. I have to deliver it."

"Give me the envelope."

She pressed her lips together and shook her head.

Horace curled his lip back in disgust. "Don't you dare defy me."

"The mistress told me to take it directly myself."

Horace grabbed her arm and dragged her into the library, where he pulled the envelope from her grip and shoved her against the desk.

"You can't take that letter!" the girl cried, reaching for the envelope. "The mistress told me to—"

He leaned over her, his fingers on her throat. "Do you know how easily I could snap your scrawny neck? Or squeeze my fingers around it until your eyes popped from their sockets?"

Whimpering, the maid shook her head, her eyes huge and frightened. Horace enjoyed seeing that fear in her eyes.

He tightened his hold, making her gasp. "Do you want to

live?" At her rapid nod, he said, "Then you must promise to leave this residence at once and never come back."

At her second nod, he released her, then stepped back as she ran to the door and flung it open. He heard her footsteps as she dashed down the hall to the front door. *Stupid maid,* he thought. *How easily intimidated those peasants are.*

He opened the envelope and scanned Katherine's letter. Just as he thought, she was going behind his back. How fortunate for him that clever Katherine wasn't quite clever enough. Striding to the hearth, he lit a match, held it beneath the letter until it was ablaze, then dropped it into the ashes.

He'd have to get rid of Katherine tonight.

Twenty-nine

Katherine lay in her bed, listening fearfully to every sound in the house, wishing for morning. She petted the cat curled at her side and tried to think about returning to America; instead she found herself thinking about Colin. She pressed her hand against her breast to soothe the ache around her heart. She should never have fallen in love with him. The pain was excruciating.

To distract her worried mind, she turned her lamp up to a soft yellow glow and reached for her grandmother's journal. Jostled by her movements, Cali stretched lazily, then hopped off the bed and went to the window to look out.

As Katherine opened the journal, the papers in the back slid out. She unfolded the top paper and was surprised to find a letter written by her grandmother, addressed to the solicitor, Mr. Firth. It was dated February 2, 1893, the day before her grandmother had died. Why hadn't it been sent? She read the letter:

> *Mr. Firth,*
> *As I draw near my end, and because your extensive inquiries as to my daughter's whereabouts have*

*proven futile, I have written a new will to supercede
my previous will.*

*It has been fifteen years since I have heard any-
thing from Suzannah, so I must believe that she is
happy and well-settled in her new life and wishes to
remain so. After much soulsearching, I also believe
that giving Ballyrourke back to its original owner is
the honorable thing to do, thereby righting a long-
standing injustice suffered by my loyal tenants. They
are a good, loyal and honest people; they deserve no
less.*

*Therefore, I am attaching a will to this letter be-
stowing the estate upon the O'Rourkes.*

Katherine was so astonished that the words danced before her eyes. It was everything Colin had dreamed of. She
imagined his shouts of joy, and the celebration that would
ensue when Eileen and Patrick and all the rest of the clan
learned the news.

But in the next breath, she felt the shock of her own loss.

Her hand dropped to her side. What would she do? She
had to build the orphanage. She'd never live with herself
otherwise. With her heart in her throat, Katherine picked up
the letter and continued, but the words made little sense to
her reeling thoughts.

*My regrets are many, among them that I will never
see the beautiful face of my grandchild. I hope she will
live her life in honesty and integrity, and I pray that
she will find happiness wherever her heart leads her.*

The letter ended abruptly with only a smudge of ink after
it, as though her grandmother had intended to write more.

Katherine eyed the other document lying in her lap. The
future of Ballyrourke lay hidden in its folds, and no one
knew it but her. She could tear it up right now and proceed
with the sale. Who would be the wiser?

Her heart thudded like a mallet as she wrapped her fingers around the stiff paper. She had the power to keep or lose

her inheritance, to fulfill her promise to the orphans or go back empty-handed. What should she do?

She was too emotional to think sensibly. She had to wait, let everything settle a bit. She started to put the document aside, but her curiosity got the better of her. She opened the will with clammy fingers.

I, Millicent Lawthrop, being of sound mind and disposing memory, do hereby give, devise and bequeath the estate known as Ballyrourke, county Wicklow, including Lawthrop House and all its contents, to the surviving eldest male heir of Sean O'Rourke, said estate's original owner.

To my daughter Suzannah Lawthrop O'Rourke I do hereby give, devise and bequeath my opal and gold pendant, a wedding gift from my husband, together with my prayers that she will live a happy, honest, and fulfilled life.

To my son Horace Lawthrop I do hereby give, devise and bequeath the sum of ten pounds, together with the fervent hope that he mend his ways and ask the Lord for forgiveness for his heinous sins.

Witnesseth this 2nd day of February, 1893.

Beneath her grandmother's neatly scripted name, another name appeared: Mary Flynn, listed only as a witness.

Numbly, Katherine folded the will and returned it to the journal. She turned down the lamp, lay back on the bed and stared at the ceiling, her mind in turmoil as she weighed her concerns against those of her relatives. One fact stood out: her grandmother had been a woman of integrity. She had wanted to do what was just, and to her that meant giving the O'Rourkes back their land.

Katherine could not destroy the will knowing how much the land meant to Colin and the others. She would simply have to go back home and find another way to raise the funds. Somehow, she would make good her promise.

A sound at the window broke into her musings. No doubt the calico, she thought, and looked up. She saw only a large silhouette, yet she knew instantly who it was.

"Colin!" she whispered.

He had climbed through the window as silently as the cat and was standing in the same pose as when she'd first seen him, his feet braced apart, head erect, shoulders straight and proud. Her heart raced madly, just as it had then, too.

"Aren't you a welcome sight, Katie," he said huskily.

Tears of joy sprang to her eyes. He'd come back! He'd risked capture to see her.

She put the journal on the bedside table, threw back the covers and ran to him, pressing herself against his warm body, her head tucked beneath his chin. "I was afraid I'd never see you again," she said in a voice choked with emotion.

"Sure, do you think I could stay away from you?"

She wrapped her arms around his waist to hug him and heard a sharp intake of breath. "Easy," he said.

Katherine tilted her head back to take a better look and gasped when she saw the gashes and blackened eye. She reached up to smooth her fingers over the bruises. "You're hurt! What happened?"

Colin took her hand and kissed it. "Nothing to worry about. Just a few cuts and a sore rib or two. Anyway, 'tis a long story, best saved for another time."

"This is worse than a few cuts, Colin."

"Now, Katie, don't make a fuss," he cautioned, as she took him by the hand and led him across the room.

Katherine pushed him down onto the edge of the bed, turned up the lamp and tilted his face to examine it. "Oh, Colin, you've been battered! Who did this to you? Never mind. You don't need to answer now. I'll go find Grainwe's salve and we'll get you fixed up. Lift your shirt and let me see your ribs."

"Don't bother with it, Katie."

"It's no bother."

"Grainwe has already tended to it. Now hush a moment," he said, taking her hands in his, "so I can explain about the paintings."

Katherine gazed into his earnest eyes and felt her heart swell with hope. "You didn't steal them from us, did you?"

"No, Katie, I did not. Those paintings from the attic are

O'Rourke paintings, and I took them only so I could buy back our land. But when it came right down to it, I couldn't bring myself to sell them. I stored them in my room, waiting for a chance to get them back inside. That's when the gardai found them. But I swear by all that's holy that I never took anything else. Your uncle planted a goblet in my room and stole the rest, then sent John Bloom to Dublin to sell them for his own profit. I met up with Bloom there and got him to confess."

Katherine was furious. "So that's why my uncle needed an assistant—to help him with his crime. We'll have to tell the police about this immediately."

"We can't yet, Katie. The evidence still points to me."

"Horace is dangerous, Colin. We shouldn't waste any more time. I'm afraid of what else he might do."

"I know, Katie. I know all about his scheme to swindle you. But don't worry. I've got a plan. Come here now and let me hold you. I missed you so."

It was typical of Colin to dismiss the danger. Katherine was about to insist that he tell her his plan, but as she gazed down at his handsome, confident face, she realized that right at that moment, what was important was just being with him. She let him tug her down beside him. "I missed you, too," she confessed, snuggling against him. She heard a slight hiss of breath, and eased back, belatedly remembering his bruised ribs.

Colin didn't let the pain deter him. He tipped her face up and kissed her, then stroked his hand down her hair. "I thought of you, my sweet Katie, of your lovely face, every night, of you lyin' in my arms, sharin' yourself with me, so trusting, so giving." He leaned her back onto the bed and kissed her, his lips firm and tender. His hand moved down to gently cup a breast, his palm making light circles over her nipple, until it tightened and tingled.

"I want to make love to you, Katie," he said huskily, kissing the smooth skin of her neck.

"Your ribs, Colin," she managed to gasp, as his hand roamed further down, pressing into the vee of her legs.

"Still want to see them, do ye? Along with a few other

parts you might be interested in reacquaintin' yourself with?" Colin wiggled an eyebrow suggestively, then rose from the bed and stripped off his clothing.

Katherine hugged her knees to her chest as he bared his magnificent body for her. Then, with only moonlight to guide him, he unbuttoned the front of her nightdress, pushed it down over her shoulders and helped her shimmy out of it.

Lying beside her, his arm around her back so that they were flesh to flesh, he said, "This is how it should be, with nothin' at all to come between us."

As Colin tilted his head for a kiss, Katherine thought guiltily of the journal on the bedside table. *Tell him about the will,* her conscience whispered. But under his passionate ministrations, her guilt floated away as though it were nothing more than a wisp of smoke. There would be time for that later, she assured herself.

She combed her fingers through his hair as he laved her breasts, circling each nipple with his tongue, sending ripples of pleasure deep into the core of her. He nibbled a line down her belly, making it tickle and tremble, then stroked boldly, rhythmically, with his fingers, faster and faster, until her body shuddered with spasms of intense pleasure.

He raised himself above her and kissed her again as his swollen shaft probed between the slick, throbbing folds, stroking her, tantalizing her until she could stand it no longer. Katherine pulled his body toward hers, arching upward, taking him in, feeling the hard length of him plunge to the very depths of her soul, a place only Colin could touch. She gasped as he rocked his hips against her, driving into her, their bodies straining together as one, damp from the heat of desire.

He raised himself up so he could see her as her passion finally exploded into waves of blissful surrender. Colin groaned as his own release came, then rolled away from her and lay back, breathing hard.

As her own breathing slowed, Katherine turned on her side to face him and reached out to touch his hair and run her hand gently down his cheek, afraid to let go of this precious moment.

Colin took her hand and brought it to his lips. "If tonight is all we ever have, it will be a night to remember."

Colin lay still at Katie's side watching her slide into a deep sleep. But why was he gazing at her lovely face and not slipping from her bed to go get the will hidden in the attic?

There's no better time, boy-o. This is your last chance.

He eased himself from the bed, took his clothes into the dressing room to dress and moved quietly to the door. He was surprised to see the chair propped there, but had no time to wonder. He moved it aside, opened the door and slipped into the hallway, pulling the door shut behind him.

The lock on the attic door cooperated for once without a squeak. But as Colin stood at the bottom of the stairwell, looking up into the blackness of the attic, he asked himself what kind of man was he that he could lay with Katie, then rob her of her inheritance?

It won't be her inheritance when you find the will.

Ah, but she didn't know that when she made love to me, did she? he argued back. What was he to do? He couldn't betray her.

Colin, you eejit, haven't you got yourself in a fine mess?

Cursing his foolish heart, he walked away from the attic and from his chance to get back Ballyrourke.

Katherine was dreaming of her grandmother when she felt something cold against her chin. She opened her eyes to see the little calico sitting at her shoulder staring down at her. Katherine cuddled her close, thinking about the man lying beside her.

As soon as Colin awoke, she would tell him about the will. She couldn't wait to see the joy on his face when he heard the news. She rolled onto her side and saw the covers turned back. She lit the lamp and looked around the room, then saw that the chair had been moved from the door. Where had he gone?

She pulled on her wrapper, lit a candle, and went to find him, searching upstairs and down without success. By chance she noticed the door to the attic staircase ajar and decided to investigate.

Katherine moved quietly up the stairwell, pausing midway to listen. She heard a scratching sound and called, "Hello? Is anyone up there?" then realized it was a tree branch rubbing against one of the attic windows.

As she stepped onto the old floorboards, she heard a creak on the steps behind her and turned with a relieved sigh, expecting to see Colin. She was wrong.

Her uncle stood at the bottom of the stairwell, a sinister gleam in his eyes. "I've been looking for you, Katherine."

Colin circled the old cottage to make sure no one lay in wait for him, then moved stealthily to the door and pushed it open, cautiously stepping inside. Instantly the stench of burned wood and thatch filled his nostrils. He closed the door and groped for the candle on the floor next to the sill, cursing the unfairness of life and the folly of love.

The candle flickered, casting the room in a dim yellow glow. At once he spied a piece of paper lying on top of the blankets. The hairs rose on the back of his neck. Someone had been there.

Cautiously, he knelt down to examine the paper, surprised to see that it was a telegram sent to Katie from her solicitor. How had it come to be there?

"Colin?" he heard Michael O Malley call softly from outside.

He went to the door. "Are you alone, Mike?"

"Yes. Open up. I've got important news."

Colin opened the door and Michael slipped inside. "Saints be praised, I found you at last. Doreen came to the pub this afternoon looking for you. She wanted you to know that Katie had given her a letter to deliver to Guthry, but before Doreen could sneak it out of the house, Ratty Lawthrop snatched it from her, then threatened to kill her if she didn't get out. Katie doesn't know, and Doreen fears she's in danger. Seems she also overheard Ratty say that Katie is a liability and he had to do something about her."

Colin muttered an oath. He'd left her alone in the house

with that devil. No wonder she had propped the chair beneath her door. "I've got to go back and get her out."

"I'm coming too, Colin."

"No, Mike. Go to the gardai and tell them you know where I am, then send them to Lawthrop House."

"They'll arrest you."

"I'll have to take my chances."

Katherine began to tremble as her uncle mounted the stairs, but she forced herself to show no fear. "What do you want?" she called sharply.

Horace tsk-tsked. "Katherine, don't play dumb. You know exactly what I want. You wouldn't be sneaking letters to Guthry if you didn't."

"Ballyrourke isn't yours. You have no right to it."

Horace's eyes glittered dangerously. "I don't want Ballyrourke. I only want the money. It should have been mine anyway." A scraping noise near one of the windows brought his head around with a jerk. He listened a moment, then, satisfied it was nothing more than a limb rubbing against the glass pane, he removed a long white glove from the pocket of his dressing gown and wound one end around his fist.

She took a step back. "What are you doing with that?"

He wound the other end around the other fist. "Ensuring your cooperation."

"You killed my father, didn't you?"

Horace shrugged. "It had to be done. He was a threat to my plan."

"You were going to come after my mother, too. That's why she stopped writing. She didn't want you to find out where we were."

His mouth curved down into an ugly grimace. "Your mother, Katherine, made a terrible mistake when she married that peasant. She tainted our bloodline and threatened the security of my inheritance. Now I'm going to rectify her error, with your help, of course."

Katherine took another step back. "I can't help you. Your mother wrote a new will leaving everything to the O'Rourkes."

"You're lying."

Seeing him snap the glove taut between his hands, she felt her skin grow clammy. "I found it this evening, in the back of her journal."

A creak of the stairs caused him to glance around. "Who's there?" he called sharply.

Katherine listened intently, praying it would be Colin.

Hearing nothing, Horace turned back, narrowing his eyes at her. "So you found a new will. Where is it, then?"

Think, Katherine. Find a way to stall him.

She glanced at the box of her mother's books sitting beside one of the trunks. If she could distract him, she could make a dash for the stairs. "I-I put it back . . . in that crate."

Horace chuckled dryly, an evil sound that raised the hairs on her head. "Katherine, you surprise me. I would have expected you to run to your lover with it. But you hid it instead so you could keep your inheritance. You've got some of my blood in you after all." He grabbed her arm, took the candle from her, and pushed her to her knees. "Find the will."

Katherine's hands shook as she removed a journal, made a pretense of shaking it out, then set it aside and went on to the next. As she worked she shot a quick glance at the stairway, her heart galloping. If she dared to escape, she'd be running for her life. She took a deep breath and tensed her muscles, preparing to flee.

Without warning, Horace kicked the pile of books, scattering them across the attic floor. She shrank back in fear at the savageness of his face.

"You're playing a game with me, Katherine. There *is* no other will!"

Clasping a book to her chest, she stood up on trembling legs. She was backed against one of the large traveling trunks, and now had no room to maneuver. "W-why would I be up here otherwise?"

"Liar!" With a snarl of rage, Horace lunged for her. Katherine flung the book at his head, then spun around and dashed behind the trunks, squeezing between the biggest of them so that he couldn't reach her. He cursed viciously as he ran after her, but Katherine was already out the other side and running for the stairs. She reached the bottom and yanked frantically on the door handle only to find the door jammed.

With a frightened whimper she swung around to find Horace looking down at her, holding the long glove like a noose. His composure had returned. "Checkmate, Katherine."

Thirty

Katherine gulped air to fight off the panic that hovered a breath away. "You won't get away with another murder," she whispered hoarsely.

"You're wrong, my dear." He stretched the glove taut. "Everyone knows MacCormack was in possession of one of your gloves. Doesn't it make sense he would also have the other? And if it's used to kill you, who will the police blame? You know they have quite a case against him already. A charge of murder will simply seal his fate."

As he started down the steps toward her, Katherine turned and yanked harder on the door, then beat her fists against the thick wood and cried for help.

"Useless, Katherine. Doreen has been sent away, and Grainwe is a bit, shall we say, tied up at the moment?"

She slid down to the floor, tears coursing down her face. Horace had planned very cleverly, and now Colin would pay for her uncle's crime.

Suddenly, the candle went out, pitching the attic into darkness. "What the devil?" Horace cried.

"Well, now," Colin said from somewhere above," I'd say the devil is about to get his due."

Katherine choked back a sob of relief as Horace stepped up onto the attic floor and called, "Show yourself, coward."

"So I'm the coward, am I?" came Colin's disembodied voice. "And you were going to pin Katie's murder on me out of *bravery,* were you? How brave were you when you stole our money, forced us from our home, and set fire to our cottage?"

"That was a long time ago," Horace sneered. "I only did what my father ordered."

"Ha!" came the reply, this time from behind him.

Horace spun around. "Damn you, MacCormack, stop playing games."

"Isn't it telling that you only like games when you're sure of winning them? I'd say it's checkmate for you, Ratty."

Katherine gasped at the sound of heavy scuffling above her, with blows and grunts of pain. As her eyes adjusted to the darkness, she crept up the stairs, where she could see the men struggling on the floor. She inched her way around them, found the candle and lit it. She turned around to find Colin straddling Horace's chest, her glove wound around his neck. Her uncle tugged frantically to free himself, but Colin's grip was stronger.

"You'll hang for this!" Horace rasped, then coughed as Colin twisted the ends tighter.

"Colin!" she cried. "Don't!"

Colin stared down at the face of the devil as deep, bitter hatred coursed through his veins. He could hear Katie's cries, but they seemed to come from a far-off place. Seeing his enemy begging for mercy, moments from death, Colin's lust for this final justice filled him with righteousness and blotted out everything else.

"Now you'll pay for your sins, you bastard—for my sister's and mother's death, and Katie's father's, and for all the people you've cheated and abused."

He twisted the ends tighter, causing Horace to claw desperately at it.

"Colin, don't kill him!" Katie pleaded. "Think! You're falling into his trap. He wants to see you hanged for murder."

Colin blinked back the sweat trickling into his eyes. He

didn't want to think, he only wanted to feel the sweet satisfaction of revenge. An eye for an eye.

"Colin, please let him go! I love you too much to see you pay for the evilness of this man."

His grip loosened just a bit as her voice finally penetrated. Katie loved him. She loved him!

"Your people need you, Colin," she pleaded. "Please don't throw away everything for revenge."

He blinked at her as the truth of her words became clear. She was right. He'd fought too hard for Ballyrourke to end his life behind bars. He released his hold, and Horace fell to the floor, clutching his throat and gasping for air.

Below, they heard the sound of feet pounding up the hallway. The door burst open from the force of several strong men and the police came charging up the stairs. Two of them grabbed Colin and one jerked his arms behind his back to handcuff him, drawing forth a string of swear words from him.

"You're making a mistake!" Katherine cried, grabbing one officer's arm. She pointed to her uncle, on his knees now, massaging his throat. "He's the one. Arrest him!"

"Save your breath, Katie," Colin told her. "They won't believe my story anyway."

"Nor should they," Horace rasped, staggering to his feet. "Captain, this outlaw tried to kill me!"

Katherine glanced around and saw Beattie coming toward them. "He's lying, Captain," she said. "You mustn't believe him! My uncle stole the gold and would have killed me if Colin hadn't come to my defense."

"Calm yourself, Miss O'Rourke," Beattie said. "One of your servants has given testimony that your uncle was plotting against you. We also have a statement from a Mr. John Bloom swearing your uncle had him sell off the gold pieces."

"You're taking the word of a peasant over mine?" Horace raged. "I'll have your badge, Beattie. I have friends in government."

"You'll need them, too," the captain muttered, throwing him an icy glare. He signaled to his men to take both Colin and her uncle away.

"Why are you taking Colin?" Katherine cried, in a panic. "He's innocent."

"We still have theft charges against him for the paintings."

The paintings! "Wait!" Katherine cried, hurrying after the captain as he followed his men to the stairwell. "A man can't steal his own paintings, can he?"

Beattie gave her a dubious glance. "Do you want to explain that a bit further, Miss O'Rourke?"

"My grandmother wrote a new will leaving everything to the O'Rourkes," she said, her words tumbling over each other in her hurry to get them out. "I have it in my room."

Colin wrenched around at the bottom of the stairs, his stunned expression twisting her heart into little knots.

"I was going to tell you," she offered, her words sounding flat and insincere even to her own ears.

By the look he gave her, she knew Colin didn't believe her. She stood frozen in shame and guilt as the police led him out the door. Why hadn't she told him sooner? She could only imagine what he thought of her now.

Beattie stroked his mustache, contemplating the matter. "I'll take your word for it. But MacCormack is still going in to answer questions, and you'll have to come down tomorrow with the will."

"Thank you, Captain."

"Now you'd better see to the old serving woman downstairs. We found her bound and gagged in the pantry."

Katherine hurried down after him, running breathlessly all the way to the kitchen, where she found Grainwe hunched over the table, her hands clasped in her lap, her face pale and drawn. In spite of her size and strength, she suddenly seemed very old and fragile.

"Are you all right?" Katherine asked, kneeling beside her chair.

"'Twould take more than a length of rope and piece of cloth to do me in, lass." But her brave words didn't match the quiver in her voice. "I shouldn't have trusted the devil, is all. Did he hurt ye, lass?"

Katherine shuddered at the memory. "Colin came in time."

"Let me make ye some tea," Grainwe offered. "Yer pale as a ghost."

"You sit right where you are. For once I'm going to wait on you." Katherine busied herself with the task, hoping it would keep her from remembering that look of betrayal on Colin's face. But as she sat at the table with Grainwe, the shock of her ordeal sank in, and her hands began to shake, spilling tea into the saucer. "Look how clumsy I am," she said, trying to laugh. She set the cup down, then put her head in her hands and wept.

"Ye'd best get it off yer chest, lass," Grainwe said gently.

After a moment, Katherine mopped her face with a napkin, took a calming breath, and began. When she finished, Grainwe shook her head ruefully.

"We suspected yer uncle had a hand in Garrett's death. Mary Flynn overheard bits and pieces of yer grandfather's deathbed confession, and shortly afterward, yer grandmother ordered yer uncle to leave Ballyrourke. Aye, that man was the devil himself. 'Tis a blessing that Colin came back tonight. 'Twould have broken me heart if something had happened to ye."

Grainwe shook her head sadly. "I never thought I'd live to see the day the O'Rourkes had their land back. Don't ye worry too much about Colin, though. He knows ye wouldn't have hurt him on purpose. He'll come to his senses soon. He just needs time to think." She patted Katherine's hand. "Didn't I say yer grandmother was a fair woman? Wouldn't she be happy now, knowing ye'd come back to live here among yer family?"

Katherine gazed at her expectant face and knew she had to be forthright about her plans. "I can't stay, Grainwe. I have to go home."

The old woman looked astonished. "This *is* yer home, lass. Ye've family here. What do ye have back there?"

"Something very important to me, Grainwe: I promised to build an orphanage."

"Well then, ye can come back when ye've finished," she

said with firm finality, belying the tears in her eyes. "And I'll not hear another word on it. Now how long have ye got afore this trip to America?"

"Mr. Firth will be here in two days to collect me." Katherine rose with a sigh and took their cups to the sink. She turned as Grainwe came up to her and put her arms around her.

"There'll always be a place for ye with yer kin, lass. Don't ever forget it."

Katherine blinked back her own tears. "I won't," she whispered, though she doubted that Colin would agree with Grainwe.

After seeing Grainwe up to her room on the third floor, Katherine dragged herself to her own room, washed quickly, then crawled into bed as exhaustion set in. She needed sleep, but she feared the dreams that were bound to haunt her. But when she opened her eyes again, it was daylight.

She washed and dressed and went downstairs, moving woodenly, refusing to let herself think about the events of the previous night. Doreen spied her in the hallway and ran to hug her, then launched into a spirited account of her crucial role in Katherine's rescue, halted finally by Grainwe's command to get on with her work.

After breakfast, Katherine made the trip to the police station to show Beattie the will. Her uncle was in jail, the captain informed her, and was already seeking a lawyer to represent him. Colin had been questioned for an hour the night before, then released. Since Katherine would be leaving before the trial, the captain asked her to provide a written statement to use in court.

Eileen and Patrick were waiting for her in the morning parlor when she returned home. Doreen had carted their baby off to the kitchen to show the cooks, and the boys were hard at work at home.

As soon as her aunt and uncle saw her, Katherine was engulfed in hugs and expressions of concern. They'd learned of her close call from Colin, who had stopped briefly at their cottage early that morning. Katherine assured them that she was fine, and explained how he had rescued her.

"He cares a great deal for you, Katie," Eileen told her.

Katherine changed the subject. It hurt too much to talk about Colin. "I can imagine you're very excited to have your land back at last."

"I still can't believe our good fortune," Patrick exclaimed. "'Tis nothin' short of a miracle."

"All thanks to you and your grandmother," Eileen said with a grateful smile.

"Grainwe told us of your plans to go back to America," Patrick said. "We want you to know you've a place with us when you're ready to come back. You're kin, and we love you."

When her company had gone, Katherine wrote a letter of apology to Lord Guthry, then attacked the one task she'd put off: a letter to Colin. She composed it in her usual, meticulous style, explaining how she had found the will and defending her reason for not telling him sooner. She read over it, then tore it into tiny pieces.

"From the heart, Katie," she could hear Colin say. She began again,

My dearest Colin,

I am sending the new will to my solicitor's office today to have it published so there will be no doubt as to its validity. My grandmother wanted the land to belong to the O'Rourkes. Now it does, thanks to her and to your fierce devotion to it. Once, I thought you were wrong to love Ballyrourke so much, but now that I know what it feels like to love with such passion, I cannot blame you for your feelings.

I have no excusable explanation for not telling you about the will sooner. I was simply afraid of losing my inheritance, and because of that, I lost your trust. Please know that I love you with all my heart, Colin, and I hope someday you will be able to forgive me.

Yours,
Katie

Katherine sealed it, then took both letters downstairs to give to Doreen. With a heavy heart, she returned to her room to make preparations for her return to Chicago.

Colin sat hunched over a table at Teach O'Malleys, drinking strong coffee and pondering the events of the past night. Michael had fixed him eggs and toasted bread, which he'd wolfed down hungrily. He hadn't slept well and now, after only a few hours of work, felt spent. But Ratty Lawthrop was finally going to be punished, and that was worth a sleepless night or two.

"So little John Bloom came through after all," Michael remarked, sliding onto a chair opposite him. "And Katie had your charges dropped."

"There were no charges; I committed no crime," Colin snapped irritably. He didn't want to think about Katie. He still couldn't get past her hiding the will from him. She had betrayed him; she couldn't have found a more potent way to hurt him.

"Colin!" Doreen called excitedly from the doorway, waving an envelope as she hurried to their table, "mistress sent this to you."

Colin took the envelope and stuck it in his pocket, much to the dismay of his onlookers.

"Aren't you a bit curious as to what's inside?" Michael asked.

"Not a bit."

"Ha!" Michael cried. "Doesn't your chin always jut up when you're lying?"

Colin glared at him from over the rim of the cup. "I don't lie."

"Mincing words, then."

"Open it," Doreen cried. "We know you want to."

"I'll open it only to quiet the lot of you." Colin broke the seal and read the first paragraph, then said with no emotion, "She's going to see that the new will is published, so Ballyrourke will legally belong to the O'Rourkes."

Doreen shrieked with joy, and Michael pounded his fist on the table. "That's fantastic news, Colin!"

It *was* fantastic. Why wasn't he happy, then?

There was more to the letter. He frowned as he read the rest. So she loved him, did she? Odd way to show it, not trusting him enough to tell him about the will.

"We need to celebrate," Michael cried, jumping up. "Doreen, darlin', will you have some coffee with us and help us plan a big party for tomorrow night?"

"I'd like that, Michael, thanks," she said, taking a seat at the table.

Michael paused to eye his friend. "For a man who's just won back the single most important thing in his life, you're certainly solemn."

The single most important thing in his life. It was true. Getting Ballyrourke was everything Colin had dreamed of, everything he'd fought for, despaired over, and now, at long last, won. The O'Rourkes were free to farm their own lands and never pay rent again. And he could do whatever he chose, whenever and wherever he wanted. What else could he possibly want?

"Who will live at Lawthrop House now, Colin?" Doreen asked.

Colin folded the letter and put it in his pocket. "Patrick is the heir. I would imagine he'll move his family in."

"What will *you* do now?" she questioned. "Will you stay on to manage the land?"

"What will I do?" Colin leaned his head against the chair back and closed his eyes, imagining. "I'll fix up my father's house, add a room or two, put in indoor plumbing, and make a fine home out of it, as he'd always wanted to do. And if Patrick agrees to it, I'll stay on to manage his lands."

"Which, of course, he will," Doreen added. "There's no finer manager than you, Colin."

He acknowledged her compliment, then downed the rest of his coffee and rose. "I've got to get back to work." He left the tavern feeling unsettled and unhappy, and didn't understand the reason for it.

'Tis yer own guilt, boy-o. Hadn't you planned to sneak past Katie to find the will, knowing there was a strong chance of her being cut entirely out of it? Knowing how

much she wanted to build her orphanage? Aren't you as guilty as she is of betrayal?

He threw himself into his work, keeping busy far from the big house so he wouldn't be reminded of Katie. He chose to sleep at his father's cottage that night rather than his room over the stable, then was haunted by the memories of making love to her there. He woke up even more irritable than before, causing a number of raised eyebrows as he worked all that day.

What was Katie doing now? he would wonder at the odd moment. Was she even at Lawthrop House? Perhaps she'd already left for home. Several times, he'd nearly made a beeline for the house, but then he'd stopped himself. What use would it be to see her again? She was determined to go build that orphanage. Would she even want to see him?

You won't know unless you try.

At the party that evening, Colin tried to smile and enjoy himself. He was a hero, after all, and there was reason to celebrate. But Kevin, Michael and Doreen sensed that something was amiss and wouldn't leave him alone about it.

"You know who should be here?" Doreen asked halfway through the evening, as the four of them sat around a table at O'Malley's.

"Tell us," Michael commanded, leaning his chin on his palm.

"My brother Kane," Colin said. "He'd be pleased with the turn of events."

"True," Doreen said, "but I was thinking of Katie. 'Tis her last night among us, after all. She leaves for America tomorrow."

"I can go fetch her," Kevin offered.

"Perhaps Colin would like to do the honors," Michael said with a wink at Doreen.

"On second thought, I doubt she'd have time to come," Doreen said with a woeful sniff. "She's busy packing. A sad sight it is, too. Nearly broke my heart to see her cry. She's not a crier, you know."

"Why was she crying?" Kevin asked her.

"I suppose because she'll miss us. Do you know, Colin?"

Colin threw her a dark glance. He knew what his friends were doing, and it wasn't going to work.

"I wonder how she'll build her orphanage now?" Michael mused.

Colin sat back with a scowl and crossed his arms over his chest. "Do you think not having her inheritance will stop Katie? When she's got her mind set on something, Michael, there's no swaying her."

"Reminds me of you," Michael remarked. "Stubborn and determined to get her own way. Except that she didn't, did she?"

No, she didn't. And Colin knew how badly she'd wanted to build that orphanage. If he thought about it, he also had to trust that Katie had meant to tell him about the will, as she had said. And what good did it do to love someone if you couldn't trust her?

What had he just said?

That ye love her, ye eejit. Ye love Katie, and there's no denying it.

Colin tunneled his fingers through his hair. He understood what it meant to want something so bad you could taste it and despair that you'd never have it. Now she had nothing, and he and the O'Rourkes had it all. But what did he truly have if he didn't have her?

After dinner that evening, Katherine stopped in the kitchen to thank the cook and her helpers for the delicious meal. She remembered the first time she'd seen the kitchen. Colin had stood in the far doorway, so handsome and proud that her heart had beat like a drum. And Doreen had sat at that table over there, folding napkins and trying her best not to show her embarrassment. The cook had been busy preparing a lunch, and she had been on a hunt for the morning parlor. How long ago it all seemed.

She wandered slowly through the house, stopping at each doorway to gaze inside. Patrick and Eileen faced a lot of repair work, but she knew for them it would be a labor of love. She wished them well.

At the door to her bedroom, she paused, recalling how

excited she'd been as she followed Grainwe down the hall that first day, wanting to learn everything she could about her mysterious relatives. With a wistful sigh, she stepped inside and looked around the softly lit room, her gaze touching on the dressing table, the elegant bedstead with its satin bedcover, the window seat—

Katherine gave a gasp of surprise. Colin stood in front of the window.

Her heart wobbled dizzily as she stared at him. She was afraid to blink for fear he was an illusion.

"Katie, don't go back to America."

Colin's plea tore her heart in two. She felt a prickle behind her eyelids and willed herself not to cry. "I have to keep my promise."

"Then I'm coming with you. We'll build the orphanage together."

Hardly daring to believe her ears, she pressed one hand to her chest to calm the excited pounding of her heart. "What about Ballyrourke? You can't leave it."

"Not right away, perhaps, but once everything is settled—and we're married."

For a moment her heart seemed to stop. "Did you say *married*?"

"I did. If you'll have me, that is."

And then she was in his arms, and he was kissing her and talking at the same time. "Ah, Katie, there I was sittin' at O'Malleys, wondering why I was so unhappy even though I'd just realized my lifelong dream, when suddenly it came to me what was truly important. You, Katie. Your love is worth more to me than Ballyrourke. Will you marry me, then, Katie?"

Her heart swelled with so much happiness she feared it would burst. "Yes, Colin, I'll marry you."

He picked her up and swung her around, laughing. "What do you know about that? We're getting married."

"You truly want to go back to America with me?" she asked breathlessly as he set her down.

"I don't ever want to be without you. Now here's what we'll do. First we'll get married. Then Patrick has said we can sell the paintings that your grandmother bought for the house, whichever ones you'd like, so you can build your orphanage. Then we'll make our plans to return to America to get it started. Now what do you have to say to that?"

That his plan was too impetuous and needed to be more carefully thought out. That it would take months to get the orphanage going, keeping him away from his beloved Ballyrourke. That she was stunned that he was even willing to leave Ballyrourke for her, and feared he'd hate being away from it.

But she didn't tell him that. Instead, she gazed up into his hopeful face and smiling blue eyes and said, "'Tis the grandest plan I've ever heard."

"Now you're learning," he said, and pulled her into his arms for a long, lingering kiss that led to much more.

Later, Katherine heard a noise at the window and rose from the bed to investigate. A little cat face peered in at her. She opened the window to let the animal in, then caught a sudden movement in the garden below. There, in the moonlight, stood Gersha. As Katherine watched, the child smiled and lifted her hand, as if in silent farewell. Katherine returned the wave.

"Who do you see, beauty?" Colin asked, joining her at the window.

Katherine turned to gaze up at the man she loved. "Just a fairy."

Irish Eyes

From the fiery passion of the Middle Ages, to the
magical charm of Celtic legends, to the timeless allure
of modern Ireland, these brand-new romances will surely
steal your heart away.